MW00988481

Josephine
A Woman of Indomitable Spirit

Elizabeth Rodenz

Josephine

Printed and published in
the United States of America 2022
Elizabeth Rodenz
Pittsburgh, PA
www.thedancingbridge.com

ISBN: (hardcover) 978-0-9722694-2-1
ISBN: (softcover) 978-0-9722694-1-4
Library of Congress LCCN: 2022904512

Josephine a novel by Elizabeth Rodenz

1. Fiction—Literary 2. Fiction—Women
3. Fiction—Historical 4. Fiction—Saga 5. Coal Mining
6. Women's Issues 7. Unions

Cover design by David Baker
Black symbolizes the mined coal
Red symbolizes the blood that was shed

To my mother, Caroline, who always inspired me by her words and passed on Josephine's legacy in so many ways.

To the miners who fought for their dignity and the welfare of their families.

To the uncommon strength and spirit of those women who stood by their husbands, fathers, brothers, and sons.

And to David who fell in love with Josephine's spirit and who was by my side throughout this journey.

"Extraordinary people survive under the most terrible circumstances, and they become more extraordinary because of it."

Robertson Davies

"There is a sufficiency in the world for man's need but not enough in the world for everyone's greed."

Mahatma Gandhi

"Not everything that walks in the guise of a man is human."

Aristotle

"If we define an American fascist as one who in case of conflict puts money and power ahead of human beings, then there are undoubtedly several million fascists in the United States."

Henry A. Wallace

I am only one. But still, I am one.
I cannot do everything. But still I can do something.
And because I cannot do everything,
I will not refuse to do the something I can do.

Edward Everett Hale

Prelude

A song claims that life is not about the breaths you take—it's about the moments that take your breath away. For the miners who worked in the coal mines, those sweet moments that took their breath away were few, if indeed there were any.

The coal company's control of everyone and everything in the patch was complete and all-enveloping—the work so difficult and dangerous that the concern was merely for survival. Imagine waking up every day, wondering if today you would take your last breath. Imagine hearing that a loved one was killed, body smashed by the fall of coal and slate. Imagine!

Josephine, a fictional tale, reveals aspects of that shameful period of industrial growth and the social injustices upon which the American economy was built. At the same time, the story pays tribute to the miners who helped build the industrial strength of this country by persevering through life's hardships.

In conceiving this story, besides exposing the injustices and hardships experienced by miners, Josephine honors the women of that time. Their courage and determination sustained their families. They were not heroines to the world, but they were heroines to their families.

We want to believe that today there are more and better opportunities for women. We may want to believe that there are more and better opportunities for non-white-collar workers. Wishing and hoping and talking about the strides made dismisses that which has stood still and what still needs to be done.

Not enough has changed in the struggle for equality for both women and non-white-collar workers. It's only about who participates. The struggles, heartaches, disregard for workers, and discrimination still exist, perpetuated ad infinitum. And that is a reality that permeates and erodes society.

I am a storyteller, as were my parents, and I have come to realize that my life's journey compelled me to write this story. My parents made me realize that stories are an effective way to give voice to history. Stories make history relevant to our lives because they are not devoid of heartache, struggles, and laughter. Stories make history relevant because they ask the reader to embrace the meaning and messages behind the events in people's lives.

Maybe if we can learn the lessons of what came before, we could keep history from repeating itself. If I believed in wishes, that would be one of them.

I hope you enjoy sitting with Josephine and those she loved in life and in fiction.

Elizabeth

February 14th 1885

Dear Reader

Words woven together to tell a story have always captured me for a few hours, sending me into a new place, a place of wonder or sadness or joy.

Sitting here on a hill behind the house where I was born, my thoughts are muddled. The life I'm living appears as a nightmare rather than a dream. The feelings and thoughts that gnaw at my very soul are crying out to be heard. I've decided to write them down not only for me, but so others might know what this time was like for people who will never live it.

Although I'm not Louisa May Alcott or Jane Austen or Nellie Bly and my story may not have a happy ending, write I must.

Josephine

April 1885

The death of Gramps was the second time in my fifteen years that my life was turned upside down.

This morning I woke up feeling captive—something I feel most days since I felt duty-bound to marry Joseph, a coal miner. His twelve-hour workday chains me to the mine as much as it chains him. For him, it is a day filled with damp and cold and danger, work that breaks the backs and spirits of men and beasts.

A week ago, four fingers were blown off a miner's right hand. A day later, an eighteen-year-old boy's leg was trapped between two mining cars filled with tons of coal.

"I can't get used to this life," I've cried to Joseph again and again, but I know I must. He says nothing, but then what can he say.

Well, that's enough of what I call misery talking—talking about what we all must endure.

This is my time of day. Joseph has gone to the mine, and I'm alone with my quiet. I'm sweeping off the front porch, but the breeze is winning, blowing the leaves back at my feet.

I see a woman, looking as if a puff of wind would blow her away, walking up the pathway pulling a wagon with two little boys tucked inside. They're bundled with an old faded quilt, their tow-heads peeking out.

She is trying to eke out a grin as they get closer. "Hello. I'm Emma. Jist move in two weeks now. Hear you've baby chicks to sell." Her voice is soft, and her accent pleasant.

"I can sell you a few. I'm Josephine."

I wave for her to come around the back of the house. She hoists the two boys out of the wagon, and they race after me. She is frail and seems to be moving with some difficulty. How did she ever pull that wagon with two little boys tucked inside?

I point to the cow grazing at the edge of the property. "Would you like to say hello to Betsy?" I give the older boy some hay. "Hold it in your hand. She won't bite."

He pets her velvet nose as he holds out the hay. His brother, not sure he wants to get close, giggles when Betsy moos. I ask Emma to have a seat on the log bench. Then hurry inside to fetch two cups of almost warm coffee and break a bun in half for each of the two boys.

"When did you come to America, Emma?"

"Six years now. Two girls born in old country. Two boys born here," Emma says, pointing to her boys who are now watching the pig grunt and twirl his tail. "You born in America?"

I nod. "Why did you come here, to this mine?"

"No scrip, no Frick," anger dripping from her words.

I understand "no scrip" and the miners' wish to be paid in cash. In most mines, instead of getting money, they receive a credit at the company store where they have to buy everything they need. Besides the long work hours and low pay, they never have a dollar in their pockets.

"What's a Frick, Emma?"

Her voice rises a little. "Henry----Clay----Frick---- Two names not enough for him. Nasty man. Cares only about money. Way we lived and mine, so bad. Better here, I think."

"Not if you talk to my husband, but there's no scrip."

"The boards were…." She puts her two fingers a half-inch apart. "Wind blew through. Could not keep warm. Patched again and again." Tears come to her eyes.

The answer for many is another mine, but Joseph believes that one is just as bad as any other. There is a sense of helplessness every minute of every day. The hardships that the miners and their families endure are difficult to imagine unless you live the nightmare.

"Emma, are you not doing well here?"

"Angry with husband," she whispers.

I chuckle to lessen my uneasiness. "Aren't we all?"

She tries to smile, revealing her dimples. "Can't feed husband and babes… food for his pail… so few pennies in pay. Need to do somethin' to git food. Had chickens growin' up. Saved and saved to buy a few."

There is sadness in her eyes. The life she is living is nothing like she would wish for herself and her children. I bite my lower lip and glance away. Why make the miners beg for a fair wage, driving them and their hope into the ground? The coal operator's greed is one answer that rings throughout the coal patch. But knowing why will not take away the struggles, sorrow, and hunger.

"Let's show your boys the peeps and pick out a few."

The boys try to cuddle the chicks wriggling in their hands. Emma cautions, "Don't squeeze too tight." I pick up one after another and put them in a basket with a lid.

Emma pulls some coins from her pocket. "Kin I buy eggs?"

"I can give you six. I'll bring you more later this week."

That's probably their dinner for tonight.

"Two dozen if you 'ave," she says, pointing down the hill to the right of the road. "We are fourth house down."

I rush to the kitchen. Six eggs can't feed that family, so I tuck a few potatoes in the basket.

I watch Emma drag the wagon down the street, the two boys fighting over who will hold the basket of chicks. The time with Emma felt comfortable, and her boys made me smile. It's sad to say that even the smallest pleasures are missing most days from my life, from all our lives. My few pleasures are squirreled away in my memory, bringing them out when I need to feel safe and loved.

Around me, all seems tranquil. The sky is still, the air fresh. Then I hear the train whistle, the sound of the cars on the tracks—a constant reminder that the quiet and peacefulness of the rolling hills are tarnished forever.

May 1885

A handful of memories come crashing around me. Memories of Gramps, who was joyful, his warmth and love in abundance. I remember sitting at his knee with my slate, learning to write the alphabet.

Sadness flows over me. I see Gramps before me, walking into the house, throwing his hat on the coat rack, and shouting out, "Josephine, up for a game of checkers?"

I imagine his hands holding my heart. As I look at the golden ball of light rising in the east, I can hear his voice, "Looks like God is baking bread." I sigh, "Oh, Gramps!"

The whistle of doom, the name I've given the long blast that rings out when there's a mine accident, is piercing the clouds of coal dust and the eardrums of everyone in the patch.

After becoming a coal miner's wife, I soon learned that the miner's day is ruled by whistle blasts. A short blast calls the miners to work or tolls the end of the workday.

When it rings out during the day, it's the sound of suffering and sadness. A miner has been injured, trapped in the mine, or crushed under the coal and slate. That will change the lives of his family forever and bring more uncertainty to their already uncertain life.

The whistle's silence means another sadness. The mine is shut down. There will be no money for food. Children's stomachs will growl, and their hunger will pierce the hearts of their mothers.

Out the parlor window, I see Betty, Gran's friend and now mine, hurrying up the path. She's the one person I can turn to when I need a pick-me-up moment. But from the scowl on her face, today is not going to be one of those moments.

She dashes onto the porch yelling, "George Mattick's been killed. He was working near my Jimmy."

Her shout turns into a shriek as she wrings her hands. "Some slate came down on top of him… crushed his chest. Jimmy was just… He was lucky he got out. Just a few bruises and injured leg."

Jimmy is Betty's son-in-law, who finds this, that, and another reason not to go into the mine at least one day a week. I turn away, thinking of George's last moments. Then I see his wife and children in tears. My eyelids close under the weight of my grief. I gasp. There is no time to mourn him. That may sound harsh, but it's a time to care for the living, Mary and her children.

I look at Betty and sigh. "What will Mary do?"

Betty slumps into a chair. "She'll do what other women have done. Move in with family, if they'll have her."

"Or she'll quickly marry again because she has to."

"Most women marry because they have to."

Knowing Betty's belief that marriage is a holy affair, I'm stunned that she speaks such truth. She, too, looks surprised by her own words.

"But who would want to marry her and feed and clothe another man's children. And no money saved?" The words are caught in my throat. "How very sad for all of them."

The image of George flickers before me like a ghost, fading in and out. He is shrouded with coal dust and slate and blood. I shake my head, trying to remove that image.

"They're clearin' away the rubble. It'll be a few hours before they get George out."

Sometimes the miners spend hours or days risking injury or even their lives to recover a fellow miner's injured or lifeless body. They do this for no pay.

Betty shakes her head and shrugs her shoulders. "The body will be ready for viewin' tomorrow night. We'll take up a collection for Mary." Her voice trails off as she moves towards the door. With no more to tell, Betty shouts, "I'm on my way to see Mary," and hurries out.

In time George's children, just like me, will have little memory of their father. I put a piece of beef with lots of potatoes, carrots, and onions in the oven for the grieving family. It won't be enough, but it's something. It was to be our supper, but Joseph will have to settle for fried potatoes and eggs tonight. Somewhat later, I walk at a snail's pace down the dirt road towards the coal patch.

Ω

The opening of a coal mine had stunned the few folks in the homes sprinkled throughout the farmland. The peaceful country life of my youth is now noisy with smoke and dirt and whistle blasts.

Beyond the miners' houses, there are rolling hills with acres and acres of wheat and oats and Guernsey and Holstein cows. A young girl hangs clothes on the line a few houses down on the right. Her mother died last year, giving birth to a sixth child.

At only twelve years of age, she cooks, cleans, and does the laundry for her father, brothers, sisters, and a babe. By the time they can fend for themselves, she will be too old or too tired to want her own family.

The laughter of three little girls playing jump rope reminds me there is some joy. Two boys are kicking a ball made of wrapped twine down the dusty path. Yet, their playfulness cannot erase or even lighten the dread I feel as I walk to the widow's home.

Sadness surrounds me as I walk through the open front door and into the parlor. Furniture, in need of repair and paint, is scattered about the room. The kerosene lamp in the corner is not lit, and the dim light from the window cannot chase away the drabness of the room.

Mary is seated on the sofa with her two sons at her side. The elder boy is standing as stiff as a board. The younger one is trying to mimic Mary's sobs. Her face is blotched, and her hair is uncombed. I cross the room to comfort her, but what can I or anyone say?

Gramps' passing had awakened me to the knowing that words hold no lasting meaning. No words of sympathy can snuff out despair or remove the heartache of losing a loved one.

I reach to clasp Mary's hands as I take a deep breath. "You're not alone, Mary." My words only cause her to sob louder as more tears well in her eyes and spill down her cheeks.

She wails, "Oh, bury me in the ground with him," and pulls a tatty handkerchief out of her bosom to wipe her streaming face.

"You have your two sons and little girl… and… there are all your neighbors."

We both know the women of the patch will be in and out for the three days of mourning, but they will not be there after those days. They have their own lives, their daily battles, their sorrows. Mary's children will become a worry, although, in time, I believe they will give her comfort.

"But where'll we go?" She puts her hand to her head. "The company'll kick us out."

"I'm making some supper. Send one of your boys in about an hour to fetch it."

Mary's hands are trembling as she pulls at the threads of the worn sofa. The expression on her face is not just despair. It's one of being alone, helpless, but don't we all have that fear at least once in our lives, if only at the end?

"Mary, in time, all will be…." My words trail off. I reach into my dress pocket. "Here's something Joseph and I want you to have."

I press money into her hand. I believe that for now, we are blessed and should bless others. Gramps would approve. I won't tell Joseph. He watches every penny, so I've given him the name, penny pincher.

Walking into the cold air, shivers run down my body as I look back down the road to the mine entry. Coal dust floats in the air in the distance. That cursed mine!

Ω

The light creeps into the small coal patch. In the willow tree, a cardinal is squawking, coaxing the newborns out of the nest to take their first flight. Then, the rooster jumps on top of the chicken coop and announces that morning has arrived. From the front porch, I look down the street at the company houses that will soon be surrounded by coal dust.

Once again, memories of my past years step on the heels of my present. My parents died a few days apart. Gran called my parents' death and Gramps' passing as fate.

"It's life, Josephine. It's just what happens. You can't do anything about your fate." I could not understand how Gran could be so… about her daughter's death and then her husband. But then maybe it was her way of keeping her heart from breaking into pieces, never to be mended.

In 1885 a law was passed that stated boys had to be twelve years old to work in the coal breakers and fourteen to work inside the mine.

In that same year, the American Federation of Labor was formed for skilled workers. Women and blacks were not allowed to join.

The miners, not considered skilled workers, had to meet in secret. Local efforts to form unions in the coal patches were pushed back, again and again, crushing the miners' voices from a whisper to silence.

June 1885

Gran and Betty had little hope that I would find "the man of my dreams" living in a coal patch. But, can any man ever be as wonderful as women dream about? That's for fairy tales.

One day while out for a stroll, my hat flew off, and Joseph caught it before it landed in the mud. I don't think he would have noticed me walking down the street, so I guess I have my hat to thank or blame for our meeting, whichever thought strikes my fancy on a particular day.

His hair is straw-colored, and he has crystal blue eyes and faint eyebrows. My deep brown eyes are set into high cheekbones, framed by a bounty of black hair. He is the day, and I am the night, and Betty believes it's a match made in heaven.

Gran and Betty had done their best to convince me that a man, once he reaches a certain age, is looking for a wife. He wants to have a woman to take care of him, and Joseph was no exception.

"So, marry Joseph and fill the house with little ones. Joseph and Josephine. His name in yours. And those blue eyes. They would make me marry him," Betty said again and again with a glint in her eye and a beaming smile.

Gran would chime in, "That'll make his Ma-Ma happy. You can cook and clean and sew. You'll make a good wife."

But will he make a good husband? A question that women are not allowed to ask. Gran and Betty never understood that I had done my own thinking about my life. To me, marriage is pushed on to women by mothers, grandmothers, aunts, sisters, and often fathers.

A woman is punished if she doesn't marry. Called an old maid or spinster. Thought of as a burden by parents and then her brothers, if she has one, once her parents pass away. So, marrying was a must, actually a decree after Gramps passed. I had to make sure both Gran and I were cared for. So, I was only sixteen when I married Joseph, the supposed man of my dreams. Six months later, Gran passed away.

Growing up, she had given me a daily dose of obedience and sweetness, cautioning me to hold my tongue, insisting, "You'll get more bees with honey." Phooey! I guess she thought it was good to pretend all the time.

Maybe I'm a foolish girl, something Gran called me often. Although quiet, not one to speak out just to talk, I can't agree when I don't, being quiet because that's what my husband wants. Maybe that's why Joseph and I butt heads now and then. Joseph wants to silence me, lose myself in him, believe and think as he does, want what he wants.

Like the embroidery thread in my basket, I will not become tangled so tight that I lose myself. Joseph thinks I SHOULD bend to his will. Well, I have a WILL of my own. I know I'm ranting, but I do that now and then, more now than ever. Maybe I wouldn't have these thoughts if Joseph were different, maybe.... Nay, I would have these thoughts.

Whew! That felt good. To write what's been spinning in my head and making me want to scream.

Ω

This coal patch, like others scattered throughout western Pennsylvania, could be compared to a cocoon. The miners and their families are enclosed in a place untouched by the outside world. But this cocoon does not provide comfort and protection.

Since eight this morning, the smell of baked bread has been coming out of my kitchen. The shine the egg wash has given to the crust on the four loaves is pretty enough for a bakery window. So, I nestle one loaf in a cloth, put two-dozen eggs in a basket, and step out the front door for my walk to visit Betty and call on Emma.

There hasn't been a day since Gran and Gramps' deaths that I haven't been grateful for Betty. She's all I have besides Joseph. My younger brothers were lost to me when my parents died when I was five years old. My maternal aunt chose to raise them, leaving my grandparents to raise me. I shake my head, trying to get those thoughts out of my head and the hurt out of my heart.

The wind blowing across the hills balloons my dress halfway up my legs. It's a welcome relief from the heat of the cast-iron stove. Ooh, it feels good to be out of that hot kitchen.

Betty lives in a nearby house. It's one of the few built before the mine buildings and company houses. Her daughter cooks and cleans for a mine supervisor's wife, working six days a week and into the evenings. Betty has to tend to her three grandchildren, clean the house, do the laundry, and cook for the six of them.

That doesn't sit well with me, asking someone her age to do so much. I don't think Betty likes it either. "I raised my children. She should raise hers," she has said to me, but we both know because her son-in-law is a lazy one, they need the money.

Around the corner, I catch a glimpse of her stark white ankles peeking from beneath the sheets she's pegging on the line. I call out, and she comes out from behind the screen of wet clothes.

The humidity frizzed her iron-gray hair into unruly curls, popping out of the bun pinned on top of her head. A dress of faded blue is snug against her body, the hem and sleeves torn and frayed. Her face appears even more wrinkled than her years. She walks towards me, hobbling like a wagon with a broken wheel.

"What did you do to your leg?"

"I fell down the steps. I've told Jimmy to fix that rotten step a dozen times. I went down like a sack of coal."

She shuffles to the back door and limps into the kitchen, collapsing into a stuffed chair. One by one, she unties the laces of her shoes and rubs her knees. "Oh, you're deliverin' eggs. Aren't you lucky to sell some?"

"I'll bring you a dozen on Saturday. A new family moved in. The peeps I sold her won't be laying for some time. I brought a loaf of warm bread, right out of the oven."

Looking around the kitchen, I am reminded that many of my neighbors live with very little—a bed and trunk in the bedroom and a few rickety chairs scattered around the kitchen. Betty's home is more cheerful than most, with curtains on the windows and hooked rugs on the wooden floors that never have a speck of dust or dirt.

"Jimmy's injuries have healed, and he's back at work." Betty's voice cracks as she cuts two slices of bread. "He could've been killed."

It's been almost two months since the fall of slate that killed George Mattick and injured Jimmy. I'm not sure what to say about a son-in-law whose injuries were healed weeks ago and who has made every excuse not to return to work sooner. Then who can blame him?

"How's that boy doing—the one who had his foot caught between two cars?"

"It was mangled but wasn't amputated. Only fourteen. His days of workin' in the mine are over."

I see the face of a young boy, his life in shambles, his hopes dashed. "It's a blessing he won't have to go back into the mine. He can do something else."

"Just one more mouth for his family to feed the rest of his life. No way he can get work."

Goosebumps appear on my arms, imagining young boys in the cold, dark, dampness of the mine, some in water up to their waists.

"There's nothing wrong with his mind. You'd think they'd build a school so the children could learn to do sums and read and write. Maybe keep them out of the mine."

Betty's knees creak as she tugs herself up from her chair. "Just because they learn somethin' doesn't mean they won't go into the mine."

"Some might want to do something else. I did." I stop and look away, not wanting to speak of that. My eyes land on pieces of cut fabric in a basket on a chair. "You're making a quilt?"

"When I can get enough pieces of cloth and have time to do it. I want to make my granddaughters a quilt so they'll each have one when I'm gone."

I'm jolted by her words. "You're not going anywhere."

I walk out the door, thinking I cannot lose Betty.

July 1885

Each day I squirrel myself away in this kitchen. A white and black iron-clad coal stove reigns over the room, not only because it's so big but most often there is something on it or in it. Every corner of every room in the house shouts out the desire for perfection that was my Gran. It was a testimony to her life. Now, it is a testimony to me, her granddaughter.

The clouds have turned black, and the wind is swirling through the branches of the trees. Lightning flashes and thunder is rumbling like mallets bouncing off a drum. Within minutes the heavens open, and rain slashes against the windowpanes.

I remove my apron and walk to the front porch to join Joseph. The rain smells fresh, and the sound is somehow comforting.

Perched on one of the chairs is a gray cat with green eyes as large as donut holes. I named the finicky cat Sally. She's licking her paws and freshening her fur.

A black and white and brown dog looks up at me, wagging her tail, her tongue hanging out. "Want a bone, Pallie?" She races to me and dances around my legs, making me smile as I pull a bone from my dress pocket.

Joseph's hair, the color of straw, is slicked back from his face. He gazes in my direction. His blue eyes are lit and sparkling like the stars. It is in these quiet moments of our day that I like him most, that I desire him most. He sits on a rocking chair, shining what is left of the leather on his best shoes. I shake my head, trying to chase away the image of my Gramps polishing his shoes every Sunday night before work on Monday.

"Those shoes don't need shined."

Joseph spits on the tip of his shoe, drawing out his words when he speaks. "Seein' mutter tomorrow."

The thought of my mother-in-law brings back memories of my Gramps' funeral. Next to Joseph stood his mother—brow knitted, smoky tinge around her eyes, and a scowl on her face. After spending a few minutes with her, I was sure her disapproving look was permanent, as though etched in a slab of stone I've seen on buildings.

A few inches shorter than her son, her clothes always look like they are on a skeleton rather than a woman's body. Her hands are always held crossed in front of her. The black babushka she wears covers her hair and is a reminder that she had immigrated. Almost two years later, I can still see her eyes looking deep within me.

Whatever I say to Joseph, he's not going to talk to his mother, get her to regard me like family. Maybe that's a good thing. Yet, at the same time, it hurts me that his mother and I will never be like mother and daughter. That's something I've always wanted in my life.

Months ago, Joseph had stopped asking me to accompany him when he visited his mother. She had said time and time again, "If you want to see me, you'll have to come to my house," so I was returning the sentiment.

His eyes widen, and he pulls on his mustache. "Mutter always told father...."

"She told your father lots of things." I pause, my stomach starting to churn, wondering whether I should be kinder towards my mother-in-law, but I'm tired of her treating me like I don't exist. It's not one of my favorite things.

My Aunt Rosie has never been kind to me, always making me feel like I'm not worth her time. Gran's love came with conditions. Now, my mother-in-law finds me lacking.

Instead of silence, I snap, "He can probably still hear her voice from six feet under and what, four, five thousand miles away."

Joseph's face hardens, his fist clenched. This turn of events surprises him. "She's my mutter, Josephine. You can't say dat!"

I feel my cheeks flush as I close my eyes and inhale. I try to swallow my words but fail. "And I'm your wife, but you choose your mother over me. You're lucky you have a mother. If my mother were alive, she would have accepted you. She would never speak to you the harsh way your mother speaks to me."

The light goes out in Joseph's eyes. I realize I have gone too far, and I look away.

The rain stops as quickly as it began. There is a warm, humid breeze drifting across the porch. Within seconds children are running out of their houses onto the street. A boy about ten is rolling a hoop removed from a wooden barrel. Tiny twin boys are jumping in the puddles left by the rain. Several girls are playing hide and seek, and others are in a circle, holding hands and singing Ring-Around-the-Rosie.

"Children everywhere. Why do they come to our house to play? There are no children here." I'm sorry for the anger in my voice. The children have nothing to do with my mother-in-law. At any other time, I'm happy to look outside and see the children playing and romping. This moment is not one of them.

"Kum 'ere cause it's away from mine, away from coal dust. Git to know 'um… their mutters." In a pleading voice, he says, "Give some milk. Cow won't mind."

"Betty says if I do that, they'll be like cats, making a home here."

I try to chuckle to chase away my…. I lower myself on the old swing that squeaks every time I sit on it. I pull out the thread for the scarf I'm embroidering and look across at the rolling hills. Pallie's bark makes me jump.

Joseph looks across at me. "You far away." He lets out a long sigh, combing his fingers through his hair. "Go to bed early?" he whispers, with the faintest hint of a smile.

I wish I could say, "It's my most favorite thing."

"Josephine, go to bed early?" This time his voice is eager. I nod. I have begun to enjoy our lovemaking, even at times craving it, but the thought of having a child in this wretched place has cast a shadow over our bed.

Joseph murmurs, "I remember da day ve met."

"What was I wearing?"

"Dark blue dress. Hair round and round," he motions with his hand and moves closer to me, "and pearl comb here." He points to the base of my neck and softens each word, "and those eyes, bright, fire."

Something in me melts, and I smile. "You do remember."

"I remember over and over," motioning again with his hand.

My mouth bends in an impish grin, and my eyes caress his face, taking pleasure in the strong line of his jaw and the mustache that frames his lips. His fingers brush against my cheek as if I were a baby chick. He tilts my chin upward, and I offer myself over to the pleasure of his kiss.

August 1885

A few minutes after Joseph walks out the door, I race out of the kitchen, leaving it in disarray. Gran is not here to scold me. I arrive at Betty's door just as the miners walk into the mine. Before I step into her kitchen, I blurt out without a good morning or even a smile, "I have no one but you and Joseph."

Betty looks up from washing dishes. "Findin' it hard to get to know the women?"

"I don't know how to talk with them. Some don't speak much English… but there's… something else."

Betty sits down on a chair, ready for a tête-à-tête. "Well, in some ways, it's because of your grandparents."

Gramps' job at the bank and Gran with her nose-in-the-air were the reasons we did not know the few neighbors who worked the land or did chores for others. Years ago, Betty had broken down the walls of Jericho by visiting every other day until Gran had invited her in.

"So, what's wrong with me?"

"Your clothes. You dress too good."

My body stiffens. "So, I'm to wear a rag dress, so the women like me? The clothes I wear are my favorites." I chuckle, but that doesn't bring a smile to her face.

"Your clothes make the men look at you, make the women think you're better than them." She gasps, trying to catch her breath. "Then, there are your words, the way you talk. Remember, some don't have any schooling, and some don't speak a lot of English."

"But most do, and I do speak slowly and use few words."

"I thought you didn't care what the patch folks say about you. You're not one of them."

But my husband is one of them. That's what's causing the split between us—one that's getting wider and wider.

"I'm betwixt and between."

Betty tries to lift herself out of her chair. "There you go with those words again."

I jut out my chin. "I don't know what to do. Are those better words?"

"That-a girl. Keep your spirits up." Betty giggles as though her feet are being tickled by a feather. I so enjoy her laugh.

What else can I do? I can sit and wail, slide into misery-talking. I can lash out. I can say what they're saying is not true or try to laugh at it, yet all the time hurting inside.

"So—what else are they saying?"

Betty's weariness and aches and pains are in plain sight as she leans forward. "Well, you throw money around. Let me use one of your big words—friv—o—lous—ly. Did I say that right?" She smiles, pleased with herself. "They don't have enough money for food and clothes. You're embroiderin' and crochetin' scarves and doilies. They'd like to do that too, but they can't."

"But what about the money I gave Mary Mattick when her husband was killed?"

"That was a nice thing to do, but it said you have, and they don't! None of the other wives could make the food you did and still give money. They thought you were saying, 'Look at me. I'm better than you.'"

I close my eyes and inhale, trying not to show my upset, close to anger.

"So, no matter what I do, they won't like me. Like my mother-in-law, and it's not going to change. They think I'm the rich witch on the hill."

Betty tries not to giggle and takes my hand in hers. "Well, I guess you've been eavesdroppin' outside their windows. It's only a few busybodies doing all the talking. Things can change. Give it time."

"Being nice to them hasn't worked." But have I been nice to them?

Betty puts the long tufts of gray hair back behind her ears. "You need to talk with them. Say something to make them feel good, get to know them."

My heart starts to pound. Betty leans back in her chair, waiting for me to speak. When I say nothing, she adds, "You need to give them time to get to know you as I do."

I hesitate, pressing my lips together. "How do I do that? But if they don't want to like me, it's hopeless."

"Maybe they don't know how to talk to you or be around you." Betty's face bursts into a big grin, and her eyes light up. "For such a little thing, you're bigger than life. But maybe you can make things better for them, help them in some way."

She pauses and moans, stretching her back. "Josephine, in your few years, you've faced so much heartache and loss. All that would make most young women collapse and give up. For that, I'm sorry. Now, there's a chance to change things for you and them."

Since I was about ten years old, I dreamed of doing something instead of marrying, stepping out into the world, but what could I do out in that world?

"How can I do that?"

"I don't know, but you're one of the few here who can. The women just don't know that yet."

I get up from the table, baffled, a lump in my throat. No words come, and my patience is gone. Poof! I've got to get out of here, so I head for the door.

Betty calls out. "Dearie, I'm sorry if I have upset you."

I wave my hand, walk down the steps, and amble toward the patch. The mine tipple that Joseph had helped build reaches into the sky and straddles the railroad tracks. I stop to watch the mine car climb up the tipple and dump the coal into a rail car.

Despite the noise, the walk down the slope always draws me into the patch. There's always something different to see. In the spring, the women and children plant a garden at the back. Chickens are scrounging for food. There are makeshift pens with rabbits. Grape arbors are growing up between the houses. Sometimes there's an outdoor oven where the bread is baked.

In the distance, I see several women who spend most of their day gossiping rather than taking care of their children or doing their chores. I wonder what filth lurks behind their doors.

Emma's front door is ajar, so I call out. There's a long pause before she appears. Her two little boys are hiding behind her. She's using the apron over her worn dress to dry her hands. "Jist got dishes washed."

"I have your eggs. How are the peeps?"

Emma pulls at the gold cross around her neck. "Growin' fast. Haven't lost any." She reaches for the eggs. "Two-dozen next week if you 'ave?"

"Yes, I'll come by, or you can stop in any time."

She takes out some coins from her apron pocket. As there is no invite, I say my farewell. I trudge up the steps to my front door, dragging my feet. The bounce has gone. It's not Saturday—the day I clean the downstairs—but I decide to do it anyway.

Anyone who knows me would never see me as plucky, ever imagine me as a woman with purpose, someone others can rely on. Yet, Betty has given me something to think about. I just don't know what to do about it, but then I'm not sure I want to go to the trouble. Or maybe I fear I can't make it happen. But then, as Gran would say, "CAN'T couldn't do anything cause CAN'T didn't try."

Throughout most of the 1800s, all forms of contraception were legal in the United States. In the 1870s, a social purity movement, comprised primarily of Protestant moral reformers and middle-class women, viewed contraception as an immoral practice and claimed it promoted prostitution and venereal disease.

As a result, contraception was made illegal in the Comstock Act of 1873, and birth control information was banned. At that time, America was the only western country to criminalize contraception.

September 1885

This morning I'm trying to set aside my misery talking and start anew. It's unlikely that will happen any time soon. The women of the patch have cast me aside without even trying to get to know me. Yet, this is not the time to grump and moan and sit still.

Betty is on her front porch and yells out as I walk up the path, "Am I forgiven?"

I try to stand as tall as my five-feet nothing and then some, not wanting her to think that she can't tell me the truth. "Nothing to forgive."

"So, what's on your mind?"

How can I say what is forbidden for a woman to say? "Do I always have to have something on my mind to visit?"

"You can tell me now or later," she says, snooping written all over her face.

After a long silence, I mutter, "How do you stop having babies? There's got to be some secret to it."

"Hah, you could lock Joseph out of the bedroom." Betty pauses, seeming to sense my bother. "Women have been asking that question ever since … well, whenever…. You know there once were ways. In 1870 something birth control was banned by law. No way to get it. Didn't matter to me. My monthlies had stopped."

"Why would the government do such a thing?"

"A group of religious people, mostly women, I think, raised a fuss. Thought birth control was causin' more prostitution."

"So, to stop their husbands from visiting prostitutes, they stopped women from getting birth control?" I pause, knowing religious groups always put their noses in this, that, and the other. They pay no mind that the Constitution says there is a separation of church and state.

"Women need a way to stop having babes they can't feed or clothe and make them old before their time."

Betty shakes her head. "Some try to get rid of it. My father's sister did. Only fifteen. She lost her life."

We are silent with our thoughts. Some women die in childbirth, leaving young ones with no mother. Often, there is no family to help the father raise his children. Out of desperation, babes are left on doorsteps, dropped off at church doors, abandoned, or end up in foundling homes.

Betty pulls out some pots and pans from the cupboard to fill the kitchen with noise. She never likes quiet for too long. "Why don't you want children?"

"I'm not sure it would be my most favorite thing." I try to smile but fail. "I didn't say I don't want them. Joseph gets paid so little. How can we raise more than a child or two on his pay?"

Betty's eyes reveal her sadness. "Women grapple every day to feed their babes. Their little faces beggin' for a piece of bread."

"And every day, there's a chance our husbands will be injured or maimed or even killed. Mary Mattick was put out of her house two days after her husband was killed. Now, she's living with ten people... some strangers... children, and adults... sleeping in two rooms."

Betty is trying to read my face. In time she says with calm, "Are you sorry you married Joseph?"

I have asked myself that many times. Were there only three things I could do with my life—get married, have children, and cook and clean and slave to take care of them? Wasn't I meant to do something else?

While these thoughts hit my head many times, I knew that I had to keep them to myself. There was no one to share my secret desires. I was alone, and such thoughts had to stay buried.

"I would have liked to work in a shop or…, but I had Gran to take care of after Gramps passed." I try to chuckle, "And then I fell for Joseph's blue eyes."

Betty's face reddens, probably surprised by my answer. She avoids looking at me as she chops onions. "So, women shouldn't get married and have children?"

I stare at my hands. "I didn't say women shouldn't get married. It's just not for everyone, and we are expected to marry at such a young age."

She puts down the knife and crumples onto a chair. "But life can't go on without children."

I whisper across the top of my cold cup of coffee at my lips. "Then let those with money keep the human race going."

"What would you do if you didn't marry and have children?"

Yes, what would I do with so few jobs for women? "Women are working in factories."

"I've heard they switch women with a stick. You don't dare take a breath or sit down. You wouldn't want to do that?"

"No, I wouldn't. Women can do a lot of work that men do. Gramps worked at the bank as a teller. Why does a teacher have to be a man? It's only in men's minds that we should stay at home, that we are helpless, that we can't do anything but cook and clean. Men make their own choices. Why can't we?" Oh my, I'm yelling.

I hesitate and gasp for breath and then continue to shout out. "I didn't want Joseph to go in the mine. He went anyway. And what kind of life is it for him, for me? Falling into bed at night, too tired to sleep. Angry because of the way we live." My words are hasty, afraid Betty will interrupt my rant.

Betty is scowling, unusual for her. "So, what are you doin' about the miners' wives?"

I take a deep breath. Betty's eyes aren't speaking to me. I want to say I don't know. I want to say I don't want to do anything or that I can't become one of them. I stop pummeling the arm of the chair and face Betty straight on.

Her face reveals only her years. "I need to find women who like me just the way I am, with... maybe... a few changes." I chuckle. "I can't change myself in so many ways to get them all to like me."

Betty rubs her hands and then her knees. "Good for you. So, what else?"

I don't want to tell Betty that I'm afraid the money Gramps left me won't last for more than a few years. I don't need to tell her about the few dollars Joseph brings home each week that are never enough.

"I must find more ways to make money and help them do the same. They're not asking for charity. I saw that when I took some eggs and potatoes to a mother whose son had done some chores for me. I made sure she knew it was to thank him because he did a good job. I didn't want her to think of it as alms."

"The miners are only asking for a fair wage, it's true. They're not lookin' for somethin' for nothin'."

Gazing out the kitchen window, I see about cows and a few horses grazing in the distance. It's a sharp contrast to the coal dust floating in the air in the opposite direction.

I sigh, "No rest for a miner's wife," as I walk out the door.

The government blessed the rights the coal operators enjoyed, a government unwilling to tackle the conditions under which the miners live and work.

Adding to the workers' misery, a law was passed in 1865, which gave the railroad companies the right to hire a private police force.

In 1866, that law was extended to the coal mines. Hired by the mining companies, men with guns and clubs, called the Coal and Iron Police, were employed to push back any worker unrest. They me to be hated by the miners.

October 1885

I stop to study the two-story building. Over the last several months, we've all watched it being built in the center of the patch. It houses the post office, the railroad station, and the general store that opened earlier this week.

The sun moves behind the clouds, and the sky is the color of slate—a reminder of the dullness of our lives, as though we need that. The wind kicks up again and sends a chill through me. Seconds later, raindrops begin to drench the coal patch.

Women and children gather on the steps of the company store, huddling under the overhang and watching the rain cascading off the roof. In front are several horses and carts tethered to the wooden rail.

Flanking the double doors are two windows displaying items for sale. The signs on the store windows catch my attention—coffee 18 cents a pound, eggs 25 cents for a dozen. A wave of pleasure comes across me, happy that I can raise chickens and gather their eggs. I can do without coffee, but not Joseph.

I grab the door handle and walk inside. A voice startles me. "Food, clothes. Not grab-all store, maybe?"

I turn and see a woman with blue eyes, similar to Joseph's. Her hair is the color of butter, her face carved with high cheekbones, but it's her voice and her smile that take hold of me. How can she be so happy with so little? Something maybe she can teach me.

I finally say, "We call them pluck-me stores." She looks puzzled. "You know, like plucking a chicken," I say, mimicking the action.

Her face becomes flushed. She doesn't seem to understand but is pretending. Twin girls with ginger hair and pink cheeks look up at me. They must have inherited the hair color from their father.

"What are their names?"

"Maria and Sophia. Girls want candy," she says, rubbing her thumb and fingers together, "but money.... I'm Annie. Come here last Friday."

"I'm Josephine," I say, noticing Annie's milky skin.

"You live up road." Annie points in the direction of my home. "I hear about you from women."

I start to turn away. "Wasn't a right way to meet!" She points to her head. "Husband says, 'stop before talking.' Tell him takes time." She ekes out a laugh and squints her eyes in thought. "Start again. I'm Annie. I like way you talk and your clothes," she says, touching the material in my dress. "Hear, there's nothin' you can't do."

I return her gaze and smile. After stroking the head of each of the twins, I say my farewell.

I turn to see women clanging pots and pans while others hold up material to their bodies. Several mothers have babes on their hips—some of them fussing and pulling at their mothers' clothes and hair. Older children are sitting on the floor playing with gadgets from the bins.

The owner, round like Humpty Dumpty, and his wife, a slender reed, wander around the store keeping a watchful eye on the children and the women fingering the items. They are acting more like prison guards than store owners. I select some sewing and embroidery threads and weave my way to the till.

"Emma, so you came today too?"

She glances up from the material she is mooning over. "Wanted to see what they have."

Her voice is so soft I have to lean in to hear. Again, today I see the sadness in her eyes, hear the suffering in her voice. There are no words of comfort, nothing I can do to ease her burdens. Most day I cannot ease my own.

"You sew?" Emma says, looking at the thread in my hand.

"Yes, it's my most favorite thing. I do chores fast, so I have time."

"Eggs so good. Boys liked cow and pig."

"Come over any time and bring them and your girls."

I take my leave and walk home in a daze, at times smiling just a little.

Ω

What a difference in the weather in just a week! The fall leaves have blanketed the hills, but they cannot erase the grime and coal dust. I step onto the front porch and notice the sun trying to peek through the clouds.

"Heard you never sit."

I jump, startled by a voice breaking the silence. I turn around to see Annie dragging her twins up the path. Only their red noses and cheeks can be seen through their hats and scarves. Annie's face is tinged pink, and her curly hair is sticking out the sides of her woolen hat.

"What are you doing out in this weather?"

"Bein' out makes girls tired, and they nap. Visit you, maybe?"

We look at each other, but no words are spoken. For a moment, I think about turning away and walking inside the house. Instead, I say, "I've got to go in and punch down the bread. It's probably walked away by now. You want to come in?"

Annie nods, and I help her bring the twins up the steps. She looks like a child who has gotten a new toy. "Just walk along the hallway. The kitchen's in the back."

She moves at a snail's pace, nudging her two girls along. The kitchen's warmth and smells are welcoming. I realize she and the girls are shivering. "Warm yourself by the stove."

"Big kitch—en. Have what you call…?" Annie points to the windows.

"On the windows? Those are curtains." I fight to get the raised dough back into the bowl. "Well, the bread only walked onto the table."

Annie looks at the stove and claps her hands as if applauding. Then, she prances around, acting like she can't believe her good fortune of being in this kitchen, maybe this home. "Big stove, big table. Sit eight… look at cupboards… all 'round. You make curtains? Sure, you did!"

"Do you always answer your own questions?"

Annie pokes her nose into the pantry with the pots and canned goods on the shelves. "How long you live here?"

"Haven't the women told you? If you spend time with me, they'll talk about you."

"Pay no mind."

"I was born here. My parents died a few days apart when my brothers and I were small. I was raised by my grandparents… and my brothers…. Well, they live with Rosie, my mother's sister…." I stop, realizing that besides Betty, Joseph is the only one who knows my story.

I hear Pallie scratching at my newly painted door. "So, Pallie, say hello to Annie and Maria and Sophia."

Annie backs away and scrunches up her nose. "You let that dirty, hairy dog in your clean house?"

"She's not dirty. I bathe her, and she's good company. So, Pallie, do you like Annie?"

The little dog gives kisses to Annie's twin girls as they giggle. What I did not tell Annie is that Pallie and I have chats daily. If she perks up her ears and cocks her head to one side, I'm saying something she agrees with. It's nice to have an agreeable dog.

"What brought you to America, Annie?"

"After Nick and me marry, we came. Four years now. Girls born here over two years ago. All my family and Nick's still in old country. You have cow, I hear. Are you sellin' milk? Buy some. Girls like."

"I can give you some today."

I butter some bread, slather it with jam, and hand a piece to each girl.

"Good," Sophia pipes up. Maria nods and then lowers her eyes.

"Girls learn just English. Want them to be American."

"How do you tell them apart?"

Annie chuckles. "Jist wait."

"Maria?" She nods. I got it right. "Sophia, milk?" I give them each a tumbler of milk and then hurry to my sewing box. I pull out a green and then a yellow ribbon. "Here, I have some ribbon. They're sweet and so pretty. You just want to hug them. Not a peep out of them," I say as I put the ribbons in their hair.

"What's peep?"

"I mean, they don't talk much. Girls are quiet."

"Just wait. What you doin' now?"

"I'm going to make some sausages and blood pudding. They're my mother-in-law's recipes."

"My Ma not a good cook."

"I cook a lot. I'd tell my Gran about my dream of getting gussied up…." I stop, seeing the confusion on Annie's face. "Dressed up, nice clothes," I motion to my body, "to go to work in town. She would shake her head and show me how to make a soup or potatoes and meat."

Annie stretches her arms out and speaks in the middle of a yawn. "How long you married?"

I wondered how long it would take Annie to ask me about Joseph. "Almost two years. His mother thinks I'm a fancy pants." I try to chuckle. "His mother heard that somewhere. She doesn't like me." I'm surprised I'm telling Annie so much, but I guess I need to tell someone.

"But he married you anyway!"

I hand Annie a wet cloth. "For the girls' mouths and hands."

I go to the chest in the hallway and return with something behind my back.

"Oh my," Annie squeals. "Girls, aren't they prett-eee dolls?"

"They'll be here for you to play with every time you come."

I get a quilt and snuggle them down with the dolls by the stove.

Annie looks at the kitchen table. "All this. Lots of work."

"Yes, everything is too much work. Men complain about the hours in the mine. I work more hours just putting food on the table and keeping the house and clothes clean. I shouldn't complain. I'm not risking my life and limb for a few pennies."

"Can me and girls come again?"

"Anytime. I have a dress my Gran wore. It's too small for me but still nice. I also have some material that we can use to make dresses for the girls."

Annie's face and bright eyes light up. "Oh, Josephine, you show me?"

"Come Friday morning. We'll make dresses for the girls."

"Josephine, how can I help? Show me, show me."

"Get a bowl out of the pantry."

I attach a grinder to the table and grind the pork butt and onions into the bowl. Then I pour the pig's blood into a pot, adding cooked rice, onions, salt, pepper, garlic, and ground pork. I put the mixture on the stove to cook until the blood congeals.

"I'll clean the guts. Messy job," Annie says, pinching her nose.

"Yeah, my mother-in-law knew that."

Over the next hour, we clean out the intestines for the casings, washing them until all the bad stuff is out. We giggle like young girls as I hold the casing, and Annie tries to fill it with the pudding mixture—often spilling some over the side.

I look over at the twins who have fallen asleep on the quilt. So, this is what it is like to have a sister, a family.

Two hours later, Annie and the twins leave. The home seems empty.

I had thought of today as a throwaway day—a day I had to get through. But, having Annie by my side made it bearable—even fun. I can't remember the last time I just felt happy. Annie and her two daughters might be the answer to my prayers, if I prayed.

November 1885

Many nights I stay up until late, baking bread and scrubbing the kitchen floor. And, because I work from morning until night, Joseph thinks I don't mind the hard life in a coal patch, that I like doing all the chores. Foolish man!

He sometimes says to me, anger in his voice, that I'm not coming to bed until he's asleep, that I don't want to make a baby. In some ways, that's true. There are times I delight being with him when he is gentle and not too hasty, but I haven't wanted.... Well, now it may be too late to worry about that.

The bare floorboards calm and cool me. I stand still for a few moments before slipping into my nightgown and crawling into bed. Joseph's body is inviting, so I cuddle up next to him.

I've been asleep only a few hours when I hear pounding on the front door. I slip on a robe and dash downstairs. Blurry-eyed, it takes me a few seconds to realize it's one of Betty's granddaughters at the door. "It's my Gran. She's sick. She asked for you."

I scurry up the stairs, clenching my fists, angry with myself that I hadn't visited Betty in the last few days. I put on a dress and wake Joseph.

"It's Betty."

With tears in my eyes, I dash up the hill, following the young girl. "She's been having pains in her chest and arms all day. She's gasping. I think she can't breathe," the young girl cries.

"She's always working so hard. Never stops."

We reach Betty's bedroom. I race across the room, grab her hands, more to calm me, I think, than to comfort her, and just in time to see that wonderful lady take her last breath.

Ω

I am clutching my heart. Tears are streaming down my cheeks as I look out the window towards Betty's home. It's been over a week since her death. Every morning, I still ask myself where will I go and who will listen to my secret thoughts?

My body shakes as I try to toss aside my sorrow and begin my day. Betty wouldn't want me to be sad, to be in tears. She always wanted me to be happy. She wanted the best for me.

Then I remember Annie and her girls are in my life, but they cannot replace Betty. No one can. But can anyone or anything replace any loss?

December 1885

The wind howling against the window panes wakes Joseph. I've been awake for hours. Although I'm tired when I fall into bed, sleep seems to escape me many nights. Silencing my head is difficult, and Gran's remedy, a cup of warm milk, doesn't help.

Joseph strains to see the clock. It's five twenty. In winter, he never sees daylight. He wakes in the dark, spends the day in the dark, and walks home in the dark, except on Sunday, his day off.

He snuggles tight against me, lingering a few minutes. I feel his aroused body, his warmth, his lips pressed against my cheek. I turn away, unmoved. He rallies the will to climb out of bed and shrieks as the cold floorboards shock his feet.

Frost has formed on the windows during the night. He blows his hot breath onto the glass to melt the ice and then rubs off the water with his hand, exposing a peephole.

"Lots of snow out dere. I clear snow and do chores. You stay warm." He fingers his mustache and scowls, "And I'll milk cow."

He dresses and limps out of our bedroom. His back is aching again. His day appears before me—the damp, the cold, the struggles of bringing down the coal to load. I release my pillow and jump out of bed.

Through the small opening, I see him step out beneath the bright moonlight. His breath forms clouds in the cold air, his boots leaving footprints in the crusted snow.

I yank on Joseph's heavy woolen socks and wrap my chenille robe around my body. I scurry down the stairs, my feet just touching the steps. The kitchen counter is lined with a squash pie and bread I baked late last night. The bread I bake every other day fills Joseph's belly and stops him from telling me he's hungry. Well, not quite!

Sally is perched on one of the chairs and greets me with a "meow." She's a chatty kitty. Pallie is curled in a ball on a blanket near the stove. She races to me and rolls over for a belly rub. Sally jumps down and wraps her body around my leg.

I hear Joseph kicking his boots against the house. His hands are quivering as he steps into the kitchen, trying not to spill the pail of milk or drop the basket of eggs. For a second, our eyes meet, but my gaze is whisked away as he places four brown and ten white eggs in the bowl on the counter.

"Good. Some look like double-yolks. Want an egg, Pallie?" The little dog sits on her haunches, wagging her tail.

Joseph puts some candle bits and chunks of coal into the stove as I cut bread for his lunch pail.

"Fed animals and gave 'um water."

Gramps had bought this house from a farmer who had built it for his son's family. The son had other ideas about his life, so it had been sitting there until the farmer decided to sell. There is an acre of land with a shed for chickens, a small barn, a bit of grazing land, and Gramps had put in a vegetable garden.

The small building that once housed the horse and buggy when Gramps was alive is now a makeshift barn for a pig and a cow. Joseph didn't want a cow and shouted, "Who gonna milk cow? Who gonna clean out stall?"

I had to bite my tongue not to scream. "I'll milk her. She'll give us milk for many years before she has to calf again. I'll make cheese and butter. I'll sell them and the milk. And the manure will be good for the garden."

One day he came home, and there she was. I named her Betsy. A pig appeared two weeks later. Within a few weeks, Joseph had made friends with the cow. He even milks her like he did this morning. In time I believe he'll be grateful for the chops and ribs and sausage from the pig, although he won't say so.

A sigh escapes my body. A fistful of memories come flooding over me—memories of Betty's laughter and of Gramps, who was joyful, his warmth and love in abundance. Before his death, I could not imagine my life without him. He had been my father since I was five years old. "What now, Gramps?"

January 1886

The word that keeps ringing in my ears is change. Change is all around me, but it has not been the change I want for myself. The change I desire would be a tonic.

Growing up in my grandparents' home, I never had to worry about money or enough food on the table. Since Gramps' death and my marriage to Joseph, those thoughts have been a constant worry. Little money on Saturday are the words not spoken. I do what I can with the few pennies Joseph brings home. The egg money I tuck away for the rainy day that is on everyone's lips.

I spend part of each day wondering how to bring about something that would make me jump out of bed. Other parts of my days, I waste worrying about whether Joseph will come home without injury or if he will come home at all. Adding to that worry is that, like Mary Mattick, I might have to raise our children on my own. That means whatever I choose must also bring in money.

How do I get Joseph to agree? Maybe I don't have to get him to agree. It's my house, not his, but maybe I shouldn't remind him of that. I cannot imagine what it was like for him to move into this house, my house. So, I have tried to be mindful of that.

I get anxious when I think of sharing any idea with Joseph. He always shakes his head no, maybe because they're my ideas.

"Why? Things good way they are," he always groans.

Talking to him during dinner will be as good a time as any. I'll make one of his favorites and hope he has a good day at the mine.

Ω

There are times when I try to picture what it was like for Joseph to come to a country, not speak the language, and not find the life of milk and honey he had expected. Now he is working in a coal mine where he is at the mercy of the company. But, most important, Joseph has lost his pride. He has no way to control or change anything, and that includes me.

Joseph had shared very little about his life before he came to America. After his father had passed away, he had grown tired of trying to eke out a living on such poor land and dreamed of a new beginning. So, in 1880, he had brought his mother and sister to America.

Although I have no reason to wonder whether he has told me everything about his life before coming to America, there is an uneasiness that gnaws at me. What has he not told me?

This evening he came home happy. He loaded more coal in a day than he had in the last three days. Now is the time to have that talk.

After placing stuffed cabbages, his mother's recipe, in front of him, I say, "Joseph, I know you worry about money."

His shoulders droop, and his head hangs down, accenting his angular jawline. "Not quit mine. Day might come…."

"You can worry until the cows come home. Worrying won't stop the day from coming."

He shrugs his shoulders, not knowing what I mean by cows coming home. I love talking in another language. Yes, it could be said that's the devil in me. It's also my way of keeping my anger inside.

I lower my voice and touch his hand. "Joseph, there are other ways we can make money. We kept this house because it's better than paying rent to the company."

"You decide—not me."

He will never let me forget that I own the house he lives in, that Gramps had deeded it to me before he died.

"Yes, I know, so why not board some miners? Single miners are always looking for a place to stay. Other women in the patch are doing it."

He glares at me and shakes his head.

"Joseph, listen, please. You worry about money. Some of this money we can save. If you can't work, we won't be hungry." I stop, my heart pounding.

I remember a few days after Gramps' funeral. Gran and Betty kept saying that I would be sad if I didn't marry and have children. Gran told me that my mother wanted me to be married and have someone by my side.

I yelled out to her, "Maybe I will never marry. The mine will soon open. There will be single miners who will want a nice bed and good food. Maybe I'll start a boarding house once the mine is up and running."

Gran shouted, "You can't have a bunch of single men with a young girl and an old lady!"

"Maybe I'll just board old men."

Betty and Gran had shouted "NO," reminding me they're not much different from young men. Then I said I could board a family. The wife could help with chores. The husband could help with work around the house.

There would still be room for some single men. Betty got in one more punch by telling me that no woman in her right mind would want to move in and have a young woman around her husband.

Back then, I knew this idea could work, but I am trapped in a woman's body—a body saying I have only one choice--marry. I fell into the trap that so many young girls fall into. I married Joseph. Now with Gran's passing and.... Maybe, just maybe, it is time.

Joseph twists his mustache. He's probably thinking money from the boarders would be mine too, just like this house.

"Men will say...."

I stop him with my glare. "This isn't about what other men will say. They're not paying for our food, our clothes. It's nothing to do with them."

I decide not to remind him that a time might come when he could get hurt and not work, or he could die under a mound of coal. Who will take care of me then?

He starts to walk out of the room. "Don't walk away! You can help me do this, or I can do it myself."

He turns and stares at me. I throw the embroidery on the chair and stand up, facing him.

"I know, don't need me," he punches one fist into the other. "Men comin' goin' all day and night."

He's right. I don't need him to do this, but I want him to go along.

"The only time they'll be underfoot is when they eat their meals. We'll still be alone."

"It's not dat."

"No, it's about you wanting to stop me from doing what I want to do. You do what you want to do. I'll do everything for the boarders. You won't have to do a thing."

I pause, trying to catch my breath. I'm sure Gran is looking down, shaking her fist at me. She believed that a woman should agree with her husband, always pretend not to have any ideas or thoughts about anything.

Joseph clenches his teeth. "No, no! I take care of us." He jerks his thumb to his chest.

"What does that mean... that I can't do anything but take care of you? Do you think I can't take care of myself?"

I clasp my hand over my mouth. That must have hurt Joseph. All he has is taking care of me. The sad thing is that I know he can't, not the way I want, no matter how much he might wish it were true. Day by day, I do one thing after another. I try to keep moving, making decisions about our lives, while he stays still.

We stand, facing each other. Silence jumping off the walls. He shakes his head, his face baffled.

He sits back down at the table. "So, how many?"

I let out the breath I had been holding. It's difficult for Joseph to say no to me. That will always be in my favor. I suggest that we start with two, then four, and maybe six in all. Then I put in front of him another stuffed cabbage and cut a piece of the pie.

Joseph pushes his food around his plate and then asks me what if it doesn't work. Then his words tail off. He knows I'll make it work.

I push two pieces of paper in front of him. "I wrote out two notices. I'll put one at the store, and you put the other in the mining office."

I thought this was a good time to try to get boarders. It's near the end of the month. They will have time to tell their landlady they are leaving.

"T'ought you might vait." He pauses and takes the slips of paper. "I know, I know, early bird ketch vorm."

I touch his cheek with the back of my hand. After we finish the evening chores, he clasps my hand in his. "Mornin' comes early." He steers me up the stairs and into the bedroom. I take out the hairpins. The strands of hair fall and tickle my face.

Joseph moves towards me and kisses my neck. He hugs me close to him. I rest my head against his chest and stroke his muscular arms.

Change is upon us. I'm just not sure Joseph will welcome any of it.

In 1848 the Married Women's Property Law in New York ruled a woman could keep her inherited property after marriage. That law was then passed in other states.

In 1872 another law was passed that stated a woman's earnings, should she be able to find a paying job, she could keep as her own.

Before those two laws were passed, upon marriage, a woman's property, as well as any earnings, the husband could claim as his own. He could spend it on anything he wished, and one day he could walk out the door and leave her and her children with nothing.

February 1886

Annie and I are meant to be sisters for life, however long that life will be. I'm not surprised as those words flow from my pen. Yes, we will be there for each other day after day. Support and care for each other, never jealous or hateful or vengeful—like sisters should be.

The clock strikes nine as Annie comes bursting through the kitchen door with her twin girls, their cheeks rosy. I notice a few stains on the front of her dress that needs mending, but then she is always busy with this, that, and the other.

"Guess what? There's gonna be a dance at the social hall. Someone has put together a band." She motions her hands as though she were playing notes and blowing into the air. "Anyway, there's gonna be music, food, drinks. They're gonna let us use it for weddings, christenings, parties."

She stops, and her mouth tightens until most of her lips disappear. She then starts to gnaw on a clump of her hair like a five-year-old.

"Spit it out, Annie!"

"Could you help me make a dress for the dance? Nothin' fancy. Just pretty. Will ya'?"

"Sewing is my most favorite thing. Stop by tomorrow morning."

"I'll give you some money for it."

"I already have the material. It will be your birthday present a few months early."

"Oh my! Thank you, thank you, but speakin' of money. Why not tell about boarders? Thought I'd tell everyone before you did."

"There you go again, answering your question." I offer Annie a spoonful of the chicken stock.

"Hmm, so good," she says, smacking her lips.

"I wanted to talk to Joseph first. I just told him last night. How did you find out?"

"Everyone's...." she motions with her hands mimicking a mouth talking. "Well, I tell you what I think. You'll take boarders from women with nice house, good food. Make boarders happy, oh my!"

"Well, I'm delighted someone will be happy. I'd be hurt if everyone hated the idea."

Annie's face beams like the sun. "Don't pay them no mind."

"There are many single men who need a room. More men than rooms."

I had not thought about what the women would think when they heard I was taking in boarders. I just want to do something with the empty bedrooms I dust every other week.

Annie snaps her fingers to awaken me from my trance. "How many boarders?"

"Six, but I'll start with what I can get. Joseph is not sure about this."

"You'll make it work."

"I have a secret, but you can't tell anyone yet."

"Promise, promise. Tell, tell!"

"I want to ask some of the young girls in the patch to help with the boarders. They can help me with laundry, cooking... other chores. I'll pay them. That'll help their families."

"You're gonna have someone in the house! Oh my! You won't be alone. You'll have help when you get bigger and baby comes."

I shake my head. I'm not like Annie. I'm fine alone. Well, most of the time, but I'm not hiring girls to keep myself from being lonely.

"It's a way to help out their families, and I could have more boarders."

"You think women will like you better for this?"

"I'm not giving the girls anything! They will earn it. The boys bring in money to help the family, so can the girls!"

"How many you want?"

"Two. One for three days and one for the other three days."

I had decided on two girls so I could help two families, rather than just one. It would also make sure the young girls wouldn't be working too hard since they would still have chores at home.

"So, know any girls you'd want?"

"Emma has two daughters. Maybe her younger girl?"

"I tell about room and board and think about another girl that might be good."

"But don't let the cat out of the bag just yet."

"What's that mean? No cat in bag!"

I cannot hold back my chuckle. "Don't tell everyone."

"Why didn't you jist say that?"

March 1886

The whistle wails, signaling the end of the workday. Joseph walks out of the mine, struggling to put one foot in front of the other. A clanging sound awakens him from his weariness, and he looks at me, surprised I'm here to meet him. We both look in the direction of the clatter to see a young man picking up the parts of his lunch pail.

Joseph touches the peak of his hat. "You jist kum 'ere?"

The miner nods as he picks up his shovel. "Yah, Gerhard Klaus. I vork vas 'ere gut."

"Yes, better here. We git dollars in pocket," Joseph says as he points to the pocket of his pants.

I add, "Your mother and father here?"

"Jist me. Wife in Austria. Want go back with money. Buy land."

I walk closer. "Where are you living now?"

"Sleep on floor," he says, pointing to one of the company houses.

The man turns to walk away, but I grab his arm. "We have room—sleep on bed," I say, pointing up the hill to our home.

Joseph nods. "Wife good cook. Kum, see room."

Gerhard nods, "I vash, kum tonight."

I'm too shocked to say thank you to Joseph. I do have the good sense to put my arm in his as we walk home.

That evening Gerhard stops by. I show him the room he will be sharing with other miners. He'll be moving in on Sunday.

Joseph and I sit down to supper when there's a knock on the kitchen door. I look up and hear the door open and a gruff voice, "Knock on other door. No one come."

Before us is a miner who is only a few inches taller than my five feet. "Billy Bowles," he says with a grin. "I hear you have bed."

"Josephine."

"I know. Your husband work in mine." He nods at Joseph.

"Could you take off your shoes and come in? Would you like a bowl of soup?" I yell over my shoulder as I walk to the stove. I fill a bowl with bean soup and cut him a large chunk of bread.

He nods in Joseph's direction again as he walks in and whistles eyeing the bowl of soup.

I point to the chair. "Sit down. Eat your soup before it gets cold. Where did you come from?"

Billy collapses on a chair, grabs the chunk of homemade bread, and dunks it into the soup, slurping and smacking his lips. "I was workin' in West Virginia. My wife died of pneumonia. My brother works close by."

I notice his eyes—eyes that say, "I'll take care of you."

"Is the price good for you?"

He nods. "Nice house, good soup."

Joseph grunts. "You born 'ere?"

Billy nods. "When do you want to move in?"

"Sunday evening good?"

"No smoking, drinking, or shoes! Not my favorite things."

I have my first two boarders. I had decided I would be fussy about who I boarded. I would ask two questions. "Do you drink?" and "Do you smoke?" The final test would be getting close and getting a whiff of their clothes. Gerhard and Billy said NO to my two questions, and they both passed the sniff test that night.

Ω

It could be said that the first few years of my marriage to Joseph had been riddled with arguments. That was meant to happen since we were strangers when we married. At times in between, our tussles had been eased by his kindnesses.

Yes, it's a morning of going over the past, along with some clearness of head. I'm still having doubts about being married. Until she took her last breath, Gran had asked again and again if I were happy as Joseph's wife. Then Betty did that. Now I do that.

I cannot admit that I have made a good match. Then I wonder if any match would be a good one at sixteen. If I had not married, I might not have the heartache of trying to live a life I believe I am not meant to live. At the same time, I struggle with why I had said no to him for months and why I gave in. So, I spend my days living in two minds.

But I did marry. So, each day, I have to plan how to be married. Yet, I have to admit, and only to myself, we do have our moments. These are the thoughts that keep spinning in my head while I work away in my kitchen.

After taking the bread out of the oven, I walk out the front door for some air. A man is hobbling on crutches up the path. His face is flecked with gray stubble. His blue eyes captivate, sparkling like stars. One eye has "gentle" written on it, and the other says, "imp."

"Hi, my name is Artie Winslow. You have a room. I do payroll for the Penn Shaft Mine down the road."

"My husband's at Manor Valley. Yes, I have a room."

It's been a week since Gerhard and Billy moved in. They are both quiet and thankful for the meals and nice bed, and Billy, bless his soul, helps me with Betsy and the pig now and then.

Artie hobbles up the steps, and I ask him to take a seat on the swing. "How long ago was your accident?"

"About four years. I was working in the Shafton mine. Load of coal broke loose and hit me. Crushed my leg. High fever. In and out of my mind for almost a week, they told me. Didn't know where I was or what was happening. When I woke, my leg was gone. Wasn't surprised. Thought I was a gonner."

"So, then, you started working in the office?"

"Worked in the company store for a few years. Someone saw

I was good with figures, so they taught me to do payroll. It's hard to find someone who can do sums and read."

"You must have been a good worker or friends with the boss."

Artie smiles, "Yeah, that too. No sense in makin' enemies."

"What made you come here?"

"My wife and baby died in childbirth." There is sadness in his eyes. "I needed to move on. I heard this was a good place."

I notice the bag he has slung across his shoulder. "You want to come tonight?"

He nods. "Come on in. No smoking in the house and no liquor."

"Don't waste money on them."

"I have a small room on this floor. Sometimes I store something in there, but it won't be in your way."

I thought Artie would be grateful that he did not have to climb the stairs on crutches and might be more comfortable on his own. Gramps had stayed there when he was ill, and often tears come to my eyes when I pass by. Putting Artie there.... Gramps would approve.

In one corner is a single bed with a quilt I had made. A table is next to the bed and a trunk at the foot for clothes. Dark blue curtains cover the windows, and two knotted rugs made from long strips of fabric are on the floor.

I rush into the room and pick up the rugs. "You may trip on them," I almost whisper. "Breakfast at 6. See you for supper in about ten minutes. Bring me your dinner pail."

A time for celebration. I have three boarders—Gerhard, Billy, and now Artie.

Ω

Why don't I have more boarders coming to my door? I checked. The notice is still up at the store. I put one in the railroad station and post office, not that the miners are often there. Maybe some of the miners are gossiping like their wives. My home is too clean, too neat. I would be too fussy with the boarders. No one could talk about the good food I cook. No one has been at my table.

April 1886

In my busy days filled with monotonous chores, I hadn't time to realize that the women in the patch would begrudge me having boarders. Now, what will they say when they learn I have two girls working for me? But Annie is right. "Pay them no mind."

At ten in the morning, there's a dusting of snow. More is swirling between the trees and houses. The wind chill feels about ten below zero, burning the children's faces out for a day of fun.

The snow crunches under my boots. The gusts of wind sting my face, yet the sun is shining on the company houses—a rare sight for a spring day. In the distance, the mine cars are dropping coal into the rail cars waiting below, spreading dust and grit far and wide, masking the outside of everything, and choking and blinding everyone.

The twelve double houses in the distance were built during the first year the mine was open. Each house is square and bare inside and out. There is a well with a hand-operated pump for every three houses. Women are always lined up, waiting to fill their buckets. They need it not only for drinking, cooking, and bathing but also for washing clothes and scrubbing the floor, walls, and windows always caked with coal dust.

My body tightens at the sound of the whistle of doom ringing out. Once again, women and children will gather at the mine. Like other families throughout the coal patches, they may wait minutes or hours or days to hear whether a husband, son or brother is injured or dead, entombed in the mine. I walk into the store and pick up some thread and a soup pot.

Within minutes there's word that several miners are scraped and bruised, one with a broken leg and arm. They have escaped death—-at least on this day.

As I walk out of the store, I hear a voice yell out, "Josephine."

I turn around, and standing before me is a bear of a man with a break-your-heart smile. "I'm Mike, Mike Gallagher. Heard you have room."

"Yes, I do. Want to see," I say, trying to keep my teeth from chattering.

We walk home, most of the time in silence. Times in between, he tells me he was raised in a foundling home and has no family. I tell him a little about Joseph and the three other boarders. It's strange, but he feels like the brother I have always wanted.

Ω

Today I'm going to honor Betty by trying to make that difference she spoke about. Yesterday afternoon I told Annie I would ask Emma's daughter, Rosalie, to help me with the boarders. Helen, Ruth's daughter, would be a good second girl, so I will talk to her too.

After Joseph and the boarders leave for the mine, I march into the coal patch, Betty's words cheering me on. Emma's eyes widen when she sees me at her back door. She's standing in the doorway with Johnny on her hip. Her wavy hair frames her deep-set eyes and the freckles high on her cheekbones. She would be so pretty, her face lighting up a room if her eyes were not so sad.

"Emma, good morning. Can we talk?"

"Yes," she says in almost a whisper and asks me inside.

"Hi, Johnny. Will you come to see Betsy and the pig again?"

He nods and smiles.

Catching a glimpse of the room, I'm again reminded of how the miners' families live. I struggle to hide my thoughts by rolling a potato from my basket to Johnny, and he then rolls it back.

Emma asks me to sit and gives Johnny a pot and a wooden spoon. She smooths down her apron and grabs hold of the cross hanging from her neck.

"Emma, I've taken in three boarders." I hesitate for a few seconds. "And I want three more. It's too much work for me. I'd like Rosalie's help."

Annie told me that Emma's daughter, Rosalie, is friendly and talks a bit—well, quite a bit.

"I need help washing, ironing, cleaning, cooking. I thought of Rosalie. She'd work only three days. I'll ask another girl to work the other three days."

After rushing through my prepared words, I take a breath and wait for Emma to say something.

"Not Violet?"

"She's the older one, right? I thought you'd want her to help you. You decide which one."

"You'll pay her money?"

"Yes. I'll bring the money to you, or you can stop by for it. This will be between us. The neighbors don't need to know," I say.

"I'll call Rosalie."

Within seconds, Rosalie and Violet race into the kitchen. Their dresses are soiled, and their faces are too thin. Oh, how I would like to see them in pretty dresses and their hair curled.

"Rosalie and Violet, this is Josephine. Rosalie, she wants you to do some work for her."

I smile and move closer to the younger girl. "I need some help with cooking and cleaning. Would you like to do that? I'll give you money every week."

Rosalie squeals and claps her hands. I notice Violet's arms across her body and the pout on her little face. She then rushes out of the house. Oh my!

I tell Rosalie that working with me is a secret and not to tell other girls. "You come on Monday, Tuesday, and Wednesday at six."

Emma thanks me and says Rosalie will be there. One down and one more to go. Now, it's time to talk with Ruth.

Ruth and I had met in the store when one of her young boys had knocked over some pots and pans. She is a cheerful woman with a full face in her mid-thirties with five children—three boys and two girls. Helen, her oldest, is twelve. From what Annie says, she would work hard, is quiet, no sass, "a good girl." With five children, the family could use the money.

Ruth, all five-feet nothing like Annie and me, comes to the door. Her little girl is beside her and says, "You play with me?"

Ruth chuckles and opens the door wider. "She's always lookin' for a playmate."

I walk inside and try to ignore the debris scattered on the counter and kitchen floor.

"Annie told me you might be stoppin' by. Somethin' about Helen workin' for you?"

"Yes, she can make some money. The boys go into the mine," I say while playing peek-a-boo with the little girl.

"She helps me out here. Doin' chores."

I feel the sweat on my forehead and upper lip. I thought Ruth would want the money for her family, but maybe she needs to talk it through with her husband. No, not Ruth.

"It'll only be three days a week. Just six in the morning until four. If you want, you can stop by on Saturday for the money, or I'll send it with Helen."

"Everyone can use money."

"Annie said Helen would be a good worker. Let her try it for a week or two. You can stop by and see what she's doing. If she doesn't like the work, or you think she's working too hard, I'll ask another girl."

I rush my words. My palms are sweaty. "Ruth, I'd like you not to tell the women in the patch. Let's keep this between the two of us and ask Helen to do the same?"

I don't want the other neighborhood girls to feel bad that I hadn't asked them. I can't give them all some work, although I wish I could.

Ruth gives me a knowing look. "When d'ya want her?"

"This Thursday at six. She'll work until four o'clock Thursday, Friday, and Saturday.

"She'll be there."

I can hear Gran's words as I walk home, "God helps those who help themselves," but I believe he wouldn't mind a little help now and then.

Ω

Spring is the time of the year I enjoy the most, smelling the air, seeing the sun coming up in the morning, watching everything turn green. The grapevines that frame both sides of the walkway are just sprouting leaves. I stroll over to the apple trees and reach to touch the puffs of flowers. There is a fenced-in area on the other side of the garden for the pig and cow and a chicken coop.

Joseph is looking at the vegetable garden where I have planted beets, potatoes, lettuce, and onions. Later on, I'll plant tomatoes and carrots and beans. The extras, and I'll make sure there are extras, I'll put in jars for the winter months or store in the root cellar. Oh, the thought of winter again. It just ended.

Looking under the cold frame, Joseph shouts, "Lettuce no up."

As I walk back towards the house, I call out to him, "I'm going inside to make sure supper isn't boiling over," and then realize he's missing. He's probably in the barn milking Betsy.

After taking the soup off the stove to cool, I walk into the parlor. I'm embroidering a pillowcase when Joseph walks in.

"What dat cost?"

"A few pennies. I used the egg money. I sold two extra dozen this week."

A look of worry appears on his face. "Need to watch money."

I grip the needle tighter in my hand. "I'm careful with the money. You're not going to make me pinch pennies. You don't want people calling you a tight-wad."

He runs his fingers through his hair. I know he isn't sure what pinching pennies mean or what a tight-wad is. I'm sure he doesn't want to know.

"No work, what we do? Can't live with egg money. I take care of t'ings and money."

Yes, he tries.

"We live most days on what's in the root cellar and what I've canned, the garden, chickens, eggs. I try to save if I can."

He continues to scowl and roars, "Must not spend!"

"Joseph, we have boarders. The hens are clucking and sitting on some eggs. I'm going to have more peeps to sell. I'm selling milk and cheese. I will do what I want!" I try to lower my voice but fail. "I won't be at the mercy of the COMPANY. The COMPANY will not run my life!" Although he allows the company to run his. But then he has no choice. I do!

He struts around the room, grumbling to himself as he pumps one fist into the other.

"You want to work in the mine, I can't change that, but I won't let them decide if we eat or not or sleep in a nice bed."

This could turn into a fight. I look up and try to smile.

"I like nice things, and sewing makes me feel good. It's my most favorite thing. Doesn't the house look pretty with things around?" That's an argument I'll never win. I don't think he cares, but I do.

He squeezes his calloused hand around mine and takes a deep breath. It's not about the money. I see fear in his eyes, fear of getting hurt, losing a leg, an arm, or even his life. What it is like to work in the mine he shares daily. His fears he keeps to himself.

On May 4, 1886, fifteen hundred workers demonstrated in Chicago to protest the killing of a striker by the Chicago police. About two hundred policemen tried to remove the workers. Someone threw a bomb. At least eight people, both police and protesters, died. Despite no evidence against them, eight labor activists were convicted of the bombing.

The newspapers called it an Anarchistic meeting and called the protesters Socialists. Those words were used by those against the union to describe workers asking to be paid a fair wage for the hours they worked, no more, no less.

Later the protest was named The Haymarket RIOT, another effort to inflame society, changing the word from PROTEST to RIOT. This event was a setback for the labor movement in America, which was fighting for an eight-hour workday and a fair wage.

May 1886

Annie walks in the door and within seconds says, "So, what's going on?"

I bite my lower lip. "Well, I'll tell you if you promise not to say anything."

Annie grins. "Me no tell. Promise! Tell, tell. You're gonna have babe? Does Joseph know?"

I hate to admit my condition to myself, let alone someone else. I'm not ready for a babe who looks to me to care for his or, hopefully, her every need. Then at other times, I imagine how it will be to cuddle a baby and, in time, have the love that died with my mother and then my Gramps.

"I told him two nights ago. He's over the moon."

Annie looks confused. "I mean he's happy. He wants lots of children." I heave a sigh. "But he can't explain to me how he's going to feed and clothe them."

"Bet Joseph'll be a good father."

Sometimes I wonder. "Just because a man wants children doesn't mean he'll be a good father. I think Joseph wants to see himself in his children." Where did that thought come from?

"I bet he wants a boy, like Nick."

Ω

Clouds are beginning to gather. Joseph, Gerhard, Mike, and Billy walk out the back door, leaving the comfort of the kitchen, ready to trudge to the mine. Joseph stoops over and rubs his cramped knees, and then stretches his back.

I walk along with them into the patch to deliver eggs before starting my chores. A gust of wind and coal dust swirls, a reminder that as we pass through the kitchen door, we are entering a different world.

In an instant, drops of rain hit us in the face and bounce off Joseph's hat, sending out a tapping sound. My umbrella is doing little to protect me.

We come alongside the other miners racing to the mine as the rain comes down harder. On some days, there is conversation, even occasional laughter, as they try to rip away the sadness and fear they feel walking toward the mine. Most days, though, they drag themselves mute, each lost in their thoughts and steeling themselves for the hard day ahead.

I notice a young boy tagging alongside his father. "So, your son goin' into mine," Joseph shouts to John, thc boy's father.

"Yah! He's gonna be a nipper."

"Ready for that, son?" Joseph puts his hand on the little boy's shoulder. The boy does not answer. "You're twelve?" The boy still does not answer and keeps his head down.

There is torment on John's face. "His mother wants him in school, but we need money."

Being a nipper, the boy will sit on a bench alone outside the heavy wooden door of one of the chambers in the mine. The rumbling sound of empty or full cars heading into the chamber signals him to open the door and then close it after the cars pass through.

John slaps his son's arm. "Long day for a young boy by 'imself in the dark. No one there to talk to, but with four girls…."

"Boys get fired for fallin' asleep. Rats'll keep him awake," Joseph ekes out a chuckle.

"Year after year nothin' changes." John sighs as he looks down at his son.

"That's why the COMPANY never show their faces," I moan, not able to stay quiet. "But even if they saw how we live, would they care?"

Joseph nudges me in the ribs. This is his time to talk. "NEVER! Don't care, look greedy," he says, rubbing his fingers together. "Laughing all the way to bank."

John nods. "And we never laugh."

Another miner comes up beside the four of us. "Another day, another nickel."

"What nickel? Another penny." Joseph flashes a grin, but they all know that the low wage they make is not funny.

"Looks like you're not movin' that well," Joseph says to Pete.

"Bones achin' and hip hurts."

"Spendin' the day hunched over in the damp," John growls.

I turn to deliver my eggs as they continue down the road to the mine. At the entrance, each miner will pick up a circular metal disc with his number. The disc keeps track of the miners when they're in the mine. It is also attached to the mine car to record each miner's tons of coal.

Every morning the disc reminds the miners of the danger. In times of disaster, it is used to identify the bodies if they cannot be recognized. It also lets the supervisors know who is still in the mine if the tag is on the mining car. Every day the disc is a reminder of their mortality.

June 1886

It is just after six in the morning. It's still 1886, but it seems more like ten years since I married Joseph instead of only two. Mike has pumped a bucket of water from the well. He fed and watered all the animals, milked the cow, and collected the eggs from the hen house.

Joseph hurt his back two days ago, so he's resting uncomfortably. Mike's not only doing Joseph's chores but some of mine as well. He is heaven-sent.

The morning light is streaming in, making the kitchen glow like a ball of sunshine. A pot of coffee is boiling on the stove. I'm frying some eggs with one hand and helping Rosalie pack the dinner pails when Gerhard and Stan plop down at the table.

Stan looks over at me and ekes out a smile. Artie brought him to my door yesterday, and he became my fifth boarder. His eyes are sunken, with dark circles underneath. His hair, what there is at the sides, hasn't been cut in months, and his gray beard isn't trimmed. His boots are worn, and his coat is tattered and frayed at the edges. His belt buckle is moved in two notches, and his pants are gathered at his waist. I look at him, trying not to imagine all the hardships in his life and what brought him here.

I pour some coffee and place a bowl of bread chunks on the table. "When do you think you'll have enough money to bring your wife and child here, Gerhard?"

Last month he decided to bring his wife and son to America instead of returning to his country. The money he can save depends on the amount of coal he can load each day and whether he can work. Two years seems unlikely, and I just wonder if he'll live long enough.

Tony, who took the last bed, wobbles in. He always walks as though his feet are hurting, and they probably are. When he arrived at the door, he asked if I could cook pasta and if I had any Italian cheeses? I said no to the pasta, no to the cheese, but he is boarding anyway.

Behind Tony walks Billy whistling a tune. When he appeared at our back door, I didn't know he would bring some happiness to the house. He whistles morning and night to my delight. His favorites are Camp Town Races and While Strolling Through the Park One Day. Yesterday, he started whistling a new tune—Good Night Ladies. Tony hums along and is trying to learn the words, so he can sing to his girlfriend.

Pretending to be irritated by Billy's whistling, I cover my ears with my hands. According to Annie, he's the best looking of my boarders. All the young girls in the patch walk past the house to get a look. He has a smile that lights up the room, is clean-shaven, and has arms that would keep a girl safe.

I bang a pan on the stove to get their attention. "So, you do want breakfast this morning?" They all look at the cuckoo clock on the kitchen wall and realize they are late.

Mike grabs the pot and pours coffee all around. "I heard you were at the Darr Mine, Tony? Wasn't that the first mine in this area?"

"Yup, opened in 1850," he says, smacking his lips on the bread he is chomping down.

I lift the burner plate and stoke the coals. "So, why did you leave?"

Stan shouts out, "Why we all leave. Tired of being paid in scrip. Thought it better here."

Artie's crutches are clicking the wooden floorboards. Joseph appears behind me and gives me a nip on my cheek. I feel a warm blush cover my face and shove him away. I believe he does that to make sure the boarders, especially Mike, know I am his.

He pours himself coffee. "So, what d'ya think of the demands we're makin' to the company?"

Billy shouts out, "Ain't sure! What are they?"

Joseph shoots him a baffled look and shakes his head. He probably can't believe that a miner wouldn't know what the miners are asking for, and some don't care. They know nothing will change.

"Want portal-to-portal pay. Got to lay track for the wagon. Got to clean up the slate after blast. Hell, spend most day doin' that. Why get paid for jist the tons of coal in car? Should pay for hours we dig and blast… load and clean up. Has to be done."

"Joseph!" Mike shouts. "They only want to pay for what makes money. Tons of coal."

Stan nods his head at Joseph. "Yeah, but Joseph's got a point, but won't we make the company mad askin' for that?"

Joseph punches his fist into his other hand. "Hell! Can't ask for anythin'. Always NO. In April, miners loaded almost 7,000 tons of coal. In May, five top miners earned $156 for 262 tons. What d'ya think the minin' company got for it?"

Stan shakes his head. "Rich get richer. Want to keep it. Don't need big house, fancy clothes, but they want it."

"Hell, I'm happy jist to have a job," Tony snaps. "Got a girl and can't marry her. Must save some money."

Mike catches my eye and winks again. We have often talked about the demands of the miners. We agreed that the mining company would never cave in and give the miners better wages and shorter hours. Portal-to-portal pay is a dream, but a good one.

Joseph waves a fist, ready to punch someone. "Mike, you always for COMPANY?"

Mike grapples with keeping quiet or not, fearing that Joseph will ask him to leave the house. I told him that he has a right to say what he wants even if Joseph disagrees. I've told him I decide who boards, not Joseph. Yet, we both know it would be easier for me if he and Joseph didn't get into a scuffle.

I shout across the kitchen as I stand at the stove, one hand gripping the edge of the bowl and the other pouring the eggs into the pan. "Remember what happened in Chicago at the Haymarket Strike. The workers decided to march for an eight-hour day."

Joseph roars, "Hell, we can't even get ten hours."

I look over at Joseph. "People were marching. Police lined up. There was an explosion. A bomb, a grenade. There was gunfire. Police and marchers were shot or killed by the bomb. Bodies everywhere." I'm surprised at how loud my voice has become.

"That's not gonna happen here. We jist want to talk to 'em, make 'em see what we want." Joseph's shouting is getting louder. He pounds his fist on the table, rattling the plates.

Mike clears his throat, and Joseph turns in his direction. "I remember now. Six, maybe seven, were sentenced to death. One didn't want to be hung, so he committed suicide in jail. They never knew who threw the bomb."

I nod agreement and put enough eggs and bread on each plate to keep their stomachs from growling until their noon meal. "Some got life in prison, and some were hanged. Those who marched were called violent, rebels by the newspapers, convicted of conspiracy."

Stan pulls on his chin. "What's that?"

Mike hesitates before speaking. "It means that they were scheming, ahhh, plotting against the company."

I nod. "The newspapers made people think the workers were in the wrong, that they were bad people."

Mike leans forward in his chair, running his burly finger around the edge of his coffee cup. "Yeah, but Joseph's right. We can't ask for anything. Josephine's right. Everyone's against us. If they aren't, the newspapers and politicians make sure they are."

Nothing Mike or I say will stop Joseph's rant once a week or more. He has said again and again that the company would never know about the conditions in the mine if the miners didn't tell them.

Joseph pulls out a handkerchief and rubs the moistness from his brow. "So, you think we should keep our mouths shut," he says, almost choking on the bread he has just put in his mouth.

I move towards him. "If you ask and walk away with nothing, then what do you do?"

I have never told him that the miners are too weak to force any demands on the mine owners. If they strike and the mine owner still says NO, then what? Walk away and let their families starve or go back to work. If they go back to work, it weakens the miners for years to come. You give in once, you'll give in again, and the mine owners know that.

Joseph shoots daggers at the boarders around the table. "So, you agree with Mike and Josephine? We should do nothin'?"

I step closer to Joseph. "You believe the company will give you something just because you ask for it. Well, they won't. So, the miners will have to walk away or go on strike and march around, hoping and wishing things will change while families starve."

He turns and limps out the door, grabbing his boots.

I shoo the boarders out of their chairs. "Well, you're not making money sitting here. Go. Give me some peace and quiet."

My upset with Joseph, even anger at times, is that he wants to cause more pain for the miners and their families. The miners are weak—not in spirit. They just don't hold anything in their hands that the coal barons can't get somewhere else.

If the coal barons paid the miners a fair wage and treated them with some decency, there would be no begging, no hunger, no unions, no bloodshed. But they aren't decent men. They need to keep the miners in line, and the miners' begging and their denying show they are in charge. Such big men pick on the poor and the hungry.

If I could have a wish come true, but when do wishes ever come true? In one way, Joseph and I agree. The miners have to do something, but what is that something?

July 1886

Once the house is empty, I sit down with Rosalie, who arrived late this morning. I put some bread and an egg in front of her. The young girl eats so quickly that she chokes twice.

She hands me her plate.

"Do you know to say thank you?"

She looks at me, puzzled. "When someone gives you something nice, you say 'thank you." It tells them you are thankful for what they gave you."

She smiles up at me and, just above a whisper, says, "Thank you."

I touch her hair. "Now go upstairs and take the sheets off the beds. Can you do that?"

She races up the stairs like a jackrabbit being chased by a fox. I'm teaching her sums in the afternoon once our chores are done. That's a secret.

Outside I pump several big pots of water and place them on the fire. After gathering all the mining clothes, I scrub them in cold water to get out the worst of the coal dust.

Rosalie joins me after collecting the sheets. Stooping over the tub, I look up into a too-thin face with deep black eyes. I stop scrubbing the clothes to stretch my back and rub my belly. In these moments, I realize I've been putting the thoughts of having a baby out of my mind.

Shocked back to my chores by Betsy's mooing, I look down at Rosalie. "Help me pour out this black water, and we'll fill the tub again."

We scrub the mining clothes one more time to remove the worst of the dirt and then dump them into a tub of warm water. We scrub the clothes again with the soap I make with lye and bacon grease.

When they are as clean as possible, we rinse them and hang them on the line. We do the same with the sheets and towels. I am thankful we only wash the miners' clothes once a week, and even that's too often. If I had to do it more, my body would buckle with pain and collapse.

With the laundry done, we go into the garden. We pick the biggest and ripest tomatoes. Using the fire in the outdoor stove, I show Rosalie how to blanch the skin of the tomatoes and peel and cut them up. Once the tomatoes are stewed, I put a small bowl of bread and stewed tomatoes in front of her and pour her a cool glass of milk. She gulps it down without waiting for it to cool, burning her mouth.

Before Rosalie leaves, I touch her head and thank her for her hard work. I then place an extra five cents in her hand and hand her a bag of tomatoes.

"This was a good day for both of us," I mutter as the young girl walks down the road.

August 1886

At three in the morning, I give up trying to sleep. Counting sheep has made me more awake, and the sun will not be up for several hours. I toss back the covers, grab my shawl, and creep down the stairs. I collapse on the settee and pick up the booties I'm crocheting.

Some of my sadness growing up came from not having a family with my brothers in it, and I would like that to change. Having decided to try and mend fences, I had written a letter asking Rosie to come for dinner with my brothers.

I wonder how I will get through the day. My aunt and brothers are finally coming to visit. Thinking about Rosie has brought on some edginess. Every bone in my body feels tense, and my head is starting to ache.

During the reading of Gramps' will, we all learned what Gran knew. Before his death, Gramps had put the house in my name and left me all the furnishings. Aunt Rosie, my two brothers, and me had been left sums of money.

Outraged at this news and convinced I had swayed Gramps, Rosie shouted I would never see my brothers again. She had kept that promise. Is there anything worse than being cast aside by your family? Is there anything more hateful?

Throughout my childhood, Gran and Gramps had always dreaded Rosie's visits. She would walk in and bark out orders to Gran and whine about how hard it was to raise two boys and take care of the house. Because Rosie was their only living daughter and had two of their grandchildren in her care, Gran and Gramps did not want to fall out with her. They believed the only way to keep her happy was to put up with her nonsense and give her whatever she wanted.

Her husband is a quiet man and always has a kind word for me. He works for the mill near Braddock and seems good to my brothers. Rosie has seldom spoken to me over the last ten years, and when she does, her voice always has an edge. I believe there is something more behind her coldness to me, but Gran had never been willing to talk about Rosie and my mother.

When I tried to explain to Rosie about the house, she snapped at me, "You're just like your mother." I smiled inside. That was the only nice thing she ever said to me.

Ω

Awakened from my thoughts by giant crows flying overhead, I look down the path to see Rosie and my brothers walking up the road. I think Frank looks somewhat like my father.

My feet cannot move, and I can speak no words as Rosie steps onto the front porch. She stares into my eyes. That glare is the way she always unsettled my grandparents.

"So, how's married life?"

"Hi, Frank and Fred." Frank smiles, and Fred's eyes peer out from under his long eyelashes, gazing at me as if he wants a hug. Such nice-looking young boys—almost men. Our parents would be proud. Although my brothers have been fed and clothed these last twelve years, they have a look of sadness, especially my younger brother.

Rosie motions to silence them. "So, you married him to please my mother before she died?"

I can't believe she is questioning why I got married. Would the reason she married be any different?

"I married him because he's nice and he would take care of me and Gran."

She looks at my belly and then turns away. "Nice doesn't put food on the table."

No words come. In time I reply in a soft voice, "We're warm and not hungry."

"You and Ma could've sold the house and moved in with us. Then you could've waited to marry."

My body stiffens. Rosie never made that offer before, so telling me now is a little late.

My grandparents were hoping I would be married and settled by the time either of them passed away, but that was not to be. So, during Gramps' illness, the three of us talked about Gran and me moving into Rosie's eight-room house.

Gran was unbending. If Rosie made such an offer, she would refuse. "I'd be afraid to make a move in her house. Hell would be cooler," she said many times.

Gramps had no doubt that Gran would give Rosie too much money for giving us a home, but it would never be enough for Rosie. They both feared she would turn me into Cinderella, having me cook and clean, barking orders. Then once Gran had died, I'd be expected to do all the chores or be put out on the street.

"So, why did you ask us here?"

I've gone over again and again what I want to say, but will I be able to stay calm?

"Let's go in." I look at the brothers I do not know as brothers. They're just young boys living with my aunt. How sad for all of us!

"Frank and Fred. Why don't you go out to the barn and meet Betsy, the cow, and the pig? See if there are eggs in the nest and give some hay to Betsy." With no dawdling, they race out to the backyard.

"Aunt Rosie, I want to ask you about my mother. Gran and Gramps told me so little about her. What was she like?"

Rosie's eyes widen, surprised by my question. Good!

She paces around the kitchen, pretending to look out the window while I set the table. "Mary was always by Mum's side. She helped with the cooking and sewing and hardly ever said a word. In the evening, she and Pa would play games and read."

"Were you close to my mother?" Again, I'm stunned that this question came out of my mouth.

"I never said we weren't close."

She glares at me. The initial upset I felt when she arrived begins to be replaced by fear. What I fear, I don't know.

"You know, Josephine, I would have raised you along with your brothers, but my parents wanted you. I guess they wanted to raise your mother all over again," her voice almost a whisper.

"Did my mother do anything to hurt you?"

Rosie is silent.

"Did she do something to make you angry?"

I'm surprised by my cheek. I walk to the kitchen door, standing with my back to her. Watching my brothers petting Betsy relaxes me.

"I took her boys, didn't I?"

I turn around and stare at her, resisting the desire to knock the silly hat she's wearing off her head. Deciding not to ask any more questions, I put soup bowls on the table and call my brothers to come in to eat.

I ask my brothers about school and what they want to do when they are grown. Frank is very talkative, answering Fred's questions as well. I chuckle, thinking of Annie's twin Sophia.

After the boys gobble the apple pie, I show my aunt my embroidery and offer her the last quilt Gran had made. It's a small gesture, but I have to offer something. She refuses. Probably not fancy enough or she wants to hurt me one more time.

Before they leave, I ask Rosie about getting together every month or two. She shakes her head. "I'm busy raising the boys, taking care of the house. Then there's Henry's family. I stop in on them every day."

She shouts for Freddie and Frank and starts to move towards the door. It's awkward, but I hug my brothers. I watch them walking down the street towards the train station. Why did she come today? Did she want to hurt me once again? The tears I have held back for so long start to flow.

September 1886

Boys and girls are playing in the streets, yelling and jousting, hopefully forgetting for those moments the hunger that gnaws at their bellies. The air is continually being assaulted by the coal dust and that damn whistle. It is now blowing to end the Saturday shift.

The miners are like a swarm of bees, whistling, laughing, and joking, glad that another week has ended without an explosion or fatality or serious injury. Like the tragedies, this time of day is played over and over in the coal patches on Saturday evening.

After six days of work, the one day off is never enough to rest their weary bodies, but it is all they have. The house is quiet and cozy, and the warmth from the stove greets Joseph as he walks into the kitchen. A large round galvanized tub sits in the center of the floor, and several big pots of water are boiling on the stove.

Joseph empties his pocket and throws the money into the handkerchief on the table. I hand a few dollars back for smokes and drink, wrap the rest, and tuck it into my bosom.

Joseph steps in front of the stove to get warm, waving his hands over the burners. "Not more pay. Lots of slate. Do a lot of blastin' to get coal."

I pour the steaming water into the tub that already holds two buckets of cold water. "This is hot enough." He unbuttons his shirt, pulls down his suspenders, and strips to his waist.

To remove the coal dust sticking to his eyelashes, he kneels on the floor and lathers his face. He cups his hands full of water onto his face to remove the soap. Then he lathers and rinses again two more times. His eyes are now stinging and red.

While I scrub his back, he scrubs his chest and arms with a brush. His muscles tighten and ripple. He removes his pants and long underwear as I pour more hot water into the tub. He shivers as he steps in and squats down.

Once bathed, I grab the towel, warming on the oven door handle, and hand it to him. While he is drying his chest and legs, I dry his back. We then hurry upstairs to get ready for the dance tonight, leaving the kitchen to the boarders for their weekly bath.

Ω

Walking into the social hall, we join the miners and their families who will make merry for a few hours. The music is bouncing off the walls, which are dark brown and plain. The only relief is from the lit candles. I see a three-man band set up in the corner and the bar about ten feet away. Several couples are strutting around the dance floor which is getting more crowded.

"I'm gonna go be with men," shouts Joseph as he walks away towards the bar.

"We only just got here," but he does not hear, or he does not want to hear.

Through the music, voices are filling the room. Hands are flying in the air. Toddlers are chasing after each other. Girls of marrying age are wearing clean dresses with ribbons in their hair. They sit on chairs with their backs straight and hands crossed on their laps.

Oh, being a young girl waiting to be asked to dance. Waiting, waiting, waiting. It reminds me of Victorian England that I read about in Jane Austen's books. But instead of lyrical music and silks and brocade, there are waltzes and polkas, and girls wearing hand-me-down drab cotton dresses washed too many times.

How sad that young girls have to line themselves up, waiting for a boy or young man to choose one of them. They don't believe they can choose whether or not to be with a man—at least at such a young age. Just like boys who are expected to go into the mine, get work somewhere to help their families, young girls are to marry, and the sooner, the better.

Men are hanging on to each other, some singing with the music. For a few hours tonight, the men will wash down the coal dust with some drink. The women will put away the dishtowels and forget their worries. Children have a chance to be children, having escaped the drudgery of their evening chores.

At the edge of the dance floor, little boys and girls are prancing around. They step on each other's feet, mimicking the dance steps of the elders. Some of the boys are rolling around on the floor. Young girls are caring for the little ones so their mothers and older sisters can dance. Shouts of greetings and conversations are heard from every corner of the large room.

The gossips are huddled in a corner, sending smirks in all directions. For whatever reason, there will always be women who band together against other women. I guess if they're talking about someone else, no one will notice who they really are.

Emma's eyes twinkle as she walks into the room. She has a lovely face with smooth, unblemished skin, and like some women, she will not age before her time. Her dress is quite snug around her middle. I hope she isn't pregnant again, but maybe she would be angry about my hoping. She enjoys being a mother, at times a little too much. She's like my hens chasing their chicks about the yard.

I smile, watching Annie and her husband Nick spin around the dance floor. Their twins are trying to mimic their dance moves. Nick's black curly hair is slicked down, showing off his high cheekbones. Where did the girls get that ginger hair?

Emma touches my arm, "Look at Annie in new dress. She said you help her make."

I gaze at Emma's boyish figure. "If you want, I can help you make one."

"Don't have money for cloth." She looks down at her threadbare dress. Her shoes are worn at the toes.

"Next time there's a dance, I'll give you a shawl to wear over your dress. I also have some of my Gran's dresses that might fit you. They still have lots of wear left in them. It would make me feel good if I could give one to you."

During her visits, Emma told me how quiet she had been as a young girl. Seeing how alone she was, her brother showed her how to throw a ball and climb trees. She was shy but thrilled, saying that she ran as fast as any boy her age and could swing an ax and chop wood. She was called what I translated into "tomboy." Hard to imagine!

At the age of thirteen, Emma decided she wanted to have children. To have children, she had to get married. At her mother's urging and wanting to be a mother, she put aside her tomboy ways and looked for a husband. After giving birth to four children, her stick shape still remains.

"Next time you come by, we'll go through the trunk. Where's your husband?"

Her face blushes pink. "John is over there by the man with a bald spot and mustache." She points to a group of men gathered near the makeshift bar.

John is tall but would not be sought out by women for his face. Emma says he is kind to their children and works hard. She didn't know her babes would be hungry all their young years.

Emma pokes her elbow in my ribs and points to Rosalie. "I've been tryin' to teach her how to dance all week. She just doesn't like boys. I don't think she wants to get married, and she doesn't want to have children!"

"She may marry and have children in time. Let's hope not soon."

"It was whispered that my gran had a sister who liked girls. I don't think Rosalie likes girls, but she isn't looking for a boyfriend either."

"The word patience comes to mind."

Annie comes running towards us, panting, beads of sweat on her forehead and lips. "Isn't this grand? It's like a wedding! The music, the people!"

"The noise," I snicker. But Annie is right.

I notice several men who've had too much to drink, tripping over their own feet. One of them tumbles to the floor, and the others struggle to help him up despite their own drunkenness.

"Look at Ernie over there with those girls hangin' on him. They better watch out," Annie barks into my ear. "He's got about ten hands. He'll have one of them up their dresses if they're not careful."

I look around and see Ernie, six feet tall and all muscles. "His eyebrows look like two fuzzy caterpillars," I say, chuckling. "I wouldn't want his hands on me. Scary!"

"These girls'll never learn. Now, I'm gonna get Nick to dance."

I see Ruth walking towards me just as Joseph grabs my hand. "How about a dance?"

"Only if it's a slow one."

His gaze lingers on my face for a moment. He pulls me close as he can, and I inhale his aftershave as we spin around the floor. "So, havin' nice time?"

I nod and close my eyes. The warmth of Joseph's body and his lips on my cheek relax me. When the music stops, Joseph returns to the men gathered in a corner. Ruth motions for me to join her and a woman whose chestnut brow hair hangs loose around her face. She cannot stop fluffing it with her hands.

"Josephine, this is Florence. She lives a few houses from me. Moved in a week ago."

"So, you 'ave any children?" Florence says.

"No, not yet. Just the one I'm carrying," I say, touching my belly, feeling the babe kick.

"I've two little girls. Made me so fat. Where's your husband?"

Ruth pipes up, "He's the good lookin' tall one over there. Light hair, mustache."

"So is my husband. He's.... Not sure...." She spies him talking to several young girls and rushes over to him. She grabs his arm and pushes him onto the dance floor.

Ruth chuckles, "She doesn't let him out of her sight."

My eyes study Florence and her husband. "I do like her dress."

"She made it. I think she's a good sewer," Ruth says. "Not as good as you but good."

I see the sorrow in Florence's face, some hurt buried deep within. So many women, so sad, so injured. Over the next hour, I talk with Ruth and Bella and meet their families. I dance with Nick and Mike and Annie and Joseph, surprised that I am enjoying myself.

Joseph walks over, motioning me again to the dance floor. "Joseph, I think it's time for us to go. My feet are hurting, and my ankles are swollen." I look around the room. "Annie's good for another two hours. Let's sneak out before she sees me."

Once outside, I look up to the stars and whisper to Betty, "Did I do right?"

November 1886

The past few months of my pregnancy had zapped my energy, but I still got up every morning and did what I had to do. I've not felt like picking up a pen, but I want to record this time in my life. Giving birth to my firstborn will never happen again.

On October 28, my water broke. Mrs. Baloh, the midwife, arrived ten minutes later and said it would be quick. "It's good it's comin' early. Won't be too big. Make it easy for you. Joseph away," she shouted.

Annie was by my side, putting a cold cloth on my head. Mrs. B, as we warmly call her, told me when to push and breathe and push again. The pains came more often, and within a half-hour, Annie shouted to Joseph, "It's a boy."

The cord was cut, and with a slap, the babe wailed. Annie placed him in my arms. I looked down at my son. He was so tiny, so in need of caring.

Mrs. B touched my little boy's head and smiled at me, "You'll git that girl."

I growled, "What's so good about a woman's life?"

Annie patted my hand. "That's pain talkin."

Mrs. B shook her head. "She's right. We clean, cook, can, plant garden, care for children, wash clothes, bake bread, bathe husband and children.... Whew!"

"Josephine likes doin' those things," Annie giggled.

Mrs. B snapped, "We all do them because we have to. No maid has shown up at my house."

She was right about my wanting to have a girl to fuss over. I'm still not sure I'll know what to do with a boy.

At that moment, I realized I had missed having my brothers in my life and being a big sister. I had put that thought aside for years. I never wanted to dwell on how my family was torn apart when I was five.

I was awake that night, feeling as though my body would never be without pain again. When my babe cried, I remembered I was a mother, and I had a son. I tossed and turned, realizing I had no idea how to be a mother.

Joseph's steel-blue eyes glowed the following morning as he gazed at me nursing our newborn son. He reached for a pillow to place beneath my head and then touched the fuzz on our son's head. "Nice boy," he said in wonder, and I rejoiced as I nodded my head.

"He's gonna be like you, Joseph. I would like to name him William after my Gramps."

"William," he whispered and then realized he was late getting up. He jumped out of bed, stripping the blanket from his body. He pulled on his worn work pants, leaving the suspenders hanging at his side. He gave me a parting kiss as I tried to get out of bed.

"No, no, stay in bed. Ask Annie to do breakfast."

"Annie in my kitchen?" My body went limp. I was too tired to care.

December 1886

The morning light broke as I lay still listening to the sound of the wind. I reach across the bed for Joseph but change my mind when I hear him purring, his arms wrapped around his feather pillow. I inch out of bed, quiet as a ghost.

After slipping into my dress, I wrap the black mane of my hair that hangs below my shoulders around my fingers and pin it high on my head. William is in his bassinet, cooing and gurgling. I pick him up and tiptoe downstairs.

Elena, my new girl, is starting today. A few months after William's birth, I decided I wanted someone to help me in the evenings for a few hours. Emma's daughter, Rosalie preferred to work supper time, so that worked out fine. Then I hired Bella's daughter Elena to help me during the day. I like the girl's laughter and how she speaks her mind.

A few minutes after I enter the kitchen, Elena is at the back door. Her dress is worn and fraying at the elbows. She looks like she has just rolled out of bed. I don't have to wonder if she has eaten any breakfast. Bella feeds her children when she has food, but often there's not enough. I hand her a piece of buttered bread.

Mike walks into the kitchen and flashes a smile at Elena. "So, how ya' doin' honey?"

When Annie first saw Mike, she said he looked like a lion on the prowl, but we both agree he's a good-looking lion.

"Now, Mike, you know my rules."

I give Elena a gentle smile. The young girl smiles back, her brown eyes twinkling. "Elena, why don't you start making the sandwiches for the dinner pails? Cut some more slices of bread."

Joseph and the boarders arrive one by one. None of them say a word to Elena as she puts some bread on the table. They are heeding my warning that they will not be given breakfast if they bother my girls. Mike is harmless and has a special place in my heart, so he's an exception.

Stan shouts as everyone begins to sit down. "Did you hear they're callin' anybody askin' for more money and formin' a union Communists?"

Tony's booming voice rings out. "Oh, the big bad Communists."

Joseph's eyes are afire. "Wantin' a livin' wage. Nothin' to do with Communism!"

Mike coughs and leans forward, his voice reassuring. "It does to some, Joseph. Some think that if you speak out against capitalist tyranny, you've got to be a Communist."

I look across the kitchen at the boarders, my stomach tightening. "Most folks don't know what that word means and why they should be afraid of it. They've just been told it's bad. Those damn newspapers."

Mike nods. "They're tryin' to get folks against the workers by calling them names. Rumor is Cleveland was once in a Communist cell. No one's talkin' about that."

I nod. "That's a rumor, but whether he was or not, Cleveland's not on the side of the worker. His heart is as cold as a block of ice. He's not a president for all people." I pause and breathe in, feeling flushed.

I had read in the newspaper about farmers in Texas losing all their crops. Congress passed a bill to give them money to buy seed. Cleveland wouldn't sign the bill. He said they shouldn't be given anything and make their own way. He didn't care that the grain prices would go up, hurting the poor folks and the country.

"She's right," Tony shouts.

Mike shouts louder, his expression twitchy, "When has any president been for all the people? President Cleveland is anti-union, and he's not willing to help anyone who needs help."

Cleveland said hardship builds character. What does he know about hardship, about character? Hardship doesn't build anything. It just tells us about that man or woman.

Some poor people steal, harm other people. Others will try to find a way to make money, to change things. They may even give their last piece of bread to someone starving.

The rich also make different choices. Some rich people are generous, give their money to others, pay their workers a fair wage. Others grind the workers' souls into the ground.

Joseph glares at me as I begin to talk. This is his chance to show the boarders that he's the man of the house. I'm to be quiet.

He straightens up to his full height and sips the dark brewed coffee. His face is red, and he looks like he's about to explode. "Coal barons makin' more money than they kin spend. Don't care people starvin' and neither does the government. Don't care about hurtin' workers. Mean devils. Burn in hell."

Tony tugs at the beard he has decided to grow. "Not soon enough."

Joseph is glaring at me again, willing me to be silent. For better or worse, I must speak. "The miners and their families are the ones living under Communist rule. If you get paid in scrip and have to buy in the company store, pay rent to the company, and everything is owned by the company, isn't that some kind of Communism? Everything is owned by the company. No competition."

Now riled, Tony's neck reddens. He shifts in his chair and lets us a heavy sigh, "No one will help us!"

Mike sits back and nods agreement, his look somber. "No one will fight for the miners."

"Not even the miners," Joseph snarls.

Seeing the time, they finish breakfast and one-by-one scurry out the door. Feeding the boarders and packing their dinner pails is the part of my day I have to endure. Once there is quiet, my day begins again, and it begins with Annie.

Her first words this morning as she walks through the door. "Heard they're puttin' a bathhouse at the mine so men can wash up before they come home. Can't wait!" She squeals so loud that Pallie runs to the other side of the room.

"It's about time. A woman running the mine, it would be the first thing she would do."

"Don't think Nick will use it. I'll make sure boarders do."

"Well, Joseph will be washing up there during the week. So will the boarders, including Saturday. By the way, how are your two boarders?"

"I've put the twins in front room on first floor. Nick doesn't want them in our bedroom. I'm jist happy the men aren't around after supper."

With the social room open at night, the husbands and boarders can spend their evenings there. They have a chance to gripe and groan with others who know their hardships and struggles. Often, they drink too much. I told my boarders if any of them came home drunk, they would have to sleep in the barn with Betsy and the pig.

I know that drinking is the only way to take away the taste of coal dust and the smell and ugliness of the mine, and it's the only way to cover up their fears. Annie and I never talk about our own fears.

January 1887

Taking care of William fills my days, but this morning I woke up early with a feeling of wanting to belong to something outside myself. Now, maybe I can get that feeling to include other women in the patch. I'm not like Annie wanting to make friends with everyone, but I want to bring women together to help each other.

A morning of decisions is what I need. Betty has been gone more than six months. She left me with a mantra to awaken the patch, do something to change the plight of the women and children! Doing something to ease their burden, brighten their days, accomplish something besides the mundane chores of the day would be honoring Betty, but what can I do?

Within me, somewhere, there has always been the desire to have some women friends, not just any women. I've watched their kindnesses toward each other's children and the laughter they share. I've always been fine on my own and enjoy my quiet time. Then Annie came into my life. Now she and her twins take up part of my day with sewing, cooking, and laughter. I would not change a minute of that time together.

I don't try to be different, but maybe I am. I cannot change myself into what I'm not, so the women will like me. These thoughts have been swirling in my head until there's a numbing pain behind my eyes. Then a wave of clear-headedness sweeps over me.

March 1887

I treasure these few moments of contentment as I sit down in a quiet space, pen in hand. It's a rare warm day in late March, warm enough to enjoy the sun and warm breeze coming across the hills. Then I see the coal dust rising in the air, the green hills of pastureland blighted by progress.

The industrial age they're calling it. The workers have other words, but the words, industrial age, are ringing throughout this country. They have taken on holiness, a beacon of what is right and good, of what this country must strive to become. Yet, there isn't any thought about those who pay with blood and sweat and sometimes their lives for that progress.

William is bundled up in the bassinet. He looks up at me every time I beat the rug with a wire broom.

"Is that your mother-in-law's head you're hitting?" Annie chuckles, peeking her head around the corner of the house.

I want to say, "Oh, how I wish," but maybe I need to put aside my feelings. After William's birth, I agreed to go with Joseph on his visits to his mother so she could see her grandson. I want to remind her that I gave Joseph his son, but nothing has changed.

With her few words of English, she asks Joseph questions without listening to the answers. That goes on for about twenty minutes. Then she starts in on me, telling me in a gruff voice about what food Joseph likes. Then she makes her daughter write out recipes, which she shoves in my face.

I look around. "Where are the girls?"

"Left them at Emma's to play. Isn't it good a school bein' built? Want the girls to go."

I sigh. "Finally! Only one big room. All the children of all ages together. How much will they learn? Better than nothing, I guess."

Annie picks up William and bounces him on her lap. He smiles and claps his hands, making her chuckle. "Some children aren't going to go. Fathers want them in the mines."

"The COM—PA—NY— will be happy. If children don't learn, they'll always have the uneducated who can't do anything else but work in the mines and the mills. They want to keep them with no schooling and hungry, so they'll do any dirty job."

I stop. They can think, and they can learn. But without a school, they won't learn how to read or write much or do sums, so they must use their backs. And strong backs are what the industrial age needs.

"So, something's on your mind, Josephine. I can tell by the wrinkles right there." She pokes at my forehead.

"Annie, I'm thinking of starting a sewing circle. Women get together and make a quilt. Then we'll sell it."

Imagine how the lives of women could be changed. Coming together for a few hours, away from their hum-drum chores. Working together. Doing something to help feed and clothe their children.

Annie raises her eyebrows. "You don't make enough money selling cheese, milk, eggs," she counts them on her fingers, "and housing boarders?"

My heart sinks. Didn't Annie hear me? I thought she would be happy for a chance to be with other women.

I try not to glare at her. "I don't do those things JUST for the money! I do those things, so my days won't be the same. I want to make the most of what I can. The sewing circle is not just about money either."

It is then I realize that everything Annie and the other wives do daily is about surviving. Nothing is for joy. They have no way to save for tomorrow. They only know now.

Annie wraps both hands around her coffee cup and holds it to her lips. I want her to share in my joy, but she is silent, so unlike Annie.

She breaks the silence when she yelps. "Where would they git material and thread and find the time? Where would you sell?" She chuckles, "So, you know."

Hmmm. Finally, questions Annie cannot answer.

"All of us will make the first quilt, and I will take it to the store to be sold. Fancy ladies like nice things. Last week I spoke with a store owner. He'll sell whatever handiwork we do for what he calls a commission. That means he'll give us some money, and he'll keep the rest."

Annie raises her eyebrows. "Will he cheat?"

I have been worried about that, but I've come to treasure and trust my feeling about people. For now, I will believe he's an honest man.

Instead of asking Annie to trust my hunch, I say, "Let's hope he needs us as much as we need him and hope for the best. I'll use my money to buy the cloth for the first quilt. Before I give each woman her share, I'll take out some money to pay me back for the material and to buy material for the next quilt."

Annie is silent, so I stay silent. It is shattered when Annie mutters, "What if they want to do it and can't quilt?"

So, that is what has been worrying Annie. She doesn't sew very well, so she's afraid she'll be left out.

"I can show them, and maybe some of the others."

I catch my breath but do not pause. I don't want Annie to jump in.

"The fancy ladies that shop in that store want special needlework, so we have to make sure they're pretty and done right. Six of us could do eight or more quilts a year.

"Once someone has a few pennies, she can buy her own thread and cloth, maybe crochet doilies and embroider pillowcases and scarves, crochet baby hats and sweaters. Then she can keep all the money. That'll give each of us a little extra money in between bigger sums for the quilts. The storekeeper will know what will sell after a few months."

"So, you think these women will buy?"

Oh my. Another question. Will this idea fail because I can't get five women? Will they be like Annie?

"The store owner thinks so. The good thing about the rich getting even richer is they're always looking for someone else to do what they don't want to do or just can't do."

"Why you askin' other wives? You could do on your own and keep money. I know how much you like money." She puts her hand over her mouth as though trying to put the words back in.

There may not be any way for Annie or others to understand that this isn't just the money. It's what money means to me. Like having boarders, it says I'm not giving in to the COMPANY, that I am not caged. I'm as free as a woman can be. It says in some ways I can take care of William if something happens to Joseph. We wouldn't have the extras, but we wouldn't starve.

I grin, hoping to relieve Annie of her angst. "A quilt takes many months. Women working together. Wouldn't that be so good to see?"

"Where will this quilt be made?"

Another nitpicking question, but I cannot let her questions stop me.

"Right here in my kitchen. We could do it in the morning for about two hours after the men go to work. Everyone could get home in time to do their chores and make supper. The other sewing could be done in their homes when they have time."

At last, the frown and confusion fade from Annie's face. "Maybe Florence and Bella will come. They're both good sewers. Bella makes me laugh, and Florence sews all her dresses and isn't that busy. Her husband doesn't want other men in the house, so she has no boarders and only two girls who are easy to care for."

Without catching her breath, she adds, "I'm in too, but you need to show me how to do that sewin' you do. I know I kin do it."

"Tomorrow morning when you come by. I thought I'd ask Ruth and Emma. Their girls enjoy working for me, and I've gotten to know them. That will make six."

When Annie doesn't speak, I ask the all-important question? "So, you like the idea?"

She nods.

"So, why did you stop by?"

"To tell you about the school and that there were two accidents in the mine. A young boy's leg was crushed, and another miner has several fractured ribs and…."

"Annie, let's stay out of the mine today."

April 1887

The houses on the street are still in darkness. The earliest risers are not yet stumbling downstairs to light the fire in the stove, if indeed they have something to cook or coal to burn. The only sound is the male cardinal high in the tree calling his mate.

The last signs of winter are slipping away. The crocuses, early this year, are peeking through the leaves of grass. It's the perfect time to begin something new.

I put on a blue dress that has some wear. I smile, remembering Florence's comment that "a dress is only worth wearing if it makes a man want to take it off." That could not be said of this dress, and hopefully, the women from the patch won't think I'm too fancy.

I pick up my hairbrush from the painted dresser and brush out the knots. I put a bun at the base of my neck. Then, pause for a few seconds, looking at my image in the mirror. Surely, the quilting bee ladies will approve. I have decided that I'm not going to change who I am, but if the way I dress makes the ladies more comfortable, there is no harm.

As I walk toward the kitchen, I hear the back door fly open. Annie is in the lead. The high-pitched voices bring life to my kitchen. They greet me with smiles and offerings of cookies. Annie had told me they were pulling all their pennies together to bake some cookies to thank me for my kindness.

Florence flounces in with a swish and sway. "Isn't this great?"

Since we had met at the dance at the social hall, I noticed that she spends a lot of time getting ready to go out—her hair is curled and pinned neatly around her face. Although her dress is not fancy or new, it fits in all the right places on her small frame.

Now and then, she has stopped to visit and brought her girls. They like petting Betsy and holding the chicks, and we have come together to sew and embroider. I find I like her. She won't be like Annie and Emma in my life, but then I have them.

Ruth rushes in as though late and greets Annie with a warm hug. She moves to hug Florence but notices her pulling back, so she turns to Bella, who is more than willing. I walk over to the cupboard to get out some coffee cups, not sure I'm ready for hugging just yet.

"This is a great kitchen," Ruth cries out once the hugging is over. "All those cabinets and that big stove."

Bella spins, her eyes darting around the room. "I'm gonna like sewing here."

The dress she is wearing is tight on her plump body because it has shrunk from so many washings or got a little snug after the birth of her children. The sewing circle could earn her some money to buy the material to sew a new one, but the first thing she'll buy is food for her children.

I say to the ladies, "Let's move the kitchen table closer to the windows so we can use the morning light."

The six of us drag the table near the windows and then arrange the chairs. "Ooohs and aahs," erupt as I pull out the material.

"I thought we'd make the star design that my Gran showed me years ago. Here is one I put together. I've already cut out the pieces to get us started." I wasn't sure how many would have scissors or ones good enough to cut the material.

Emma's visits have given me time to show her some embroidery and crochet stitches. From the minute she first picked up a needle, her fingers just flew, but she is timid and unsure. In time she'll be fine. For a few hours each week, these women can escape the humble dreariness of their own homes and create a thing of beauty. That thought makes me smile.

For the next half hour or so, there is silence. Everyone is working hard to get the stitches just right, asking others to make sure. I get up and pour each a glass of water and suggest they rest their hands.

I touch Bella's hand to get her attention. "Bella, I hope you don't mind my asking, but how did your boy lose his leg?"

Sadness comes across her plump face. "Henry is his name." She pauses and sighs. "I didn't give birth to him. He and my son, Walt, played together when they were little. They're twelve years old now. When Henry was four, a wagon tipped over and crushed his leg, and they couldn't save it."

Bella sighs again, and I see a tear in the corner of her eyes. "Anyway, his mother died a few months later in childbirth along with his baby sister. His father wanted to send him to the Poor House or a foundling home, letting someone else take care of him."

Emma blesses herself, and Annie shouts, "What a horrible man!"

"Maybe, but he couldn't take care of him. I liked the little chap. No Mom. No Pa who wanted him. No leg. He needed to be loved. He needed a family who could help him. I said I would take him in, raise him as mine. I couldn't ask for a more loving son."

I nod. "When I see Henry, he smiles and tips his cap."

Bella smiles a thank you. "I just wish I could get him to just enjoy being a boy. He wants to help me, and he doesn't want to be a burden. This year he became twelve. He wanted to get work. Pestered my brother until he got him work on the railroad.

"He's doin' odd jobs, cleanin' up and helpin' out. It isn't easy for him, but nothin' keeps him down. He wants to work in the tower one day as a switcher—you know someone who switches the tracks."

I resist asking why not want more for him, but how do I say it without offending Bella, so I say, "Maybe he could get a job in the office if he went to school."

"He's not much for learning, and I can't help him much."

"And you took in a child that wasn't yours," Emma says, almost in tears.

"But he is mine! Not the usual way, but he's mine!"

Florence sighs. "My neighbor is going to have her tenth child. Imagine that!"

I stand up and look at the women gathered around the table. "Without ways to stop it, women will always be trapped. 'Barefoot and pregnant,' my Gran called it."

Emma's eyes glaze over. "The church says it's God's will we have children. To stop having them is a sin."

Annie glares at Emma. "Isn't it more of a sin to have a child you cannot feed, who dies in your arms? I haven't seen God putting food on my table."

Bella growls at Annie. "Maybe he is, and you don't know it!"

Emma's face shouts out sadness. "Well, I like havin' my babes, but you're right. Not enough to eat."

Emma, with four children, miscarried the last time she was pregnant and twice before and is not yet thirty. It saddens her when her children look up at her with hunger in their eyes. Her worst days are when she has to give them broth with hardly any vegetables and no meat and no bread.

I feign a cough before I speak. "I hear there were ways to stop having babies."

I see everyone's confusion, so I continue. "It was first in Germany. It looks like a cap, and you put it inside to keep from getting pregnant. It was allowed here in America, but not anymore. The law now says you can't do anything to stop from having a baby."

Ruth shouts, "So, there was something, and now there isn't?"

Then Florence jumps up. "Bad enough husbands demand it. Now the law is telling us we have to have children."

Emma groans. "Government's doing nothin' to help us feed those children. They don't see our babes' hungry faces, hear stomachs growl, hear their cries for food."

I nod. "Wouldn't it be a blessing if women could have children when they want them? Think what women could do if they weren't pregnant every year and could choose when and how many. Just imagine!"

Annie looks away. Maybe she does not have to imagine.

Bella chuckles. "Do they have something to keep our husband from crawling on top of us when they want"

Everyone tries to eke out some laughter, but it's not funny for many women.

I offer them coffee. "Maybe someday it will change. Maybe."

The two hours pass quickly, with the women talking about their homelands, husbands, and children. They all groan when we need to stop.

"I can't believe it's time to go," Bella says. The others nod as they scurry, clearing off the table, putting the pieces of cloth and thread into a large basket. Once the table and chairs are back in place, they rush out the door, mumbling their thanks.

I'm now alone with Annie, who cannot stop smiling. "So, Josephine, what do you think? Do you like women? I was surprised Florence wanted to join us, but she's good with a needle. I think it went fine."

Laughter erupts from within me. "Will the day ever come when I answer your question before you do? But yes, it was a good morning."

February 1888

Every day, during the evening hours, Joseph complains about the mine. Not one day is he silent. He's grousing again tonight, but only to me, about the thickness of the coal seam. "Only two feet thick today. Wasn't much coal to load."

I've learned the thinner the seam, the more work he has to do to get the coal and the less coal he can load onto the wagon. This tells me there will not be much in his pay envelope.

The tools were not enough today. They had to blast. Joseph is always eager to explain every detail, wanting to show me that mining takes cunning and bravery.

"Begin undercuttin' coal with pick. Then take augur and breastplate. Bore a 'ole in the rock face… deep as undercut."

He doesn't stop to explain what's an auger or a breastplate, so caught up in the telling.

"Then make cartridge with newspaper jist less than 'ole… fill with powder. Put cartridge on tampin' needle, pushes it into 'ole with tampin' bar." He stops seeing my confusion. "Heavy rod. Tamps the cartridge with clay or wet coal dust, pushes in the squib, blastin' fuse, into that."

I shake my head, mulling over his words. He has to talk, so I must listen. "Can't you use something that takes less time? Something that doesn't seem so dangerous?"

Joseph meets my gaze and scowls. "Cheapest way, Josephine! Other ways cost too much. Light the squib. Run like hell to safe place." He mimics with his fists clenched.

"Flame goes through squib—gives time to get away. Blast explodes. Wait till dust and smoke clear. Then git back to work. Had to use picks, wedges to free coal. Hard to get at… lie on back."

Joseph's anger now can be seen in his eyes as he paces around the room. The miners don't get paid for all the time it takes to free the coal. After the mine cars are loaded, they place their metal discs on a hooked nail driven into the side of the car.

Then they push their cars to where the mule driver waits to couple them to the other cars and haul them away. I've never understood how the disc really works, but Joseph says it does, so I need to let go of my confusion.

When he tells his tales at the supper table, many of the boarders often join in, each adding to the stories of the others. The sound of their voices and their brief agreement relaxes them, and they can get ready to slog and grind another day.

When I'm the only one listening to Joseph, I find myself trying not to listen. In the depths of the mine, the miner's soul is choked and smothered day after day.

In 1888 the payroll figures for the Denmark Mine near Claridge indicated that 140 Czech miners and several "day diggers" were employed.

The miners were paid 60 cents for a ton of coal for general mining and 74 cents a ton for particular mining. This was a sharp increase from the 30 cents they were paid when the mine first opened.

The length of the working day was still twelve hours, and a day digger worked for $1.50 for a twelve-hour day.

April 1890

Thoughts of sorrow and raising a son on my own have brought up some misery talking. Over the last year, I haven't felt the need or had time to write. Sometimes the days crawl by like a turtle. Then I look up. A week, a month, and then a year has gone by. I'm still a miner's wife, no matter how I beg Joseph to do something else.

Some people live their months and years taking at least one step forward now and again, but in the last five years, the miners haven't taken a single step in the direction they crave. They're still working twelve-hour days. They're not getting paid enough to keep their children's stomachs from growling. They work in unsafe conditions, and accidents often occur, with deaths now and then.

Most of my time is spent doing my chores, so one day seems to meld into the other. The sewing circle still meets every week. Those weekly gatherings around my kitchen table and watching William grow up make my days so worth living.

The sewing circle is doing well, giving us a chance to do something we want to do and earn money. We made eight quilts last year. We are now making baby sweaters, caps, and booties. The lack of birth control helps our sales. I guess we should be grateful.

Ω

Joseph was hoping for another baby, but I miscarried last year. William has become my world and brings me joy every day.

Soon he will be four years old. He's sitting at the kitchen table with his slate and a piece of chalk. Pallie is by his side. I scratch behind her ears.

"What is 2 plus 2 Pallie?"

"Ah, Ma, a dog can't do sums."

Hiding a piece of chicken in my hand, I point my finger, and Pallie paws the floor four times.

"How did you do that, Ma?"

"Pallie did it. If she can learn, then you can too."

I hope he doesn't ask me to have Pallie read.

When I was four years old, Gramps taught me to count and add and subtract at age five. That same year he taught me the alphabet. Memories of Gramps are everywhere this morning. But, instead of making me sad or bringing tears to my eyes, I smile.

I tell William about Gramps now and then. By speaking his name and telling stories of his life, he will never die. He must live on, not forgotten, and he lives on in William and through me.

Joseph is always cross when I mention Gramps. I think he was hoping he would replace him as the most important man in my life, that I would put Gramps in a chest, lock it, and throw away the key. NEVER! Teaching William letters and numbers isn't making him any too happy either.

"Why are you teachin' the boy all that? What will folks say?" Joseph shouts when he hears me talking to William about the early settlers and showing a United States map. I can't believe that he has one mind about learning.

"Just a little is good enough," he tells me again and again.

He doesn't think that in time he might be proud of William if he got an office job or was a teacher.

None of my pleas sway Joseph. He always says, "He should be doing what boys do, not sittin' here with you learnin' things he doesn't need to get a job."

Again and again, I ask why it has to be one or the other?

Joseph never has an answer. I believe wanting something different for William makes Joseph feel ashamed of how he takes care of his family. But I cannot stop fighting for my son.

Maybe our fights are not about our son getting some learning. Perhaps he's afraid William will become too much my son and not his.

H.C. Frick Coke Company purchased the Mammoth Mines in Mount Pleasant Township for over $1,000,000. Frick operated the mine for a little over a year when an explosion occurred on January 27, 1891.

Over a hundred men and boys were killed. Some were suffocated by afterdamp, the gases left behind after the explosion. Others were mangled beyond recognition by the blast.

Thirty-one of the men were married, seventy-eight were single men and boys. Seventy-nine miners were buried in a mass grave—one big hole in the ground with no names.

January 1891

I see Annie marching down the street with a newspaper in her hand. She wails as she bounds into my kitchen. "At the railroad station, I heard there was an explosion at the Mammoth Mine. Somewhere near here. Over a hundred dead, even the boss."

She shoves the newspaper under my nose for me to read. I glance at the paper. A sudden buildup of gas in one part of the shaft caused the explosion. Just that morning, the fire boss had said the mine was safe.

"The paper says the explosion was caused by after-damp."

Annie is still standing, too fidgety to sit. "What's after-damp?"

"Caused by too much gas in the mine. In the end, the company will blame the miners. And Frick, he'll not help the families of those who died." I pause, not wanting to be sad or get angry again. "Annie, do you have any good news?"

"Ruth's daughter Helen wants to get a job workin' as a clerk in a store. Rosalie's talking about workin' at the post office right here."

"Yes, they talked with me about that. I have to start again with new girls, but it's time."

"All these years, you've been teachin' them to read and write and talkin' to them about working and not getting married."

"I never talked against marriage. But there are worse things than not getting married. Besides, who would they marry? These girls are smart, and most men don't like smart women."

She giggles. "And they always think they're smarter."

I nod. "You have girls. Doesn't it bother you that they are not wanted? That men and even women want sons and not girls? Imagine girls learning at a young age that they are not as good as boys. The very words, 'boys are better,' say that. Daughters.... Well, they can't wait until some other man takes them off their hands."

"Nick likes the girls, but I know he wanted sons."

"Girls could work in the office doing bookkeeping and writing letters, tellers in banks, teachers. They could do those jobs just as good as men, maybe better because they have to work harder than men to prove they should have that job. Men don't have to do that."

"My mother never said 'get work.' She just talked about getting a husband."

"And they'll be doin' that a hundred years from now. That's not going to change soon. For centuries mothers have taught their daughters to accept being a wife and mother. Never wondering if their daughter would want to do something else or could do something else. My Gran taught me to cook and sew and clean and told me to go along with whatever my husband said. When I talked about working, she laughed. I'll always be grateful for Gramps that he thought I should get an education."

"But you don't go along with Joseph!"

"No, and he doesn't like it. Some women are fine with men ruling over them. They think women like me are wrong."

Annie's sharp eyes bore into mine. "Do you think Emma is one of them?"

"I think Emma loves her children and wants them not to go hungry. But I also see that she takes pride in her boys. Her girls she wants married with grandchildren."

"Men want to run the world!" Annie shouts so loud Pallie hides under the table.

"Want to. Men do! Then some women think they should. I don't know why it has to be this way, but it is."

William runs into the kitchen, his choirboy voice shrill. "Ma, Ma. I'm hurt."

Pallie greets him with kisses. "Oh, my," I say, looking at the scrape on his knee.

"It hurts, Ma. I was on the swing and jumped off. I thought I could do it. I fell hard."

"It's only a scratch. You'll be fine," I say, washing off the dirt. "See—all better." I kiss my fingers and touch his knee and then push his hair away from his forehead.

"Now, go on and meet your father."

Annie tries to hug him as he races out the door. "Speakin' of smart. Girls tell me you're teachin' William sums and reading. He's so young."

I continue to knead the bread.

"So, Joseph not like, right?" Annie bursts out laughing.

"Joseph thinks William will get too big for his britches. You know, too smart for his father. If he learns, maybe he won't think so much of Joseph. He'll not want to go into the mine. Joseph thinks the mine is good enough for him, so it should be good enough for William."

I throw Annie a tea towel to dry the pot I just washed. "Did you always want to get married, Annie?"

"Nick asked, and I said yes."

I pause a moment and close my eyes. "I think some of us marry because mothers, fathers think we should. Because it's time, and because we have no choice."

"You're right. Never thought I had any other choice. Everyone getting married or wanting to." Annie pauses, and when she's quiet, she has an idea. "I wanna know if you'll teach me and the girls. Some other women would want to learn too. You don't think it's too late?"

"Never!" I stop mixing the bread and smile. "Maybe we could get mothers to bring their daughters."

"Whew! Won't that make the men angry? But Josephine, why didn't you get a job and not marry?"

The words catch in my throat as I start to speak. "Too many things, and like you, I didn't think I had a choice. My Gramps was gone. No parents to take care of me, help me." I pause, wanting to tell Annie the main reason, but I couldn't.

"So, how do we start learnin'?"

I wipe off the table and throw the crumbs out the kitchen door for the birds. "Let's start with the mothers we know. We'll spend a few hours or so a week on what's easy."

"What's that?"

"You know some of it already. You count money at the store when you buy something. We'll do sums and then read and write. Maybe... just maybe, Ruth and Florence could teach English to those just learning it. Even a half-hour a week could help. But everyone must keep it a secret."

"You like keepin' this from the men?"

"It's best they don't know about the reading and writing and sums. So, let's get together this Friday at ten after the morning chores are done."

February 1891

Dashing into the kitchen, William trips as he pulls up his trousers. Joseph and the boarders are already at the table drinking coffee and mopping up the egg yolks with big chunks of bread. I stand at the stove cooking sausage for their dinner pail, jumping back now and again when the grease splashes.

"Twenty or so houses built," Joseph says. "Another mine bein' open right down the road."

I bang the fork on the stove. "You could be building those houses instead of working in the mine." I look at the boarders gathered around the table. "So, are any of you going to work for the new mine?"

Mike walks to the stove to pour another cup of coffee. "Better to stay with the devil you know than the devil you don't."

Joseph shouts out, "If it's safer and better money, I'd go."

"William, don't sit there like a bump on a log."

"I'm not a bump, Ma. I'm a boy."

I try to hide the smile that comes to my face. "Go outside and collect the eggs and be quick."

"Do I have to? I'd rather milk the cow."

"You can do that later. Then after breakfast, we'll deliver the milk and eggs in your wagon."

William grabs the basket and steps outside onto the back porch. He puts on his shoes and runs to the chicken coop, with his shoelaces dragging in the grass.

When he comes back into the kitchen, he yells, "Eight eggs, Ma!" He spies some scrambled eggs on a plate that I have set aside for him. The boarders and Joseph have already left for work.

I sit him down at the table, tying a dish towel around his neck. "Ah, Ma, I won't spill nothin'."

While he eats his egg, I check out his ears. "Eh, Ma, that hurts."

"You could grow potatoes in there. They're so dirty."

"Ah, Ma, a potato won't fit in my ear."

I smile as I write down this tale of William. This is my way of recording how we spend our days.

On March 25, 1891, the H.C. Frick Coke Company and McClure Coke Company posted a new sliding scale of wages for the next three years. The other offerings were a nine-hour day, no strikes, and the contract signed by each miner. Labor leaders said that by posting the scale late at night, the companies tried to trick the miners into believing it was agreed to by the union. It was not.

A group of miners held a protest march on April 2. With Andrew Carnegie's support, Frick brought in Pinkerton detectives who evicted miners' families from their homes, causing more unrest. The early morning clash with deputized agents of Frick Coke Company began with words, and then shots were fired by the deputies. Nine miners were killed. This labor-union conflict became known as the Morewood Massacre.

When Frick learned about the killings at Morewood, he wrote: "I have no further particulars. This will likely have a good effect on the riotous element up there." In early May, the defeated miners went back to work. Frick notified Carnegie of their complete victory.

July 1891

Soon William will be five years old—a year from going to school. Next month I will be twenty-three. On some days, I feel more like forty. I'm dusting the furniture and fluffing the cushions in the front parlor when Joseph walks in.

"I'll have supper on the table in about ten minutes."

He follows me into the kitchen, and one after another, the boarders amble in, their boots lined up outside.

Mike calls out. "I smell chicken."

On Sunday I do a roast with potatoes and carrots or beans. On each of the seven plates, I put a piece of chicken and vegetables. I put scraps of meat that have fallen off the bone with the trimmings on William's plate and mine. I never allow myself a whole piece of meat. Because the men are in the mine doing such hard work, the meat is for them, although that's unspoken.

It hasn't been the same the last few months. Gerhard, after five years, had enough money to bring his wife and son here. They are living in the patch. Tony married his sweetheart. She waited six years for the Mrs. They live next door to Gerhard in a double company house. Mike, Billy, and Stan are still boarding with me. Earlier this year, we lost Artie to pneumonia. I guess I can't hold on to them forever, but it was a good five years.

Mike has a gleam in his eyes and a lilt in his voice. "That looks so good, Josephine."

Joseph plops down on a chair and scratches his head. "I was talkin' to Ange Ribis yesterday about a union."

Milos, a new boarder who has spent the last five days competing with Mike for my favor, steals a glance from me and then speaks up, "Men won't join. Too afraid! Need money. COMPANY needs miners. Miners need company."

Not what Joseph wanted to hear. Everyone at the table knows that miners in other coal patches are asking for an eight or nine-hour workday. What no one can say is that there is little they can do. Yet, the union is thought to be the only hope the miners and their families have for a better life.

Joseph shouts, "Ask for better workin' conditions. They say NO! Safer mine. NO! Want paid for time spent gettin' the coal. NO!"

Mike glares at Joseph. "They did give us a ten-hour day."

Joseph looks as though he's been slapped. "Give us! Right thing to do! Should be happy, not say anything? Union is the answer."

I raise my voice too. "But look what happened at Morewood. The union didn't win there. Frick didn't give in. He's a tough...."

Mike stops eating and then finishes my sentence. "Bastard. It was just like other strikes. The miners and kin put out of their homes—all their bits and pieces dumped on the road, awful conditions, homeless, without food."

Billy groans. "Heard the miners started to picket, jeered at men who went back to work. Pinkertons started shooting, and men were killed."

I try to stop myself from shouting. "Nine miners were killed. It was a warning to anyone who wants to strike. If you march and protest, you could lose your life."

"Nothing changed. Frick declared he won. Coke works started up again. They didn't have a leg to stand on," Mike adds, pulling out his pipe and filling it with tobacco. I glare at him, and he blows out the match and puts the pipe on the table.

Joseph, who has been silent, shouts, "Why go over this? Must stand up for our rights. Must be strong."

I look into his angry eyes. "That's the problem. You have no rights. My guess is most men in the coal patch don't want anything to do with the union. They have wives and children."

Stan nods. "Takes every penny to feed them. Won't spend money on dues. They fear losing their jobs. It's hopeless."

I press my hand down hard on Joseph's shoulder as the vision of putting my hands around his neck appears before me.

Joseph stares long and hard at those at the table and makes a fist. "You sayin' it has to stay like this?"

Again, silence. Stan clears his throat and speaks in a somber voice. "Miners have no money saved for a strike. Their families will starve. Joseph, you think striking will get the bastards to listen, but it won't."

Billy looks up when he hears the shrill chatter of hail against the window. He hates arguing at the table, but sometimes…. He speaks in a soft voice. "Just like Morewood, they'll throw the miners out of their homes and bring in other men to take our jobs."

Stan nods. "Yeah, that's the worst thing."

I stop scrubbing the pot. "No, the worst thing at Morewood was that nine men were killed, and as yet, no one has been punished for those deaths."

Early in the 19th century, mining companies brought men to America from English-speaking countries, England, Scotland, and Wales, to work in the mines and the mills. By the 1840s, chiefly the Irish were working in the mines.

Once the surface coal was gone, the coal had to be mined deeper, bringing more accidents and deaths. The miners, unwilling to work for low wages or tolerate the living conditions, chose to leave the mines.

The coal operators then decided to bring to America men who were desperate for work, who would work for almost nothing, and couldn't talk back. The answer was non-English-speaking men. So, they brought in immigrants from Southern and Eastern Europe with the promise of the American Dream. But nobody told immigrants, for people like them, the dream would forever remain just a dream.

October 1892

Today is the 400th anniversary of Columbus Day, according to my calendar. The leaves are just starting to turn russet and gold. I look out the kitchen window, wondering if that means a colder than usual winter. Now that William is six and at school, my days are quiet, and most of the solitude that I had enjoyed before his birth has returned.

I'm still meeting every Tuesday and Thursday morning with several women and their young children, teaching them to read, write, and do sums. Some mothers are now teaching their other children, and I'm hopeful this will continue for years to come. I also asked them to get groups together in their own homes. All of this is being done quietly, with the children finding it fun to keep a secret.

The whistle of doom rings out for the second time this week.

William looks up into my eyes. "D'ya think Pa is alright?"

I look away from my son's gaze. I've tried not to pass my fears on to him, but he's anxious about his Pa at only six years old.

"So, how was school today?" I say as William starts drinking the milk and munching his cookie.

With his mouth full, he whines, "Ma, you ask me that every day."

"And you must answer it every day, so how was school?"

"We had to recite a pledge. We have to do it every day. Some can't read, so he keeps sayin' it, and we keep sayin' it. That's how we're gonna learn it."

"Do you know any of the words?"

William's face beams as he gets off his chair and stands up with his arm out in front of him, hand straight out, high in the air. "I pledge a-lee-gence to the flag of the United States of America…. is all I remember. I jist don't know what pledge or alleegence is, Ma."

I wonder how I can explain those words to a six-year-old boy.

"You are saying that you care about where you live." I push William's hair from his face. "Are there any new children?"

"Three girls and one boy."

I'm surprised there's even one boy. If young boys are sent to school, they attend until they are old enough to work in the mines and sometimes not even then. They are given chores around the house, sent to pick pieces of coal from the slate dump, scavenge from the nearby farms, any odd job…. They do whatever to help their families while the girls work in the house scrubbing floors, washing clothes, and taking care of the younger children.

"Did any of them speak English?"

"Only one."

They cannot learn and keep up with the lessons if they don't speak English. Does the government not want them to learn? They're just children of immigrants. How sad for all of us, for our country.

William's voice brings me out of my trance. "One boy talked about a cave-in. Two of his brothers workin' in the mine. There was a loud noise. Took over a day to find them. His father found 'um under rocks and everything. They were dead, Ma. Will that happen to Pa, too?"

"Did you play games at recess?"

"Yeah, but three boys got in a fight. The teacher told them to stand in a corner for an hour. We all laughed. Sam and I are gonna…."

"Sam and I are going…."

"Pa says gonna."

I stop, realizing I am asking too much from such a young boy. He lifts his shoulders up to his chin. "Ah, Ma. I want to meet Pa at the mine."

I can't help but smile. "Go on, but you'll read before you go to bed."

William sprints out of the house, passing Annie in the hallway.

"D'ya hear? Of course, you haven't—stuck in this house all day. Lester Newcomer was killed. He was tightening the brake on the mine car when the chain broke. Oh, Josephine, he fell, and the mine car got loose. The wheel passed over his head. Just forty."

He would be considered old if you count how many boys and young men are killed or maimed, but I decide it's best to be silent.

"Annie, I don't want to hear anything about a miner dying so horribly. Oh, I didn't mean it that way, but when is this going to stop?"

"Not in our lifetime!"

January 1893

The year arrived with a foot of snow, burying the coal patch.

I haven't written during the last few years, although my mind hasn't stopped. William is doing well in school, and I enjoy our moments together. I miscarried once again. Every time I can see the disappointment in Joseph's eyes.

I hear Joseph's footsteps in the hallway and feel the chill from the outside air. A candle is flickering in the front parlor. I'm in shadow when he finds me sitting on the couch staring into space. He takes off his cap and holds it in both hands in front of him as he sits down and looks into my face. "You don't look good. Should get to bed early."

I put my hand to my mouth, my forefingers and thumb pinching my upper lip. "I'm going to have a baby." I rest my head on the back of the settee, turning my gaze to the ceiling.

He leans back in his chair and stretches out his legs. "When the baby comin'?"

"About four months."

The three miscarriages since William's birth have left us wondering if we would ever have another child. Joseph drops to his knees in front of me. "You knew. Didn't tell me."

"You were in my bed." My words are clipped and bitter. I touch his hand, and my voice softens. "Something could have happened. It's been almost seven years since William was born."

If I had told Joseph sooner, I would have had to endure more months of hearing what I should and should not do, adding to my worry.

There are no words of happiness, no smile on his face. As for me, there's a tightening knot in the pit of my belly. I fear I will not only lose another child, but I could lose my life too. Many women do. "I'll ask the girls to work a few more hours and on Sunday."

This evening we spoke to each other very little. The silence between us is louder than any words spoken. This is the first time in our marriage that there is coldness, drawing a divide between us. I'm not sure why. I can only believe that Joseph has given up having another child and fears another child will be lost to him. I wonder if he thinks that I might be lost to him. The baby growing inside me remains in my thoughts until sleep overtakes me.

May 1893

This morning at the post office, I heard that something happened in New York, causing panic. The clerk chuckled when he told me that rich people have lost a lot of their money. Doesn't mean anything to working folks. They have no money to lose.

The newspaper said the panic will bring on a depression, and those with money will suffer. I would laugh if it weren't so sad. The miners and their families suffer depression every day of every year. How much more can there be?

Above ground, the temperature has dropped quite suddenly, and there is dampness in the air. This evening Joseph and Mike came home late and told me what happened below ground.

Mike grips his cup of coffee. I'm surprised it doesn't break from the force of his hand. Then he begins. "The walls shook, and then a young miner comes running. A wooden rafter collapses just ten feet away. We drop our picks and run. The slate roof comes down over the boy, pinning him to the dirt floor."

As Mike speaks, I can see them below the earth. Their faces smeared with coal, only the whites of their eyes seen. A flicker of a kerosene lamp hanging from a timber. Their eyes squint as they work a few feet apart. The only sound is the "tic, tic" of their picks hitting against the slate.

Joseph takes a deep breath. "The young man. Chest up and down. Dust and dirt all 'round. Stay in corner. Don't know what to do. We scared more slate would come down." Joseph chokes on the words. "Watched him, afraid to move."

Mike drops into a chair at the table. "We waited for the dust to clear, couldn't believe what we jist saw. Waitin' for the mine boss...." He shrugs his shoulders. "Don't know how long. When safe, he and two miners came down to check the damage. We were trying to remove the rubble from the boy's body."

As they describe this cave in, the black dust and grime on their faces cannot hide their fear and anger.

The young man who was killed was a mule driver, age 20. He had run a loaded mine car into a post and knocked down the roof. The collapse nearly killed Joseph and Mike. On this day, death came knocking on our door.

June 1893

I buried Pallie today in her favorite quilt. I had let her out this morning, and

when she didn't come back, I went looking for her. She was near the barn. I spent the morning digging her grave, William by my side. She's been my comfort and companion all these years. I will miss her every day.

September 1893

My babe came too early. The birth pains frightened Joseph. I heard Mrs. B whisper to him that she didn't think the baby wanted to come into the world. Finally, at four in the morning, she awakened Joseph and told him I had a little girl.

He crept into the bedroom and saw tears in the corners of my eyes. "We have a girl, Joseph. She is so tiny."

Joseph told me that his Ma is sick, so he wanted to name the baby after her. "She'd like havin' a babe of mine named for her."

I wanted to say no. It would be a constant reminder of the woman who hates me, but I held my tongue, saying nothing.

Ω

My babe remained frail throughout the following weeks, not gaining weight and showing few signs of thriving. Then two days ago, the life went out of her. She is gone, buried the following day with only Joseph, Annie, the twins, William, and the sewing circle ladies by my side.

Following the burial, I stayed in my bedroom, not speaking to anyone. If Joseph tried to take me in his arms, I shoved him away. Emma took William to her home for a few days. Annie and the girls who worked for me did the chores and cooked the meals.

After three days, I was back downstairs and doing my chores. But I was still not looking rested in the eyes of those who cared about me, and the feeling of loss has not left me.

October 1893

I'm pulling out pots and pans from the cupboard, when I hear the front door open. It takes several seconds before I realize my brothers, Frank and Fred, are standing in the doorway. Aunt Rosie had passed away two months ago.

"You two are so tall and good-looking," I start to get up from the floor.

Frank gives me his hand and pulls me up. "You look good too, Josephine."

Their suits are well-made, their hair slicked back, Frank's cheeks plump. "What are you doing here?"

Fred steps towards me. "I'm getting married. We're both working for Westinghouse in East Pittsburgh."

Frank jumps in. "Now that we have a car, we can drop in for a visit."

"I want you to be at my wedding," Fred says. "Maybe we can see each other more often."

"I'd like Willian to have family in his life."

Fred nods. "It would be good to have a little chap about. My bride-to-be loves children and can't wait for some of our own."

Tears form in the corners of my eyes. Since Gran's death, we have seen each other once or twice a year. "I think our mother and Gramps would have liked that."

Frank bows his head, and Fred looks at me with sadness in his eyes. He had a Ma—Rosie. I want to ask if they had a good life with Aunt Rosie and Henry. They had a comfortable home and good food and schooling, but I often wonder if they got enough caring.

During their visit, I believe we all realized we didn't have much to talk about. We spent so many years apart—our childhood together taken away from us. At the same time, I realize I like the men they have become.

I am of two minds after my brothers leave. I was happy to see them, but their visit brought up thoughts of all the years we spent apart. They were under my aunt's thumb for all those years, but now they seem ready to be my brothers.

A few minutes after they leave, Annie walks in.

"Who are those good-lookin' men drivin' down the street? I saw them comin' out your door."

"They're my brothers, Frank and Fred."

"You've never said much about them, even after you visited your aunt."

I lower my head and attack the carrots with a peeler. I guess it's about time Annie knew.

"Not much to tell. Remember I told you that after my parents died, I was raised by my grandparents, and my brothers by my aunt and her husband. My aunt never liked me. Always thought I was too much like my mother. When my grandfather died, he left this house to me. Rosie thought he should have left everything to her. She got angry, so she kept my brothers away from me."

"What does that mean?"

"It means that the house is mine."

"Yours and not Joseph's?"

"That's right. The law was changed some years ago. A married woman can now own property. My grandfather gave the house to me so I would always have a home. Before that, if my grandfather had left the house to me, it would have become Joseph's when I married. He could sell it, take the money, and leave."

It never made sense that men had the right to a woman's property once she's married, that everything that was once hers or should be hers became his.

"All these years, you never told me."

"My aunt never forgave me. She's been punishing me by keeping my brothers from me. I hardly knew them when my parents died. I was just five, and they were one and three. Now Fred is twenty-three and Frank twenty-one I believe."

All those years apart. Now we are grown. Still no chance to be together, day in and day out, but still time to make some lasting memories.

"How sad. So, tell me about your brothers."

"They're like strangers to me, Annie. We never got to know each other."

"What does that mean?"

I pick up a pair of socks to darn. I need to do something to calm me. "I'd like to change that. My child should have uncles and aunts and cousins."

Joseph's sister married about three years ago—late in life. Still no children, but maybe in time.

Annie lets out a giggle. "So, what has Joseph done this time to make you mad?"

"Who said I was mad?"

"The way you're stitching those socks. Every time you and Joseph fight, you punch the bread hard, beat the rugs senseless. Whatever is around gets battered. I knew years ago you two…." she mimics a fighting motion. "Who doesn't, but you…." Annie dances around the floor and motions for me to give her the words.

"Yes, Annie, we have rocks in our bed, but most of the time, we dance together without tripping over each other's feet."

"Rocks in your bed. That's a funny way of saying that. I thought over the years you liked the bedroom as much as you liked the kitchen."

I hold back a smile. "Who said I like the kitchen?"

"So, Maria is doing good in school. She came home and told me that the women in Colorado have been given the right to vote. She said her teacher wasn't happy about it."

"Yes, men don't want it. Wyoming, another state out west, already did that. They're both far away—thousands of miles. Probably not enough women there to make a difference in a vote anyway."

"So, you're sayin' it doesn't matter if it happens here?"

"What I'm saying is that women will be voting for men, even if we could get the right to vote. And it will be many years to get a woman nominated and then many more to get one elected to any office."

"Why you say that?"

"Because men won't let it happen, and neither will a lot of women. They too think men should run things."

"Aren't we glad we're not two of them?"

January 1894

What a wintery day, yet, the sewing circle ladies have arrived early despite the eight inches of snow that came down during the night. Bella arrives with her cousin, Izabelle, who is visiting her, and Annie, followed by Emma and Ruth.

Despite the money we're making with our sewing, their dresses are more threadbare than ever. Emma and Ruth are still thin and frail, their eyes sunken in. They work long days, and there's never enough money for food, even though a few of their young sons are working in the mine, bringing in a few pennies.

"Did you hear the news?" Ruth shouts before Annie gets a chance to talk about the accident. "Another miner fractured a leg. A post wasn't set right... down came the coal."

No one says a word. No one wants to talk about an accident if the tale faults the miner. Besides, why waste our voices moaning about safety in the mine. We leave that to the men.

When I started the sewing circle, I hoped for light-hearted banter from the women to ease all our struggles. I was surprised when they talked about personal problems, not leaving out much detail. More surprising is they all drop by for a visit or a sympathetic ear.

Emma says just above a whisper, "Izabelle, do you have any children?"

Izabelle takes a deep breath. "I was ten when I fell out of a tree. A thin stump was sticking out the ground. It hit between my legs… smashed my inners. Doctor said no children." She brushes a strand of hair away from her plump face. "I have no one. My parents had four children. But I'm the only one left."

Annie moans, "Oh, Lord! What happened to them?"

Izabelle's eyes became wet with tears. "It was so very sad. One of my brothers fell off a log in the river... taken away, drowned. He was only four. The baby died of pneumonia at a few months old. Another was a toddler. Jumped off the roof. Thought he could fly like a bird. He hit the ground. Smashed his body into pieces. Died a few days later. He was only three." She pauses and then whispers, "I should've been watchin' him."

Bella gasps. "Your poor mother."

Before crossing herself, Emma gazes over to make sure Annie is not looking at her.

Izabelle shrugs. "My poor father. He loved the boys so. I think he wished one of the boys had lived instead of me." Tears are now streaming down her cheeks. "I was the last one my mother thought about if she thought about me at all. My father started drinkin' more. Lost one job after another. My mother kept to her bed. I took care of them until my father drank himself to death and my mother wasted away."

I can hear Annie's voice. "Where was your God while all this was happening?" Izabelle's life is a reminder once again that hardships and suffering are everywhere and sometimes a constant in one's life.

In the late spring of 1894, the United Mine Workers, with a membership of thirteen thousand miners, called a strike in the bituminous (soft coal) mining industry. They asked that wages return to the level they were on May 1, 1893. More than one hundred eighty thousand miners went on strike in Colorado, Illinois, Ohio, parts of western Pennsylvania, and West Virginia. Most of Westmoreland County was not included in that strike.

On May 23 near Uniontown, Pennsylvania, fifteen guards armed with carbines came face to face with fifteen hundred strikers, killing five men and wounding eight.

The depression continued, and the miners could not hold out for a wage increase. By late June, the strike failed. Most miners had returned to work, and the United Mine Workers Union was shattered.

August 1894

The heat is more stifling than I remember of past summers. Annie's daughter Maria comes running into my kitchen out of breath. "Auntie, please come now. Ma needs you. Sophia's sick."

Over the years, I have seldom been to Annie's house, usually because I'm stuck in my own. But mostly, Annie loves to spend time in my kitchen and the front porch, away from the coal dust.

Racing down the road, it takes too many minutes to get to Annie's house.

Maria cries, "Auntie, she's so sick. They're in the bedroom."

Walking into the bedroom, I am shocked by the pale skin and the black circles under Sophia's eyes. Annie had mentioned that Sophia was complaining of being tired and achy. I thought she had lost some weight and remarked about that a month ago. Annie had chided, "Oh, she isn't eating as much, afraid she'll gain weight and get plump."

Annie cries, "Josephine, look! She has purple patches on her skin. She's complaining her tummy hurts."

"We must get a doctor," I shout, although I know Annie can't afford it. My rainy-day money is just for times like this. I shove a few dollars in Maria's hand. "There's a doctor in Harrison City. Ask him to come here, no matter what the hour. Tell him it's urgent."

Ω

The doctor and Maria arrive two hours later. Annie is crying and talking as she tries to explain Sophia's illness. The doctor stops her by waving his hand and asks her to give him some time to examine Sophia.

I drag Annie out of the bedroom and downstairs into the kitchen. I turn to Maria, trying to read her eyes. She needs to be kept busy. "Maria, go and get Emma and then make sure your father comes home when the whistle blows. He should be here."

Between sobs, Annie whispers, "He's always said they're my girls."

"Of course, they're your girls, but Nick watches over them. He loves them."

"But Josephine, you know they're not his girls, really."

I had always wondered where the girls got their ginger hair. Then one day, Annie told me the story of the twins. When they first arrived in America, Nick couldn't get work. So, Annie worked for a couple cleaning their house and cooking and minding their two girls.

One day when the wife was out, taking care of her mother, and the girls were next door playing, the husband came into the kitchen. He forced himself on her, his hand cupped over her mouth. She tried to fight him, but he was bigger and stronger. He told her if she said anything to his wife, she would lose her job.

After that day, Annie made sure his wife or one of the girls was always with her and always carried a knife in her apron pocket. She didn't tell Nick because she was ashamed and needed to work. Nick still hadn't found a job that could take care of both of them. But then Annie became pregnant. They had been married three years and still no children, so she knew Nick couldn't be the father. He knew they were not his girls when he saw the ginger hair.

I listened that day, her telling me what she would. We never spoke of it again.

"But you stayed together all these years."

"All we had in this country was each other. We couldn't make it on our own. Together, maybe we could. He's good with the girls, but we've never been able to have our own children. I never gave him a son."

My hand tightens over Annie's. "Not all men want a boy! They're his girls."

I've seen Nick's kindnesses to the twins. The love in his eyes. When they were little, he would pick them up and toss them in the air, making them giggle. And as they grew older, he watched after them, protecting them from the bullies on the street.

"I knew one day I would be punished."

"Punished! For what? You didn't do anything wrong. You love your girls, and you give them what you can."

The kitchen door opens, and Maria and Emma walk in. We hear shuffling feet in the hallway. It's the doctor, his stethoscope dangling from his neck.

"I'm sure your daughter has a rare blood disease. Her lymph nodes… those are glands in her neck…. They are swollen, and those purplish spots…."

The concern in his voice causes Annie's body to shake. "What can you do?"

"There's no cure. Nothing I can do. She will become weaker. She will be in pain."

As the doctor speaks, Annie collapses into my arms, sobbing.

Annie cries out to the doctor. "So, she's going to die?"

Maria touches her mother's head. "We'll take care of her, Ma!"

Swallowing hard, I whisper, "Yes, we'll all take care of her. We'll make her days as happy as we can." I hug Annie to me, tears starting to run down my face. Neither of us wants to ask how long before she passes away.

Emma stands nearby, struggling to find the cross around her neck. She conquers her tongue-tied state. "God is always with you and Sophia. You're not alone."

"You and your God! Your God is taking my Sophia away from me," Annie screams, her fists clenched and her eyes crying out.

The doctor starts to speak, "Death will…."

I glare at him and pull on his sleeve, "Doctor, let me walk you out."

Annie screams after him, "You're wrong. My daughter doesn't want to leave me."

The doctor shrugs his shoulders, and we walk out the front door.

"Doctor, surely there is something we can do for the pain. Something to make death easier."

"There is something, but your kind can't afford it."

"Let me worry about that." I know he's thinking how can we afford medicine if we live from pay to pay, hardly enough food to keep bellies from growling?

"Keep her warm. Keep her drunk."

"And…."

"There are drugs like opium, morphine, but it costs. Too much could kill the girl." He pauses, "But then death will be a blessing."

"Where do I get it?"

"If you get the money, go to Pittsburgh. Some doctors there pass it out like candy."

He writes on a piece of paper and shoves it in my hand.

Ω

Two days later, Maria and I took the train to Pittsburgh. I asked to be the one to call on the twins' father at his restaurant, hoping he still owned it. If not, we would go to his house. Given Annie's description of him, I believed when he saw Maria, he would know she was his daughter.

As we entered the restaurant, a man with curly red hair was talking to a couple having their noonday meal.

He came forward, offering to seat us. I waved him off. "I'm a friend of Annie Sevchick. Do you remember her? Maria," I nodded in her direction, "is one of your twin daughters."

I swore later to Annie that I believed in some ways he knew that as soon as he looked at her. He tried to walk away, so I raised my voice, "Sophia, her sister, is dying. She's...."

He grabbed me and pulled me into an office. Maria followed.

"You know what I'm saying is true. The girl you fathered is in pain and will suffer badly before she passes. The doctor suggested morphine to help with the pain. Annie and Nick don't have the money."

He shook his head and turned away. "You never got punished for what you did. This is your punishment. I want you to give me money to buy medicine for Sophia's pain. If you don't, we will call on your wife."

He growls at me, "She won't believe you."

"Like you, once she sees Maria, she will know I'm telling the truth. Do you want that for your wife, for your children?"

I did not have to say anymore. He went to the till and pushed dollar bills into my hand. "That's all I have now. If you need more...."

"I'll write, and you'll send money?"

He nodded, and we rushed out of the restaurant.

He had given me over $200. I could not believe it was so easy, but something had to be easy in this time of sadness. As we left, Maria broke down in tears. "That was my father. Well, not my father, really. But wouldn't you think.... He looked at me with...."

"I'm sure he was shocked to hear he fathered twin girls. He never knew, and he never had to think about the two of you all these years. Fear that we would tell his wife, seeing how desperate we are, was all he could think about."

"That man who hurt Ma is part of me."

"The only thing he gave you was your beautiful ginger hair. You are your mother's daughter. Don't forget that."

When Annie told Maria Nick wasn't her father, Maria said that Annie was wrong. Nick was her father. The other man was a stranger. When I told Annie I should make the trip to Pittsburgh, Maria was quick to say she should come with me. When he saw her, he would know I was telling the truth. We thought it best not to tell Sophia, who was suffering so.

With the note I had from the doctor, we got the morphine. In about five hours Sophia was resting without pain.

October 1894

The days are going by at a snail's pace for those who love Annie and her twins. We are all watching Sophia die more than a little each day. The sparkle in Annie's eyes is dim, her face saying, "The time is near."

The morphine had little effect these last few days, so I told Annie to give her a little more. I don't want to cause her death, but we must ease her pain. I have talked about Annie's sadness to the sewing ladies. "She's not going to be the Annie we love, but she does long for our visits. Stop by with your embroidery or just drop in."

The ladies assured me they would visit and take something for supper when they had extras, pulling together whatever they could. Believing that Annie is so numb that she will not resist any kindness, I remind Emma that Annie needs people around her at this time. I caution in a soft voice, "Just keep God out of it. I know you find comfort in knowing that God is all around us. It doesn't give Annie any comfort right now."

Emma doesn't give up trying to console Annie and visits at least once a day. There are times when Annie has an edge to her voice, so we sit in silence. Often, Annie does not say much. Yet, she never once asks any of us to stay away.

I love Annie as much as I love William, and I love her girls. Instead of fussing to find the words to express my feelings, I make food for them and wash their clothes. I try to reach out and provide comfort, but no words come. I pray for Sophia and Annie, hoping I have God's ear.

I want to cry out every time I see mother and daughter together, but I must be calm and comforting. I quiver and tremble several times a day but never in front of Annie. Tears are not going to heal Sophia or lessen Annie's pain. It would say to both of them that death is as close as they imagine.

In the late evenings, I made a white nightgown for Sophia to be buried in when the time comes. It took weeks before I dared to show it to Annie. I thought she and Maria could embroider flowers on the front. Annie cried and hugged me, bringing me to tears.

Ω

Sophia is laid out at home in the parlor. On the first night of the vigil, the sewing circle ladies came early with food and a white blanket they had crocheted to put over Sophia. Emma and I have been by Annie's side during the last three days.

I touch Annie's hand, seeing Nick holding Maria as she sobs. "Nick has been here for you all these months."

"I didn't know how much he cared about the girls. Why did Sophia have to die so young for me to know that?"

Emma put her palms together as if praying. "We don't know why God took your sweet little girl into heaven."

Annie's eyes glaze over, and she takes a deep breath as she struggles to speak. She is close to collapsing. I close my eyes. Under my eyelids, I see Sophia as a toddler with Annie and Maria.

"So, it's God's will?" Annie spits out the words. "So, God needs my little girl more than me? I can't believe that. He doesn't want me and Maria and Nick to have sorrow for the rest of our lives. I see God in tears."

As Annie cries out, Emma walks away, her head bowed and her body trembling.

November 1894

My heart is aching, not only because Sophia is gone, but it's so sad to watch Annie in such sorrow. She seldom stops by for a visit or joins the sewing circle. I drop in on her and clean every two or three days, but I see no signs that my dear friend who has brought me so much joy will be herself any time soon.

She will never heal if she doesn't talk about Sophia, share stories about her, keep her alive. Her eyes say that she aches every time she looks at Maria, but Sophia lives in Maria. She needs to reach out to her living daughter, but instead, she seems to be moving farther away from her.

Maria visits me every day, needing comfort since her mother is absent in spirit and words. She shares that Annie does not speak to her or her father most days and often doesn't get out of bed.

Outwardly over the years, Annie has appeared strong and always positive. Inwardly, I believe Annie's disguises are just blustering to make us all think she is happy. Within, Annie suffers more than she wants others to know.

March 1895

The days, weeks, and months have been a blur, much more than usual. After watching Annie ignore her living daughter, I told her, "Annie, by being so sad, you're telling Maria she doesn't matter. You're mourning one child and losing sight of the other. Is that really what you want to do?"

"But I miss Sophia," Annie had cried, her voice trailing off, tears trickling down her cheeks.

I was struck by her sadness, missing the joy that was Annie. "And Maria knows that. In time you may lose her too, and that loss will be just as great. You must know that Maria loved her and misses her. She's in pain too."

The twins were like night and day. Like her mother, Sophia couldn't keep her words in her mouth and had difficulty sitting still. I remember telling Annie that I thought her favorite daughter had ants in her pants. I feared that Annie would be offended. Instead, she laughed.

Maria seldom spoke and spent time alone reading, thankful for my teaching and the quiet chats. From an early age, she was happy alone and didn't play with anyone but Sophia.

I finally got the courage to tell Annie that now she has a chance to give Maria the attention that she had never given her while Sophia was alive. And that, if she didn't show Maria how important she was to her, in time it would cause a break that would haunt her for the rest of her life. During the last few weeks, Annie has spent more time with Maria due to my nudging and has taken her shopping to buy some cloth for dresses.

Annie probably never realized that her face always lit up when Sophia walked into the room or spoke. She was never harsh or mean to Maria, but she did not give her that approving look she had given to Sophia.

I would never say it out loud, but often I wish Maria were my own daughter. I shiver, trying to regret that thought. She has Annie, but then my face lights up when I see Maria.

November 1896

The last year passed at a turtle's pace, and this year has started the same—without nothing to celebrate. Some part of my day has to be something I choose to do, not have to do. Teaching has become one of those things. The mothers and their children gather around the kitchen table, eager to learn. Those times together and the sewing circle help me get through my days until Joseph and the boarders come home. But to my dismay, every evening, there's talk of the mine and accidents.

"It was a bad day," says Joseph, staring at the food on his plate. "We'd stopped to eat and heard a terrible cry. Hearin' a young boy screamin' out in pain and can't do nothin'. We heard he was mangled in the machinery." He heaves a sigh. "John Bott's boy, Joe. Only fourteen years old. Died in minutes, his father said."

Mike shakes his head. "At the Crabtree mine, a breaker boy slid down the chute. No one knew he was missin' until he was found, smothered, dead."

I don't want this mining talk every night, but Joseph and the boarders cannot leave the mine and forget. I shake my head, trying to remove the image of a little boy dying alone in a heap of coal. "That's why we don't want William in the mine. That's why he needs to learn and go to school."

"No, we jist got to change things," Joseph growls, his face twisted. "We need to make mine safer. Someone has to mine the coal. Not doing nothin' means it will be this way—always!"

This time I smother my words. Whenever I speak, Joseph has cotton in his ears.

I agree with better wages, but what does a safe mine look like? Mining can never be safe. There will always be mine cars loaded with tons of coal on a track. Men and boys will have to stop them by sheer force. There will always be slate coming down that the miner didn't know would fall. Working underground with the unknown above their heads will always mean accidents and deaths.

Two incidents convinced the miners they had to strike. A mining superintendent had beaten a young mule driver over the head with a hand ax calling it "work discipline," and the miners saw another reduction in their pay.

Fifty million tons of bituminous coal were produced annually in the Pittsburg coal district. Seventy-thousand men and boys were employed. The price paid for thin-vein coal dropped from 79 cents to 47-54 cents per ton and for thick vein from 65 cents to 28-30 cents, ensuring miners and families were starving and cold most of the time.

The strike was called for July 4, 1897, by the United Mine Workers of America. At the time the union had less than 10,000 members, but 150,000 miners went out on strike, urged on by the horrible conditions in the mine and the constant reduction in wage for several years that brought the miners and their families on the verge of starvation. Mother Mary Harris Jones and Eugene Debs were among the famous labor organizers.

August 1897

At nine o'clock in the evening, I wake from a deep sleep on the couch in the sitting room. Two miners are trapped under coal and slate. Joseph and the boarders are helping with the rescue and will probably not be home for several hours, if then.

If Joseph comes home and finds me out of bed, he will say, "You need rest. You want to have this baby?" Every time I'm pregnant, it seems he worries more about the baby dying than he does about me.

I decide to go upstairs to rest. Before I reach the landing at the top of the stairs, I realize I'm in labor. In a few minutes, the pains worsen, and my water breaks. I try to steady myself from falling backward. Within seconds I start swaying. Moonlight trickles in through the window at the end of the hallway. I want to collapse on the floor, but I cannot give in to that urge to slip away.

The pain inflames my body. I cannot make my way down the steps without falling. My hands start to tremble. Fear sweeps over me. I yell out to William, but he doesn't come. I drag my body down the hallway to his room, kneel beside his bed, and shake him.

"Get Mrs. Baloh."

The last thing I remember is his running by me. I'm aroused and see Emma's face. I feel a cool cloth on my head. "You're here. Where's Annie?"

As I speak those words, I know Annie is not able to share in my joy. She is still grieving, and if the baby is a girl, it will cause her even more pain.

"Josephine, I need you to move down in the bed. Can you?" The sound of Mrs. B's voice calms me but doesn't lessen my pain. I wave my hand, signaling yes.

My eyes catch sight of the full moon outside my window. Then I start to count the stars. The light from the heavens cloaks me into a blanket that feels like downy feathers, comforting me, a tonic for the pulsing pain.

"Good, now when I count to three, push."

I summon the iron will I have left in my drenched body. I grit my teeth and make a dogged effort to push every time I hear the number three.

"Push, Josephine, one more time. I can see the head. Soon it will be over, and you and your baby can nap."

The light on my dresser casts a shadow on someone else in the room.

"Joseph," and before he can respond, I hear Emma, "One more push, Josephine."

"You keep saying that!" I yell and do not regret my bad temper. Then I hear a cry.

Emma reaches for the baby. "It's a girl. A little girl."

Hearing those words, my body collapses. I desire to hold my baby girl, nestle her beside me, but my tired body cannot carry out my will. I close my eyes and whisper, "Clara," and then slip away into the world of sleep with the image of Joseph looking down at our baby girl and smiling.

Ω

The following morning Joseph finds me in the parlor. I had made my way down before he woke. Eleven years after William was born, we have a little girl. Joseph's hands are thrust deep in his pockets. He's rocking back on his heels as he stands in front of me.

"Joseph, what's wrong?"

"Nothing." He tries to smile at me. "I git you some breakfast."

"No, I can get up." I try to move and then collapse back on the cushion.

"This birth not easy."

"No, but she's fine and healthy, isn't she?"

"From what I kin tell.... She's not tiny."

"Maybe she'll be tall like you and William. I just want her to put on some pounds so she can fight off any illness."

Joseph's mouth curves into a grin. He always says I believe I can cure anyone of anything with food.

"So, you want to name her Clara?"

"Yes, I think it's a lovely name. You don't like it?"

He shrugs his shoulders and walks toward the kitchen.

Ω

Being an only child, William never had to share anything. He got all my attention, so will he be happy having a baby sister? Probably so. He has a kind heart.

Emma insists that the delivery has left me weak. Still, I'm up within two days, cooking for the boarders. Joseph and I spend hours rocking Clara to keep her quiet. In the evening, I sit by the bassinet, crocheting a tiny sweater and booties that match.

Clara goes with me into the garden, to the store, on my deliveries. At times I feel guilty that I am so happy while Annie is still sad. She needs something that will make her smile. She is still young enough to have another child, but that will not happen, so how can I help her?

Ω

"Oh my, Josephine, what a beautiful face," Ruth says, her pink cheeks shiny and scrubbed. "You named her Clara?"

"She's so sweet, like an angel," Emma sings like a bird.

Bella reaches into the bassinet. "Can I hold her?"

A smile spreads over my face. I finally have the baby girl I wished and hoped for, but my happiness fades when I look at Annie.

September 10, 1897, In the anthracite coal mine of Lattimer, Pennsylvania, 19 men were shot in the back by deputies and 38 wounded. It started as a peaceful march when the miners were accosted by the sheriff and his deputies. Words were exchanged. The miners began running away, fearing for their lives.

The Detroit Free Press wrote, "Laid Low by Bullets, the Men Fell Like Sheep Before the Murderous Winchesters of the Officials."

The Boston Daily Globe wrote, "Dead in Heaps, Deputies Fire on Miners at Lattimer, Men Were Huddled and Slaughter Was Terrific."

Slovak newspaper, Amerikansko Slovenske Noviny "Massacre of Slavs—In the Freest Country Under the Sun, People Are Shot Like Dogs—Slavs Are the Victims of American Savagery."

Philadelphia Inquirer called the massacre "a human slaughter in which men were mowed down like grain stalks before a scythe, by the deadly bullets which stormed for fully two minutes...."

"If the courts of justice shield you
And your freedom you should gain,
Remember that your brows are marked
With the burning brand of Cain.
Oh, noble, noble, deputies
We always will remember
Your bloody work at Lattimer
On the 10th day of September."

— The Hazelton Daily Standard, Sept. 17, 1897

On Sept. 11, 1897, miners in Pennsylvania, Ohio, Illinois, Indiana and West Virginia ended a ten-week strike after winning an eight-hour day and abolition of company stores. As a result of the strike, the United Mine Workers became the nation's largest trade union.

October 1897

Thank heaven for the sewing circle ladies who arrive early. After the sweet baby-talk is over and Clara is asleep, we all get out our threads and start quilting.

Maureen, who joined us a few months back and is often silent, stops sewing and looks around the table. "Well, have 'ya heard the news?"

We all keep sewing, not saying a word.

"My daughter's pregnant and only thirteen."

Emma covers her mouth with her hand.

Annie turns to Maureen. "What's your daughter doin' about the baby?"

Maureen shrugs her shoulders. "What's she doin'? It's what I'm doin'. Gonna do what other mothers have done. Raise the babe as mine, I guess."

Ruth shakes her head. "So, who's the father? Can't she marry him, or has he left and gone workin' in another mine?"

Maureen burst into tears, "I think it's my husband."

Bella jumps up, shaking her head so hard I'm surprised it's still on her shoulders. "You think he raped his own daughter?"

"She's not his daughter. She's mine. I got pregnant. No husband. Bob was my brother's friend. My father gave him some money to marry me and take me off his hands."

I ask a question we probably have all been thinking. "So, are you sure it was your husband?"

"She didn't say no when I asked her."

Annie clenches her fists, ready to hit someone. "What are you gonna do about Bob?"

There are beads of moisture on Maureen's upper lip and forehead. "If I say somethin' to him and it's true, then what I do?"

"Throw him out," Florence shouts.

A look of panic crosses Maureen's face. "Throw him out? Then what?"

With no way to earn any money, she is stuck in a bad marriage, or she goes back home, hoping her family will take her in. Unlikely, since he got rid of her once.

"What happens if he does it again and again?" Emma snivels.

"So, you're sayin'...." Ruth squeals, scaring my little dog, who skids across the floor to her bed near the stove. She brings a smile to everyone's face. I treasure the little dog the ladies gave me for my birthday. I named her Daisy, Gramps' favorite flower.

Fists clenched, Annie bellows, "Yes, kick the bastard out the door."

"What if he gets angry? He could beat me, even hurt my daughter."

I throw my handiwork on the table. "So, you think you have to stay with your husband no matter what he does?"

"She'll have to do what other women do," Ruth sighs. "Put up with it, watch her daughter, and raise the child as her own, so her daughter doesn't have the shame."

"Or take a knife to his body parts so he can't do it again," Florence shouts.

No one could laugh. Deep down, it's what we all would want to do.

Maureen stops untangling the pieces of thread in her hand. "She wanted to get out of here, get a job in town when she got older. Now she's gonna have a baby."

I choke on my words. "You could get down on your knees and pray day and night to get out of here and then wait to be disappointed."

Ruth nudges me in the ribs and chuckles. "I thought only you got on your hands and knees to scrub the floor. The rest of the time, Joseph is on his."

I feign my upset. Over the years, Ruth has become fond of teasing me, and once again, I don't disappoint.

I put my finger to my mouth to shush them. "Now, let's not wake Clara. She's been cranky all morning." I sigh. "And I'm angry with Joseph. This is the third day he has taken William into the mine as a helper. He says a lot of men are doing that. William will hand him his tools and supplies, fill his lamp with oil, load the wagon. Do anything he can to help Joseph work faster, load more coal."

"Is he old enough?"

"Old enough to go in with Joseph. William told me he's never been so cold. His teeth chatter and his hands hurt. I have goosebumps up and down my arms every time I imagine him knee-deep in water, crawling on his hands and knees."

Emma touches my arm. "So, he'll have to quit school?"

"No, no. William will only work during the summer break and on Saturday. I told Joseph if he didn't keep his promise, he would be sleeping with the boarders."

The rest of our time we spend in silence, leaving all of us in quiet with our thoughts.

Ω

A week later, Maureen and her daughter left Bob and moved in with her brother and his wife. They cannot have any children and will be happy to help raise the child.

In February 1898 the sheriff and his deputies were tried for murdering one of the strikers following the Lattimer Massacre. Nineteen strikers had been shot in the back, thirty-eight wounded. Innocent was the verdict.

The defense used the country's prejudices against the immigrants, calling the miners "invaders from the Steppes of Hungary," who had come to America to destroy peace and liberty.

Articles had been published nationally using racist language about the miners and stated the miners had attacked the deputies. It swayed the public against the strikers.

Strikers, supervisors, and other miners who supported the strikers lost their jobs. The nineteen immigrant miners that had been killed came to represent the miners' plight and struggles in that area. Like all memories of loss and heartache, there was the desire to honor those miners by remembering and the need to forget what caused their deaths.

January 1900

Day after day, like most women in the coal patch, I am never still. When nothing much was happening, Gran would cry out, "Josephine, keep putting one foot in front of the other." I don't need her to nudge me along. My life does that.

The last years have not been memorable in a good way, which saddens me, but they haven't been memorable in a bad way, for which I am grateful.

My one joy is teaching the mothers and their youngsters who show up at my door two days a week, eager for their lessons. Word has spread. Ruth and I also spend some time helping children struggling with speaking English or reading. They are eager to do chores for both of us, grateful for our help.

The new decade has been ushered in just like any other year. I sit here watching the snowflakes flutter against the windowpane and wondering what the new century will bring.

"What's been gay about the last ten years?" I've asked the sewing circle.

The ladies agree that those who coined the phrase The Gay Nineties never visited the coal patches to see how the miners and their families live with tattered clothing and not enough to eat. The depression ended for the rich, but there is always a depression for the poor. It's a constant in their lives.

The ladies of the sewing circles still make quilts, and I have found another store willing to sell what we make. We are still taking orders, and we are now making curtains that match the quilts. I bought a sewing machine with the money I had tucked away and have taught Emma and Ruth to use it, so they can help.

While waiting for the ladies to arrive, the whistle of doom sounds out. Annie will not come until she has gathered all the news. A few minutes later, she races through the kitchen door and starts to share every detail.

"Annie, enough! Enough! No mine!" I pause and take a deep breath. "I've been thinking. Maybe we could teach Maria to quilt. She's been embroidering and doing a great job. We can make room for her at the table."

Annie's face beams. "I'll bring her next time."

"Good. Now, I've been wondering all these years about Emma. I know she's more religious than most, but you're outright mean sometimes. It's a miracle she's still talking to you."

Annie frowns and starts to twirl her hair. "Do you remember years ago when you asked me if Nick was the first man I loved?"

So, there is something more. "Yes, and you said, 'No, but I hope Nick's the last.'"

"Yes, and that's the truth. If Nick is the last, he'll be with me for a long time, but he wasn't my first love. My first love was a boy I met in church when I was ten years old. We were always together. I thought we'd marry. When I was fifteen, he told me he was going to become a priest." Annie pauses and sighs, a sign that this pain has been with her all these years. "You think it's silly that I'm still cryin' over him?"

Not even the bread I've taken out of the oven catches her attention. I fumble as I butter a roll. Eating always calms her. "I think the two of you never lived together. You never had to go through the tough times. The feelings you had for him never burned out. You remember him better than he might have been. Your time together seems sweeter than it really was."

Annie grabs the roll from my hand and chomps down hard, speaking with her mouth full. "But the Catholic Church kept us apart."

"His wanting to be a priest kept you apart. Maybe he didn't want to be with a woman. Some men don't."

I recently learned that my boarder Mike has no desire to be with a woman, something I guessed years ago. I can't understand it, but he's the brother I wished I had in my life. But then, in many ways, he is.

Annie scrunches her face, confusion written all over it.

"And yes, it's a wonder why priests can't marry. Maybe that's why he made that choice. Maybe he didn't want to marry and have children. Marrying was only in your head."

Other reasons come to mind, but I hold my tongue, so I pause, keeping my thoughts to myself.

"So, you're sayin' he didn't care for me?"

"I'm saying either his calling to be a priest was too great, or he cared more for himself or both. He chose the life he wanted. It didn't include you. You can't continue to blame the Catholic Church for that."

Annie dries her tears as she tries to speak. "I've just come to wonder if there is a God.... The devil, I'm sure of! Evil is all around us—the way men treat other men."

I nod, and as I do so, Bella walks into the kitchen fifteen minutes early for the sewing circle. Right behind her is Ellen, a new lady in the second sewing circle we started a week ago.

"Ellen, are you OK?" I say, noticing the absence of her smile and puffiness around her eyes.

"My son Billy is workin' as a breaker boy. Now, I've got two boys in the mine. My husband got him up yesterday morning, dressed him, and off he went to the mine. I was hopin' he could stay in school. He was good at readin' and sums."

I have a special place in my heart for Billy, but that can be said about all the children I teach. I want to help them all, protect them from the world they were born into.

Ellen sighs. "Hands and back hurt. The boss uses a stick or broom across their backs when he sees them dozing or talking or daydreaming."

Bella sighs. "When my son was a breaker boy, the boss would stomp on his fingers. The boys would throw pieces of slate or rock at him when his back was turned. They also threw slate in the machine to make it break down. It gave them a rest."

I gaze out the open kitchen window into the dull sky, feeling the cold air sweeping over my body.

Bella grabs a frosted bun off the counter and tries to speak between bites. "Day after day, Billy will come home with fingers bleeding, his skin dry and cracked open. You'll see."

Emma looks up from the fabric she's cutting. "Get some chicken grease from Josephine to use on his hands."

I draw in my breath and speak my words slowly so my voice won't shriek. I don't want to add to Ellen's upset. "The boys have to be twelve years old to go in the mine. That's the law now!"

"He's twelve," Ellen whispers. "He's just so tiny."

Bella shakes her head, pulling the thread out of the quilting piece she is putting together. "Yeah, but when my husband wanted my boy in the mine, he went to the notary. He paid him fifteen cents and got a piece of paper that said he was twelve. Money talks."

"Why can't our boys do something else?" says Emma, who now has her two sons in the mine.

I bristle and stretch my neck to release the kink. "It's the family birthright. Just like the rich pass on money, our men pass on mining."

"I know he's frightened in that dark, noisy hole," Ellen mutters, looking up from her sewing, tears in the corner of her eyes. "He's not his brother Tom. Tom wanted to go into the mine, be like his Pa. He was bigger and stronger at that age. Billy is afraid. He's heard stories about losing fingers. When they tip the coal out, it rains coal dust all over him. He came home yesterday with coal dust in his eyes, up his nose, in his hair. It breaks my heart."

Bella nods. "It's worse because they're not allowed to wear gloves."

"His fingers are so swollen. Already they're bleedin' like you said. They'll never heal."

I bang down the coffee pot. "I don't understand why you and Emma have two boys in the mine."

Annie sits down at the table and joins in. "According to Nick, wages went down again."

Ellen's twisted face reveals her anger. "If they wouldn't keep climbing in our beds, they wouldn't have so many mouths to feed."

Bella throws her quilting piece on the table. "Try stoppin' him. Even dead tired, my husband has enough energy to crawl on top of me."

No one can laugh. They bear the heartache of that one act every day, looking into the faces of their starving children.

In the latter part of the nineteenth century, many children were swallowed up by the demands of industry. Every day, coal mining put not only children's bodies—their arms, fingers, legs at risk—but their lives.

In Pennsylvania, in 1900, between ten thousand school children under fourteen years of age were reported to be working in coal mines, possibly more. How many more? There is no way to know. Often a boy was taken into the mine to work beside his father. Or the father had lied about his son's age to get him hired as a worker.

So many children trying to help their families survive.

The causes of most deaths in the early 1900s were pneumonia and tuberculosis (TB), plus diarrhea, enteritis, and diphtheria, which caused one-third of all deaths.

Of the deaths, about one-third occurred among children five years and under.

May 1900

When William was twelve years old, and after much arguing, Joseph had agreed that our son could attend school and only work in the mine on Saturdays and during the summers. In some ways, I'd thought I was giving Joseph a reason for not sending his son into the mine.

Now that William is fourteen, my time and William's have run out. Joseph has a job for him in the mine. After I did all the caring and feeding for fourteen years, he now believes he has rights over our son. I'm to remain silent.

"Joseph, you don't care that I will worry every minute if William goes into the mine. He gets good grades. It would be different if he weren't clever, but he is. He could do something else." I spit out the words.

Joseph just shakes his head and glares. Oh my! Maybe he thinks I'm saying he's not clever. Or maybe I'm shaming him. Oh my!

"He's gonna be a spragger."

"He could get his hands and fingers caught or sheared off, or the cars could fly out of control and run into him."

"He's quick. He kin get out of way. He'll be good at it. The boys work in twos. How you know so much? Ahh, those biddies, you know. They talk too much."

"But William's not a bit like you. He can't stop the train of cars rolling down the hill." I punch him in the shoulder. "And don't call women biddies!"

He scowls. "He's not stoppin' them. Each boy holds long pieces of wood. Spraggers run alongside the cars. Jab the sprags in wheels. Sprag locks wheels. Slows down cars."

"How many cars?"

"Sometimes six, eight."

"Two young boys using pieces of wood to stop tons of coal? Oh, Joseph! That job is dangerous. If you said that to make me feel better, it hasn't! Can't he be a mule driver or something?"

Joseph shakes his head. "You don't know much about the mines. Mules are mean creatures. Have killed miners and drivers. Kick them in the head or the chest or...." He points to his stomach. "Job not easy."

I try to turn away, but Joseph grabs my arm. "William needs to go in mine. He wants to go in mine, be a man."

Joseph has no patience for any softness from his son. To him, any signs of weakness or laziness are sins against his family, a family that needs him to pay his way. Anyone that does not pay his way, he calls freeloaders, living off others.

"He doesn't need to go into the mine to be a man. You want him to go into the mine. You think if it's good enough for you, it's good enough for him. Don't you want anything better for your son? We have some money. He can stay in school."

William has strong legs and arms, but where Joseph is broad with muscles that bulge through his shirt, William is slightly built. And yes, as Joseph said, he is wiry and quick and sure on his feet. But Joseph is handing down a life sentence for William without his consent or mine. I want something else for him. I believe my son does too. In time, when he's older, maybe William will be brave and go against his father and make another choice.

Joseph starts to walk out of the kitchen. "Do what you always do. Walk away when you don't like what I'm saying, when you know I'm right. I can't believe after seeing Charlie Peterson die right before your eyes, you'd still want your son to go into the mine. All those years of seeing young boys lose their fingers and get their hands crushed. Oh, Joseph, don't you care about William?"

"He starts Monday."

Ω

Thinking about William in the mine takes my breath away. He keeps a brave face during his first days. I believe he holds back his tears and anger until he is alone in some darkened corner of the coal seam. Then, when he comes home, we give each other a knowing glance, his face covered with coal dust. He knows that I tried to keep him out of the mine, and I failed.

Not wanting to hear his father bellowing and seeing his disapproval, William doesn't complain. He knows it will not change anything. So, instead, he faces the mine, trying his best and keeping his resentment to himself. My gentle boy is becoming a man, but there are other ways for that to happen.

November 1900

Annie comes tripping up the steps onto the porch. The whistle of doom rang out about ten minutes ago.

Her voice is filled with horror. "Josephine, several miners are trapped. Joseph is one of them."

I repeat the words in my mind, "Joseph is one of them." I feel I've heard that before, but maybe I've imagined it, dreamed it. All these years, I hoped I would never hear those words. I look up to the ceiling, trying to clear my mind.

"What about William?" I almost whisper. I am not ashamed that my concern is more for my son than Joseph. William has so much life yet to live. And I guess I feel guilty that I've not been able to keep him out of the mine.

The miners are trapped behind fallen slate and coal. This is the first time, surprising Annie, that I race to the mine, Clara on my hip.

Already a crowd of women and children have gathered. A thick cloud of dust is still pouring out from the entrance. Some women are huddled together, chatting, probably trying to ease their worry and making the time go more quickly. It's true. Joseph and William are in the mine, and it will be hours before they reach them. I walk home and wait.

Ω

It took almost a day to clear the rock, coal, and slate from the collapsed area. All the men had been found alive. Some had cuts and bruises, and others were injured with broken bones. Joseph and William were among the first miners out of the mine. I rushed to William and then Joseph. They were banged up, but nothing serious. No words passed between Joseph and me for several days.

I wonder how often William will replay this accident in his mind, remembering the horror he was feeling. I don't have to wonder about Joseph. He pretends it was nothing, and he still wants William in the mine.

September 1901

Clara is now four years old. Her latest tirade has made the blood in my head throb. She flails her body back and forth as if she's been hit by a lightning bolt.

"Clara, Clara," I cry, wishing I could snap my fingers and quiet her in an instant.

I worry every day—afraid Clara will have what Gran called a tantrum, that tears and blubbering will spew. Her face will turn blotchy and red, and she will throw her head back. I wonder if she's possessed by the devil. Then I dismiss the thought. I'm just foolish. I know some children are like this, although William was gentle and quiet.

She rages when she is denied anything she thinks she should have or I make her do what she doesn't want to do. So, what to do? Give her everything and not make her do anything. That will spoil her rotten, more than she seems to be. Oh, that's a terrible thing to say, but I can't help myself.

"Please sit and eat your breakfast," I demand, but she stands frozen in place. I know if she doesn't eat now, she'll stomp her foot in a few minutes or an hour and cry out for something to eat. It's always something I won't have or don't wish to make.

I tell her if she isn't eating by the time I count to three, I will lock her in a room. She doesn't move and starts screaming, "No. Want to stay here." She grabs my hair as I carry her to Gramps' old room. It will always be Gramps' old room.

My hands are shaking, and my heart is pounding so loud as though it were outside my chest. With Clara safe inside, I close the door and bolt it. She is finally quiet, probably surprised I carried out my threat. Silent for how long?

Over the last year, I've wondered what I've done to raise a child with such fury, such meanness. So unlike William.

For years I wanted a daughter to dress in pretty clothes and teach to sew and cook and love as I had been loved by my grandfather. Then a few months ago, I decided that Clara's anger was put there by some other force, a force I cannot name. Perhaps I've made it worse by what I did or did not do.

With thoughts of Clara still spinning in my head, my mind jumps into the bowels of the mine, and I see Joseph. Is he thinking of me too? I keep imagining what it is like for him to spend the best hours of a day below the earth's surface. As winter approaches, once again Joseph will only see daylight on Sundays.

For some unknown reason, images of how Joseph spends his day keep popping into my head today. I see Joseph's face soiled from the coal dust, water up to his waist, and the smell of musty odor from the dirt on his stained clothes.

Maybe these images appear more often because Joseph looks older and doesn't move as quickly as he did. Maybe I worry because we've settled into a comfortable marriage, although we still don't agree on some things.

Despite Joseph's yelling and badgering, he gave in. I've sent William back to school this year. He will not be a miner—not yet or ever, I hope. While William was working in the mine, my thoughts of him tormented my days. He tried to be brave and do what was expected of him, trying to earn his father's approval. He is my son, not Joseph's, at least not his alone.

I have tossed and turned many nights after the accident that had trapped William and Joseph. I kept hearing Annie's voice. "Josephine, there's been a horrible accident. Several miners are trapped in the mine. Joseph is one of them."

May 1902

Again, it's been way too long since I've written down my thoughts. I say too long because I need to write. I could say my running after Clara and teaching William and some children and their mothers take up my time. All that is true, but sometimes my spirit isn't willing.

But perhaps those are excuses. Maybe I can't write some things down. Writing makes everything so real—at times slapping me in the face. So, then I must struggle with what I can do, and most of the time, there is nothing, just like the miners.

Since the coal strike of 1897, there have been several other strikes in the coalfields. This year the United Mine Workers once again called a strike in the anthracite coal fields of eastern Pennsylvania. The miners are quiet here, except around the supper table.

October 1902

The anthracite strike has dragged on through the summer, and now it's late fall. Businesses and schools have been forced to close because of a lack of coal for heating. The strike threatens to shut down the winter fuel supply to major American cities.

Miners were given some hope when Clarence Darrow decided to speak for the anthracite mine workers in the eastern part of Pennsylvania. On the other side, Baer, a spokesperson for the mine operators, said, "These men don't suffer. Why, hell, half of them don't even speak English."

Darrow spoke of the horrible working conditions, the child labor abuse, and the plight of the miners in a touching plea. "They, the coal companies, are fighting for slavery while we are fighting for freedom. They are fighting for the rules of man over man, for despotism, for darkness, for the past. We are striving to build up man. We are working for democracy, for humanity, for the future."

When I read Darrow's plea to the boarders from the newspapers, Joseph sputters, "He's right. Capitalist king! Workers? We aren't even peasants. We're slaves. Just because they're paying us doesn't change that."

Finally, my husband understands what I've been saying. Or does he?

Ω

The mine owners could give the miners a fair wage and still have a life filled with everything that money can buy. The miners and their families believe they are too greedy to change their ways, but it's much more than that, at least I think so.

I can't help but believe these men take pride in cutting into the hearts of the workers and their families. It shows their power, and they use that power to hurt others. They believe that money and all that money can buy tell the world that they're above others, smarter, better, but what is better?

We are a better people when all are paid a fair wage and can live without fear and hunger. We can all hold our heads high when everyone has food, clothing, and a roof over their heads. Then, the American dream that is shouted from the rooftops has a chance of coming true. We can be proud of our country. We can then say as a country we are good and just and care about each other. We can then hope for a place in heaven, but the actions of these men never show they believe in God or heaven or hell.

The strike has ended. Most of the miners in the eastern anthracite fields were given a ten-percent increase and a nine-hour day. They had asked for a twenty percent wage increase and an eight-hour day.

The mine operators would not recognize the United Mine Workers. Instead, they agreed to a six-man arbitration board with an equal number of labor and management representatives, giving them the power to settle labor disputes.

The United Mine Workers called it a victory, and the miners returned to work on October 23, 1902.

March 1903

Snow is pelting on the window panes, showing no signs of lessening. It relaxes my whole body to watch it cling to the tree branches and cover the bleakness of winter. Children come out of their houses, making snowballs out of the wet snow.

The bubbling from the large soup pot is steaming the windows, starting to block the view of the outside world. I wipe the windows. I don't want to lose sight of the children, who are always hungry with sad faces, now laughing and playing. The smell of the soup combined with the bread baking will welcome Joseph and the boarders as they drag themselves in the door.

After a ten-hour shift, I see Joseph outside the window trudging through the heavy snow, slipping and sliding. His gait is hitched. His back looks stiff. Every day I see more lines on his face, his body hunched lower, and he's not yet fifty.

During the last few months, his anger has increased. He's not moving as quickly as before, and the amount of coal he can load in a day is decreasing. I wonder how long can he work in the mine and what will he do when he can't.

The force of the wind brings flakes of snow in the kitchen as Joseph opens the door. In slow motion, he bends down, taking off one boot and then the other. He is shivering as he heads for the coal stove. "I can't wait for summer," he growls.

Yet, in summer, he complains and stays out of the kitchen, insisting we eat on the porch on the days I use the oven for baking. He looks in my direction. I cast my eyes down at the snow-covered boots and the trail of snow on my kitchen floor.

"Josephine, it's cold out there," he shouts as he picks up his boots and puts them on paper to soak up the snow that is melting. A few minutes later, William arrives and goes to the pantry. When he walks back into the kitchen, Billy grabs the cloth from him to wipe up the melted snow. The other boarders soon follow.

All gather, and I put a pot of beef vegetable soup and hot bread on the table with a large glass of milk for each. With the bit of oomph Joseph has left, he kisses me on the cheek and touches my belly before he sits down to eat.

Happy I'm having another baby and hoping it's a boy, he helps with the chores and sends out his happiness daily. I shake my head, embarrassed by that thought. I know he's a good man.

I sigh as I cut large chunks of bread. "I heard there was another death in the mine today."

Words spew out of Mike as he swallows hard. "It didn't have to happen. It was bad. Charlie was killed by a fall of slate. His chest and legs were crushed. He was only twenty."

Joseph drills the knuckles of one hand into the palm of the other. "We need to walk off the job for a few days."

"Wantin' to bite the hand that feeds you," Mike mutters.

The other boarders keep on eating. They know that not all accidents are caused because the mine isn't safe. Falling slate just happens because mining has dangers. Maybe more posts should have been set, maybe? Accidents happen because the miners are in a hurry. They earn only if they load coal. Anything that delays their doing so is not often done.

The muscles in Joseph's cheek twitch, and he glares at Mike, pulling on the corner of his mustache. "You and Josephine said that many times last twenty years. That means because you feed a dog some scraps, he shouldn't bite you even if you beat him again and again with a whip."

I raise my eyebrows. "The mine owners can starve the miners and their families, fire them. What harm can a strike do to the owners? They will still eat and be warm. Hire other men. Striking won't hurt them." There is a bitter tone, an edge to my voice.

Joseph knows those around the table disagree with him, but he will not be stopped. "If you need work, shouldn't ask for nothin'?" He grits his teeth and points at Mike. "Think one day they're gonna care about how we're sufferin' and do somethin'?"

Stan shouts, "No, because they don't need to do anythin'. Men and young boys, hungry and waitin' in line for our jobs."

Joseph cries out, "You've been listenin' to Josephine too"

I glare at Joseph and shout in return. "You think because the union declared a win last year, the mine owners will give in here? They won't! They're like the birds that feed on dead meat. You just refuse to see that, Joseph."

Mike adds. "If we go on strike, they'd be glad for us to be gone. They wouldn't have to listen to us complain. They could hire people who wouldn't or couldn't talk back—at least in English."

A similar discussion happens at least once a week, and no one ever says anything different. Miners, like Joseph, rant because they feel helpless. Doing something, even if it doesn't work, is better than doing nothing.

Miners still remember the Morewood Massacre in 1891. It was rumored that Henry Frick told the miners they were welcome to pick up a coal shovel and go to work. But, if they dared ask about money or safety, they would be reminded that other foreigners with strong backs would take their jobs.

Mike sighs. "How can they watch people suffer?"

"Because the coal barons don't watch the suffering. Too busy spending the money you make for them." I bow my head and say just above a whisper. "Accidents and deaths are part of our lives, not theirs."

January 24, 1904
TWO HUNDRED MEN -- *Imprisoned at Bottom of a Burning Coal Mine.*

EXPLOSION BRINGS DISASTER
PITTSBURG, January 25, 1904

Between 125 and 150 men were entombed by an explosion in the shaft of the Harwick Coal Company near Cheswick this morning, shortly after 8 o'clock. Not one man was rescued at 11 o'clock, and it is believed many of them were killed outright by the explosion or have been suffocated by the gas....

RESCUE PARTIES PERISH*—Brave Men Urged on by Scenes at Mouth of the Shaft Die in an Attempt to Save Lives of the Unfortunates Below. PITTSBURG, January 26, 1904*

Nearly Two Hundred Dead.
Between 180 and 190 miners were in the pit when the dread fire-damp ignited, blowing the cages clear out of the shafts and burying the inmates. Of these miners, two have come out, one dead and one-half dead from injuries and effects of the deadly afterdamp.

Even the rescuers have not escaped, and SELWYN M. TAYLOR, the mining engineer of this city, who planned the mine and led the rescuers into the dark depth, is lying dead, while his companions escaped with their lives only with the greatest difficulty.

January 1904

The question on everyone's lips is whether there be an explosion in the mine here? The explosion at the Harwick Mine, a few counties away, wrecked the tipple built of iron. A mule was blown out of the mine shaft and over the tipple… forty feet in the air, falling to the ground. Three men on top of the tipple also fell. Imagine how much gas had built up in the mine to cause such an explosion.

All those men and boys—within seconds, poof, and they were gone. The mining engineer and a miner lost their lives rescuing the miners. The only survivor was a sixteen-year-old boy who was severely burned.

Smelling the bread baking in the oven, I'm struck by the guilt I feel at this moment. I have a warm home, good food, friends that gather around my table to sew, and children to teach.

Ω

Annie and Emma are early for the sewing circle and see me ruffling the pages of the newspaper.

Annie touches my hand. "Josephine, what's happened? Another accident?"

My cheeks feel warm. I shake my head, trying to muffle my sadness. "I was just reading about a woman…." I search for her name in the article. "The paper says, 'She haunted the hospital and the mouth of the shaft all night, just as she had done all day yesterday since the explosion, as she was still doing this morning, looking for her husband and two sons who were buried in the mine and whose fate, like all the rest, is the most profound mystery.

'She procured a lantern when night came on and went about with it trying to find her missing ones. During the night, when a couple of the rescuers had thrown themselves down on the cot in the schoolhouse, Mrs. Sumoskie went up to them and, lifting the lantern to their faces, peered into them to see if they were her men....'"

Emma sobs, "How horrible. That poor woman. All those families.... Do they know how many died yet?"

I shake my head. "The paper says around one-hundred and eighty. It happened 220 feet below the surface. How will they ever get the bodies out?"

Emma, through her tears, mutters, "What will those families do?"

"A relief fund is asking for money. A senator gave a check of $1,000. Nothing from the coal company that I know about."

Again, mothers will be tossed out of their homes, without money to feed their children or bury any survivors. Families left behind in the old country will never know what happened to their sons and brothers, maybe husbands and.... If this is a sign of things to come, it will be another bad year.

Ω

This morning I woke up shivering, the cold going straight through my bones. Many miners and their families are perhaps sharing one bed. On winter days, the children run down the cold stairs and push and shove each other for a spot right next to the stove if there is enough coal and wood for a fire. Mothers pack dinner pails with one hand and put bread, sometimes stale, on the table. There's much more hunger in winter. There are no gardens with vegetables, no berries or apples to pick, and wild game is scarce.

Once the house is quiet, and my chores are done, I remember how I enjoy putting my thoughts on paper. Then I wonder if I have much to say that anyone wants to read. No matter what, I need to write.

I walk over to the cradle and check the diaper of my baby boy, Lucas, born on October 8, 1903. William is now 18, Clara 7, Joseph 48, and I'm 36. Joseph was shocked when I told him I was pregnant, almost six years after Clara's birth. I have to say I was annoyed. Clara is enough for one lifetime.

Before leaving the bedroom, I look around. Everything is in its place, just as I like it. I smile, thinking of Joseph teasing me about always having a paintbrush, a broom, dustpan, or dust cloth in my hand. But I know he appreciates that I keep the house clean and tidy.

I pick up all the laundry I've collected from the bedrooms the day before and throw the huge bundle down the stairway. As I walk down the steps, I pick up the pieces that have not made it to the bottom. My girl for the day is ill, so it will be a hard day of work alone.

After feeding the animals, Joseph comes through the back door just as I walk into the kitchen. Over the last year, he's lost some of his hair, but he still makes a woman look at him. A bit of the sparkle is missing from his eyes, but they are still warm, pulling me into his arms at the most unexpected moments. I shake my head, dismissing those thoughts. I have laundry to do.

July 1904

It has been ten days since my fears came true, and I'm still numb. I have thought about those days again and again. Live-over moments I would prefer not to live over. Maybe writing them down will help ease my sorrow. Maybe.

I was in the kitchen, Lucas by my side in the bassinet. When the whistle of doom rang out, he started to cry. I picked him up in my arms to dry his tears, and a shiver went through my body. "Why don't they stop blowing that whistle," I muttered to my little boy.

While he was resting on one hip, his tears almost gone, I started to measure the flour and salt for bread. I was putting the bread in the bowl to rise when Annie raced into the house—her face flushed and tears appearing in her eyes. I was struck by the horror of what I knew I would hear.

"Josephine, it's Joseph." Annie did not need to say anymore. I looked at Lucas's face and saw the face of his father.

William and the mine boss came into the kitchen as I was about to speak. "Josephine, you've heard," the mine boss said, gazing at Annie. "It was quick. A mine car hit him."

He stopped speaking as I glared at him. I can still hear my words, spoken in an even tone, without tears or anger, "I don't want to hear any more! I don't need to hear anymore."

My defiant stare told them to leave me alone. I could not speak or cry. I collapsed on a chair, Annie's voice in the distance.

Joseph's body was delivered to our home an hour later. The sight of his body, all bloody and broken, made his death real to me. Annie and Emma were by my side, helping me remove his clothes, wash away the coal dust and blood, and dress him in his only suit. We did it all in silence.

Ω

Joseph was laid out in the sitting room. For two days, mourners visited and shared stories about their families. Throughout, I tried not to imagine life without Joseph. The despair of his death was like a strong wind whipping through my life.

Yet, I could not let his death put out the fire within me. I have seen other women fall apart, not taking care of their children, hiding away. That won't happen to me. Instead, I will become stronger.

Several times during the wake, I looked at Joseph in the casket, trying to hold back the tears that well up in my eyes and stream down my face. I felt alone and, at times, fearful. I wanted Joseph to be alive again, bellowing throughout the house, and my sadness to be gone.

William stayed by my side, his eyes often moist and his grip tight on my arm. Clara's expression revealed no sadness, but I believed she loved her father. At least, that's what I wanted to believe. He had doted on her and never said a harsh word. He left that to me. "I take care of William and you, Clara," he had said when she was about two.

Annie had walked over to the casket and touched my arm. "Clara hasn't... She never seems to...." and her words trailed off, possibly realizing she would bring me more sadness.

Maybe Clara was protecting her heart. If you don't love, you can't have pain and loss. I shook my head, thinking of her, and tried to stop myself from sinking down on my knees. I realized then I was not concerned about Clara's heart. It was my own heart I was thinking about. Clara was too young to understand death, to miss her father like I would. She might never know the meaning her father's death will have on her and her life.

I turned towards Annie. "When she was a toddler, she'd coo and snuggle on Joseph's lap. She always wanted him to play with her, and he did that. I paused, trying to swallow my lump of sorrow. "I waited so long for a little girl." My voice was choking with grief.

"Well, she's only seven years old," Annie said above a whisper.

Yet, we both know that her age is not why Clara cares only about herself. She can hold the same hard stare as Joseph's mother and Rosie.

When the lid was closed on the casket, the rain stopped outside. The gray clouds still hung low and heavy, blocking out the light. Water was still dripping from the leaves of the trees as the mourners arrived at the gravesite.

The neighbors who attended the funeral were miners and their wives and children. They stood still with blank stares. I winced, realizing the wives are picturing their husbands or sons or fathers in a coffin one day. The sadness on their faces was for themselves—the uncertainty of life, the fate that awaits them.

Joseph's mother stood across from me at the burial site, her usual stare piercing my inner being. She had not spoken more than a few words to me over the three days, although she broke her promise and came to our home for the vigil. She sat by Joseph's casket, not leaving his side or speaking to anyone, not even me.

Instead of listening to the priest's words, the realness of Joseph's death was beginning to enter my body. My mind was buzzing with thoughts of what my life will be like without Joseph by my side. We had been together for twenty years, and we had never spent more than a workday apart during that time.

I glanced at the faces of my brothers and their families, women in the sewing circle with their children. Then, I noticed a tall, angular woman who I did not know arrived. She walked over and stood between Joseph's mother and sister. The woman's blue-gray eyes, watchful and intense, grabbed on to mine. The bond was uncomfortable but genuine. Her stare sent shivers through my body. The look in those eyes told me she understood my heartache. For those few seconds, I forgot that my husband was about to be lowered into the cold ground.

I awakened from my numbness when I heard dirt hitting the casket and the priest saying, "Ashes to ashes, dust to dust...." I shuddered and cupped my face in my hands.

William's voice startled me. "Ma, let's go back to the house. That's where Pa is, not in this ground."

As I turned, I noticed William looking in that woman's direction before taking my arm. On the way back to the house, I was silent, but before we arrived home, I said to William. "You noticed that woman at the gravesite with your grandmother? Do you know her?"

William bent his head and cast his eyes downward. "William, did you hear me?"

For a moment, he glanced away and seemed to want to escape. Then, just above a whisper, he said, "I saw her at Gran's house. She was there almost every Sunday when we visited."

"You and your father never said anything. I always thought it was just his mother and sister's family. Why didn't you tell me?"

He hesitated, pressing his lips together. "Pa said there was no reason to tell you."

Tears pricked behind my eyes and were ready to spill down my cheeks. I pulled them back and breathed a deep sigh. "He's not here. I can't be angry at him. But who is she?"

William hesitated for several seconds, his eyes squinting in thought. "Pa knew her from the old country. She spoke like him. Pa said he had known her since he was little. I think she was the wife of a friend of his who died. I didn't tell you because Pa asked me not to, but I always wanted to tell you. She was always nice," he said and then bit his bottom lip.

"What's her name?"

"Clara, but I don't know her last name."

I felt as though I had been slapped. Was that the reason Joseph wasn't happy about the name Clara for our daughter? My stomach churned with emotions going in all directions.

"His mother. She never liked me, never thought I was good enough for her son." I realized my voice was rising. "To her, I was always the wrong wife. It didn't matter that he had a good life with me, that I gave him three children, that I cared for him."

William's eyes flashed a look of disbelief. I had not shared those thoughts with my son before. My voice dropped to a whisper. "When was the last time you saw that woman?"

William lifted his head and gazed back at me, his eyes dull and sad. "A few weeks ago."

I released my hand from William's arm. He had betrayed me, kept Joseph's secret. I had not expected that of William.

Ω

Like my Gran preached, I resist crying in public. Grief and sorrow are to be suffered in silence. If you want to fall apart, you have to do it alone, behind closed doors, so I worked to keep calm although my heart was in pieces.

At the house, I sidestepped the mourners. I didn't want to be pitied or hear the words, "You have my condolences" or "He was a good man. He'll be missed."

I walked up the stairs to check on Lucas. A neighbor had been watching him. A smile came over my face as I watched him stretch and gurgle. "Thank you, Meg. I'll stay with him now."

Our bedroom brought back so many memories, throwing me off balance. The stillness of the room was overwhelmingly sad.

I could smell the dampness and carbide of my husband's hair. My first impulse was to escape, but where could I go?

I then felt Joseph against me. A smile appeared on my face, waiting for him to touch my hair and kiss my neck. Then I remembered that he was no longer walking on this earth.

"Is it alright now, Gran, to fall apart?" I whispered, collapsing on our bed.

Ω

No misery talking this morning. This is about my life and the life of my children and the one yet to be born.

Night after night, for twenty years, I had fallen asleep comforted by the presence of Joseph next to me. I can still hear his breathing and feel his arms wrapped around me. Now, next to me are memories that disturb my sleep.

There are moments when I want to be still, frozen in time, not thinking about what to do next, but my mind cannot be silenced. Day after day, I awaken, knowing that I am on my own. I have no time to grieve, no time to grumble.

Hoping that my life will be different would keep me stuck in place. Hoping would fool me into thinking that my life could be changed by someone or something, that everything about my life is in someone else's hands, not mine.

The loss my children and I are suffering is ever-lasting. Wishing to marry someone I would come to care about is using time—time I cannot afford to waste. Hoping and wishing will never change anything.

There is no returning to when Joseph and I sat on the porch and enjoyed quiet moments. My head is telling me I have to accept this loss so that healing can begin. But, how am I going to get my heart to come along on that journey?

Ω

The fire in the hearth in the sitting room is growing dim. Bits of candles are flickering. William is sitting slumped deep in a chair in the corner of the room. Seeing the sorrow and misery on his face, I touch his shoulder. "Can I get you a cup of coffee?"

My son rakes his hand through his wavy hair and then shakes his head. A sudden change in his expression, a tightening around his lips and eyes. "Ma, now I'm the man of the house. That's what Pa said. If anything happened to him, I'm the man."

I cannot hide my surprise. To put that on the shoulders of a young man.... Now eighteen years of age, William has Joseph's blue eyes and straw-colored hair and chiseled jaw, but that is where the likenesses stop.

In my quietest moments, I always thought that Joseph never gave our son the approval he needed. Even when William was a little boy, Joseph tried to make him into a man. He had never accepted the boy William was and the man he would come to be. Our son had grown up without his father ever seeing him.

We sit together in the silence and gloom of the darkened room. I have to move, to keep busy. I ease out of my chair, yet wanting to give in to my weariness. "I'll make some bread."

William's face shows no reaction as he leans forward. Trying to keep me still.... His father gave up early on, and my son learned a long time ago that I follow my own path.

"Ma, do you think Pa is walking beside us? Gran told me he watches over us."

"He did that while he was here. He walks on this earth in you, Clara, and Lucas. He lives on in all of you. I think that's the most we know."

August 1904

The rain is bouncing off the window glass. Moments later, I hear the boarders walking up the steps to the back door. The men arrive one-by-one at the table. In between the mouthfuls of food, I hear the mutterings about the mine.

What could crush your spirit more than working in a coal mine and living in a coal patch? I close my eyes, and a pang of fury runs through my body. I open the oven door and start to pull out the casserole. I'm doing my best to give the boarders a good meal without Joseph's pay.

John gets up from the table and rushes to the stove. My newest boarder has made himself part of the family during the past few months, playing with Lucas and chatting with William.

"Can I help you, Josephine?" He grabs a towel, takes the hot pan from me, and puts it on top of the stove.

Before Joseph passed away, John had told him that he was blessed to have such a fine wife and son like William. Joseph had just mumbled. I don't think Joseph ever thought about it. He just took it as how it should be.

John had watched the two of us on the porch or in the garden, content and at ease with each other most of the time. Yet, the harsh words that spouted from Joseph's mouth seemed to make him uncomfortable. John would walk away or busy himself with something or smile and nod approval when I spoke up. Like Mike, he seems to like my spirit.

Ω

The late afternoon sun is sending a shadow through the kitchen window. I imagine Joseph sitting next to me. The image is so vivid I believe I can reach out and touch his hand. I'm not surprised by his constant presence in my life after his death, showing up in my quiet moments. The banging of the kitchen door brings me out of my trance.

Annie walks in and takes a towel to dry the pots and pans. Over the years, we have forged an affection for each other that I never expected from anyone. Annie has been a gift I gave myself the second she arrived at my front door with her twins in tow. I can still hear the twins' laughter and the pitter-patter of footsteps on the porch and Annie's voice calling after them.

A thought that often washes over me is that Annie was sent to me to make my days happier and lighter. Daily she walks into the house, and we meld into one, gabbing, enjoying each other's company. Besides her bubbly ways and laughter, Annie always oozes a sense of warmth and caring.

"If I had a penny for every time you walked into my kitchen, I'd be rich." I pause and notice the hurt behind Annie's eyes and add, "All these years, I wouldn't have laughed so much. I wouldn't have the sewing circle ladies as friends."

She plops down on a chair and smiles. "And I wouldn't have learned so much. It's good we have each OTHER, and this OTHER is worried about you. I always thought that if anything happened to Joseph, you would pick up your life and move on."

How can I come to grasp that I am still on this earth, but Joseph is not?

"You did, did you? Well, that's what I've been doing."

I don't want to remind her how long it took for her to stop mourning the loss of Sophia if, in fact, she has ever stopped.

"You're just doin' what you always do, Josephine, but you're somewhere else. Why not have some faith? Why not hope for things to change? Doesn't cost anything. Speakin' of that, why don't you hope to marry again? There are lots of single men hangin' about."

Over the years, my feelings for Joseph had deepened. Still, of one thing I had become convinced, love and marriage never change anything, never solve anything. Marriage turns some women into silly ninnies who expect someone else to take care of them, tell them what to think, and make decisions for them. They are needy, looking to their husbands for.... They never get their wings.

I'm not soaring, but at least I've taken flight. I spent the last twenty years resisting Joseph's efforts to put me under his rule, and I don't want to face that again.

Sorrow bubbles up around me, swift and crushing. "I don't want to rely on someone else to take care of me. I have my children and me. I thought that was enough, but Annie, I'm going to have another baby.

"Oh, my, Josephine, another baby. You must marry."

"Where would I find another Joseph?"

"So, you came to love him more than you thought."

I want to say that marriage isn't always about love. It's about a need or doing what is expected. Instead, I say, "I came to care for Joseph in a special way. I'm not sure he cared for me the way I thought he did. If you love someone, you don't hide things."

I'm trying to calm my voice. "To Joseph, love meant 'I will tell you what to think, tell you what you can and cannot do. I want you to take care of me, raise my children, and keep my house. I trust you to do that. I just don't believe you can do anything else, to think for yourself! I can do whatever I want, but you can't.'"

"Whew! So, you found out who that strange woman was at the funeral?"

Sadness mixes with anger. "You know I went to see Joseph's sister about that woman." Before Annie can speak, I add, "I lived with him twenty years, and I didn't know."

"What didn't you know?"

"That Joseph was married before."

As I say those words now, I still can't believe they are true. Yet, from our courting days, I suspected there was something Joseph was not telling me. I had no proof until now.

Annie's eyes widen. She looks dumbfounded, just like me. "Joseph, married before? And he never told you?"

A cold chill grabs my heart. "Yes, back in the old country."

Annie starts to bite her bottom lip. "So, who was the woman? His first wife?"

My throat starts to close, and my words sound hollow. "Joseph's first wife and child died in childbirth before he came here. His wife's name was Clara. That woman is his dead wife's twin sister. When her husband was killed, she came here. That was about five years after we were married."

"Oh, my." Annie's voice falters. "And he kept that from you, all those years."

Joseph's face appears before me. His eyes are sparkling, and there's a smile on his lips. "I guess we all need our secrets."

"All those years, every time he saw her, he looked into the face of his dead wife."

And only Annie could understand. Every time she looks at Maria.... Annie's touch brings me back. "I'll just never know why he didn't tell me about his other life."

"Maybe he thought you wouldn't understand. Maybe you'd be jealous of his memories of his wife."

"Or it was painful to talk about her. Whatever Joseph's reason, he has taken it to his grave."

Annie has no words. When she finally speaks, her soft voice drops. "There's another man out there for you."

I rub my temple, trying to rub away the headache that has started to add to my irritation.

"Not if that man has more children attached to it."

I shoo Annie away. I hope she doesn't feel the sting of being dismissed, but she's snooping where she shouldn't. Yet, she got me to talk about Joseph, something I have not been able to do since the funeral.

Ω

Almost two months have gone by since Joseph was killed. Last night I drifted into a deep and troubled sleep—nightmares of being alone, trapped in a hallway, in a room, in a train car. A sense of urgency and helplessness awakened me again and again. When I woke up this morning, my nightgown and sheets were soaked, and then I realized I was indeed alone.

September 1904

I sit down in a chair with a cup of coffee that is now cold. Low black clouds are casting gloom over the coal patch. Sadness often overtakes me and gobble up my oomph without warning.

Over the last several weeks, whatever I do to move on, my anger and sorrow return when I look into the eyes of my fatherless children and touch my belly. At times I feel trapped in a web. Every time I try to wiggle myself out, I become more entangled.

Then I realize that I've never overcome the worry that has been my constant companion over the last twenty years, the fear that if Joseph were killed in the mine, my children would suffer.

I keep reminding myself that I have to go on, I will get through this, and one day I'll be….

Yet, I cannot forget the hole in the ground that is now Joseph's resting place. During this time, I'm grateful for Annie, who reminds me often that Joseph had been one of the lucky ones. He had a wife who took care of him, a home, good food, and two sons, who in time would make him proud. Yet, her words do not comfort me.

Knowing Joseph had a better life than most does not stop the hurt of William and Joseph's betrayal. I cannot forget the strange woman who was my husband's companion all those years and forgive my son's silence.

For William, there is an empty space his father left. He wakes up in the middle of the night and sees his father's broken body. I have no words to comfort him. I cannot comfort myself.

Ω

As I walk through the front door after my walk to the store, I'm struck by the quiet and darkness of the house—all without realizing what I'm doing. Joseph's hat is still perched on the hall tree. I run my fingers over the brim, bringing a cloak of sorrow over me. Footsteps on the porch startle me, and then I hear Emma's voice.

"So, another death?"

She nods. "The rock ceiling collapsed, and Paul Partley was killed. His partner escaped."

Paul emigrated from Poland, and he and his wife recently had a baby. Another widow struggling to raise a child without a father.

"He was setting a row of posts, and the ceiling collapsed. Another senseless accident. Why aren't they more careful?"

I know Emma regrets those words as soon as she says them. We all know the miners try to be careful, but they are always in a hurry. They don't get paid for setting posts—just the coal they load, so everything in between is done in haste.

A few seconds later, Annie rushes in. "Oh, Emma's already told you about Paul."

I nod. "No more mine."

We collapse on the chairs on the porch. Again, I can't help but imagine Paul's last minutes in that wretched mine. Joseph's last minutes.

Annie stares at me for a few seconds. "You have a secret. I can tell. What is it?"

I shake my head. Does she read minds too?

"You know I've been helping Mrs. B deliver babies. I've delivered fifteen with her over the last year. She's getting too old to go out at all hours of the day and night.... So now she wants me to take over. I'm going to be a midwife."

Annie claps her hands. "So, everyone's tryin' to give you somethin' to do."

"With all the heartache I've had, she said I could help comfort any woman who loses her baby and any children who lose their mother."

Annie shouts out. "Smart lady!" She then looks over at Emma, holding onto that cross she never takes off. "Did you hear about Pope Pius the tenth? He's banned low-cut dresses in the presence of churchmen."

I love it when Annie pops out with these tidbits, often making me smile.

I chuckle. "The Pope is just another man trying to tell women what to do?"

Our laughter cannot replace the sadness I feel for Paul's family, for my family.

October 1904

Andrew Carnegie is now living the good life in New York City, away from the people whose lives he and Frick have made a living hell. I just read that he created the Carnegie Hero Fund Commission. Touched by Lyle and Taylor, who had sacrificed their lives to rescue the miners after the Harwick explosion, he had medals minted for their families. He's established this commission for heroes of other disasters and funded it with five million dollars. I've heard nothing about giving the miner's families money to pick up their lives.

You can't put food on the table with a medal. Imagine if a few hundred dollars had been distributed to each of the miners' families from that five million. It could have made a big difference in their lives. Still, Carnegie cannot look beyond putting his name on something, anything, not caring about the poor people he and Frick and others have made suffer.

Ω

I drag myself back into the kitchen and find John, my second favorite boarder, sitting at the kitchen table.

"John, what are you doing up early? Want to eat?"

He walks towards me and takes my hands in his. I can feel the warmth and dampness. As I look into his deep brown eyes, I'm baffled. I try to pull my hands away, but he holds on to them.

"Marry me? I kin help with the house. Lucas is still a babe and needs a Pa. Could help raise him. Maybe we kin have some?"

Silence falls between us, and I look down at my bulging belly.

When I say nothing, he says, "Watch and help Lucas grow."

Over the two years that John has been a boarder, I've been grateful for his help and find his gentleness comforting. Yet, in my quiet moments, I never thought his attention was anything more. I'm sure John notices the worry on my face. For not knowing me that long, he knows me.

He waits a few seconds, but I still do not speak. "You think it's too soon?"

I remove my hands and move backward. "I just don't know," I mutter. The freedom I feel since Joseph's death I have welcomed. I miss having him about, but there are times when he had consumed the air I wished to breathe.

"You like me?"

John's smile sends warmth throughout my body. Over the last few weeks, anyone paying attention to us would probably say we had more than just a boarder and landlady relationship. The knowing glances, smiles, and kindnesses could mean that something was between us, but that could be said about Mike and me for years. Even Billy serenaded me with his whistling.

Part of me wants to be on this earth alone, free, not chained to a man. Oh my, what a word, chained, but I guess that's how it feels sometimes. The other part of me would like someone by my side, the comfort of someone in my bed every night.

I soon recover from John's words but remain silent while John stands still, his lips so inviting, waiting for an answer. Beads of sweat are in the folds of his eyes and on his forehead.

"John, you need to know, I'm going to have another baby. Are you sure you want to marry a woman who's having another child? Want to raise another man's children?"

He touches my face. "Two little ones!"

With some hesitation, I say, "Well, maybe. I need time. Maybe you do too."

"I do what you need." He gives me another smile that would charm the devil and walks out of the kitchen.

When I think about marrying John, it might be said that I needed his paycheck. Yet, it would also be a marriage that would be good for both of us. He would live in the house as my husband, not a boarder. He would have a family, and I would have extra money to raise my children and someone to help with the chores. I'm jolted by those thoughts. All my reasons are about what is practical and not about our feelings for each other.

Ω

The following morning, no words are spoken between us, and then there is the absence of his smile. He's not pouting, just giving each of us time.

Ω

I yawn and clap my hands to my cheeks, trying to bring life back into my weary eyes and tired body. Last night I was called out to a miner's house to help his wife give birth to their first child. I gasped when I saw a frail body collapsed on the bed. The sheets were drenched in blood, telling me she was already bleeding out.

The bedroom was clammy and depressing. Dust was on every surface, and the floor needed scrubbing. The drabness of the room made me long to be back in the warmth of my own kitchen, but I had to push aside my thoughts and feelings and help the mother give birth.

I put a wooden spoon in her mouth and told her to bite. So sad she did not have the strength to push as hard as needed. After a lot of tugging and pulling, there was the sound of a babe screaming. After being ripped from a safe nest inside his mother, his face was puckered, skin bruised.

The young mother reached with her last bit of strength, touched her baby's head, closed her eyes, and stopped breathing. I want to believe that she heard me say, "You have a son."

When I told her husband, an overweight man with a gray-flecked beard, he had a son, but his wife has died, he cried out, "Don't want it! What I do with babe?"

I was too tired to argue, so I brought the little boy home with me to clean and feed and give him warmth. It would give the father time to calm down and speak to family members or neighbors who might help take care of the baby.

At six this morning, the neighbor lady knocked on my back door. "He doesn't want the babe. If you take him back, he'll probably drown him or put him on someone's doorstep," she cries. She then explained that he had come to America with no family, so he had no one to care for his son.

I look at the little boy asleep in the bassinet at Lucas's feet. I'm happy both babes are quiet and sleeping peacefully, so I begin to peel and cut up carrots. But before that chore is completed, I start another never finishing one—my mind awhirl. I have asked myself several times in the last hour, "Where's Annie?"

When she appears breathless, the babe starts to stir.

"I heard you have a baby here. What are you thinkin'?"

I try to get up from my chair, but my body is limp. I finally get the will to stand up, but a cramp goes down my left leg. I hobble to the bassinet, pick up the newborn babe and bounce him in my arms. "I wasn't. I was too tired. This baby needed fed and someone to take care of him."

"I heard the father doesn't want him." She then grins, "So, are you going to keep him, raise him as yours?"

I scowl at Annie, irritated by such a ridiculous notion. "No, I thought you could do that. I have enough children to feed. This tiny boy will never know his father or mother. Nick has always wanted a son, and it could be just what you need in your life."

For a few seconds, we look at each other, our thoughts reflected in each other's eyes.

Images of Sophia race across my mind, and the light in the corners of Annie's eyes fades away. "You think my life is so bad?"

"No, I think.... NO, I KNOW you're lonely. This little boy will bring some joy to your life and take away that loneliness. Having someone who needs you might make you...."

Annie's eyes glaze over. Those words, although true, probably have pierced her heart—a heart that will never be whole again. I can't imagine raising a child for ten years and then having to watch her waste away, with no way to save her.

"I'm too old to take care of a baby. I should be a grandmother, not a mother again and not the mother of a boy."

"Well, that's a fine thing to say to me. I've got one in the bassinet and one inside me."

Annie gasped. "Oh my, I didn't mean it that way!"

I avoid looking into Annie's eyes. "We can raise the two boys together, and maybe there will be a little girl as well. We can make their clothes, and they can play together."

"I'm not sure Nick will agree," she says, pacing back and forth, not wanting to look at the babe in my arms.

"You won't know unless you ask him, Annie. The babe is not wanted by his father. He needs a good home."

Tears form in the corner of Annie's eyes as she walks towards me and takes the babe into her arms.

I smile and touch the few strands of hair on his head. "He has no name. He has no one who wants him. Take him home with you, spend the day together, talk with Nick tonight."

Annie sits down on a chair, holding the baby in her arms. "He's so little."

"It's a miracle he's alive. His mother was so frail. She didn't have enough to eat while she was pregnant. She was too weak to live. She lost so much blood. You can change him and then rock him while I feed Lucas."

Annie puts her face against the baby's face and smiles.

Clara comes running into the kitchen, her chubby legs jiggling. She glances over at the babe in Annie's arms. "Clara, you want to hold the baby?"

She straightens her back and scowls at Annie. "I don't like babies. They're smelly and wet all the time."

"Be nice. This little one has no mother. No one who wants him." There is tightness in my voice, and I try to stop spitting out my words.

She shakes her head and stomps her foot, "I want cake."

"I don't have any chocolate cake."

She walks out of the kitchen and slams the door.

"What am I going to do with her, Annie?"

"You're doing everything you can. Clara's young. Maybe you're expecting her to be older than her age. Maybe you're expecting her to be like William."

I say, but only to myself, "And you want Maria to be more like Sophia."

"In time, I'm just hoping she'll not be so… mean."

Maybe I've given her too much, never asking enough of her. Other children will do anything to bring in a few pennies. The older girls help take care of the younger children, but not Clara.

Annie stutters. "All I can say is nothing, no nothing seems to make her happy."

I look out the window at the farmland in the distance with fields of cut wheat, stalks of corn turned under.

"Oh, she's happy, but only when she gets what she wants. When I say no, she talks back or walks out and slams the door like she just did."

Annie chuckles, "Maybe she needs lots more brothers and sisters so…." and races to the other side of the room. She pretends to duck from what I might throw at her.

Mentioning more children would have angered me, but this conversation only saddens me. "I think it's something more. She thinks she should get whatever she wants. She wants good food put in front of her. She demands pretty dresses. Despite all I do, life with Clara isn't easy."

The newborn stirs and gurgles as Annie hugs him to her. "He's sweet."

"He needs you, and you need him." Good. This time she doesn't scowl but smiles.

"I'll take him home and talk to Nick."

"I'll give you some diapers, and I'll feed him."

Annie looks so good with a baby in her arms.

"I've got some news. John has asked me to marry him."

"So, what did you say?"

"I told him I needed to think about it."

"Why? Nothing's going to change. You need a husband. You're going to have another babe. Why think about it? From the first time he walked into your kitchen asking for a room, you know he was smitten. Is that the word? Always polite and smilin', with a twinkle in his eyes."

She chuckles. "You two can make a good marriage. But more than that, John will help you raise Lucas and the babe. Maybe he'll even help with Clara, put her right."

She smiles and looks into the face of the baby in her arms and sighs. "John is so handsome and rugged and those muscles and black wavy hair. You'll have beautiful children. You could do worse, but I'm not sure you could do better."

"I need more than muscles to keep me happy, although that's not a bad thing. A strong back helps, but more children? I don't know. But, another miner—worrying about whether he will be injured or die in the mine...."

"Who else is there around here but miners?"

"There's the old guy at the company store—the young one working in the post office."

Annie tosses her head aside and chuckles. "John's what—ten, fifteen years younger than Joseph? He's got a lot of life in him, and you're just gettin' into that time of life."

"What time of life?"

Annie winks. "You know...."

"Annie, you're being...." I pause, seeing Joseph before me. "I always thought if Joseph died, I wouldn't get married right away, if ever. That's why I worked hard and saved money, but with three little ones.... If Lucas and Clara were older... and I wasn't having another baby, maybe I would never marry again."

"You know you've thought about this. You want to be married again. You haven't fooled me all these months. You want to say YES. You just want me to push you into it."

The first time I got married, I believed I had no other choice. Now, I am having the same thought—what other choice do I have?

"You're wrong! I don't want to be married again. Believe me, if I didn't have to raise my children on my own or if my life were different.... When will I be able to do what I want?"

Annie shakes her head, probably thinking I always do what I want. "Look at how good the sewing circle is doin'. You taught the children and mothers, hired the girls, started the boarding house, and now a midwife. You did a lot of things these last twenty years. I always thought Joseph was just along for the ride."

Yes, I've done everything I could to take my life into my own hands. Yet, things continue to happen that keep pushing me into a life I would not have chosen. But, at least now, there is a calmness that had not been there when I married Joseph.

"Having a younger man by my side could make a difference—maybe not better but surely different, and I like his gentle ways and kind voice."

"So, you're going to say yes!"

I believe that he will be kind in bed. But at this time in my life, I don't want more children. Well, no more after this one. I was grateful that Joseph was less interested, amazed when I had Lucas and now pregnant again.

Annie looks around the room. "John's not been married before, right? Any women?"

I've never heard his name linked to any of the young girls in the patch, yet he would soon be thirty-one years old—five years younger than me.

I try to laugh. "One good thing. John's mother is still in the old country." I lift the lid off the pot of soup. "He has a married brother who came here last month. That's all I know."

"Well, I hope he knows that you like to get your own way."

I sit down and stretch my legs. "John seems easy to get along with. I think we're alike in those things that matter. In the years he's lived here, he's never missed a day of work—no matter how he felt."

I want to add, "What will the neighbors think? Marrying so soon, marrying someone younger." Still, any woman trying to eke out a life for her family will understand.

Ω

On a warm evening, I married for the second time. William, Clara, Maria, Annie, and Emma were by my side. Some may think it's too soon. I would agree if I were living a life where choices were many, or I could choose otherwise. But in the end, I would marry him, so why not marry him now.

November 1904

In the first few months of our life together, John's kindnesses provided comfort. Yet, as the weeks went by, I realized I did not have enough time to grieve Joseph. Twenty years with him was just too big, too important. That time could not be forgotten simply because I had married someone else. The loss will always be there when I feel my baby kick or look into the eyes of Joseph's children.

In the window glass, I see my reflection. The years have been gentle on my face. My black hair is pulled back and piled on top of my head. My body has become more rounded, but Joseph always said it was in the right places.

I walk around the house, startled at times when I realize I had talked myself into this marriage, that I believed I had no other choice. Then I imagine that I could have made my way without marrying John. Neediness and fear can make anything seem right. Now I have to chart my course day by day, living with my loss while starting a new life with John.

January 1905

Almost five in the morning, and I lie awake listening to the wind outside the bedroom window. I remain in bed by John, feeling his warmth. After a few minutes, I raise my plump body out of bed, pull a printed dress over my head, and then ease it over the belly that is getting larger, it seems by the hour.

John wakes up a few minutes later. He reaches over for me and finds me standing in front of the mirror. He's used to my crawling out of bed at all hours. Often, he will find me sitting alone in the kitchen. Fortunately, my somber moments are few. Instead, our home is filled with calm and, at times laughter that ripples through my throat and body. John does that for me.

He slips out of bed and rolls his head to stretch his neck. He buttons his shirt and pulls on his pants, raising the suspenders over his shoulders. His burly hands sweep through his tussled hair. I open the door, and we tiptoe along the hallway, down the stairs, and into the kitchen.

He places a kiss on my forehead, and I raise my eyes to meet his. We will have a few minutes together before the boarders come down.

About twenty minutes later, the smell of ham in the air and the sound of coffee dripping call out to John and the boarders will soon be eating. Sensing John's nearness, I look up from cutting bread, and he pushes strands of hair back from my face. Even though I'm eight months pregnant, I show no signs of discomfort, and John says my eyes are always bright.

He grins and kisses my belly. William walks into the kitchen with Lucas racing behind, his tiny feet just touching the floor.

"Take Lucas with you when you give the chickens some feed and water."

William walks outside onto the porch and pulls his tasseled hat down over his ears. He bangs his hands together to keep them warm. He then picks up Lucas and carries him to the chicken coop.

The front door opens. I know it's Annie shuffling down the hallway. "Why are you here in this cold weather? Where's Nicky?"

"Maria is taking care of him. She's such a good little mother."

"So, she likes children more than you thought. I wish I could say that about Clara. She's paid no attention to Lucas ever since he was born. She'll do the same with this one," I say, massaging my belly to calm the baby that seems anxious to be born.

"Lucas is going to be tall like Joseph," Annie says.

"And John will be the father Lucas needs, but I'm not sure that's enough." I hear the pain in my voice. "And more each day, Clara reminds me of Joseph's mother."

"That's a scary thought."

February 1905

John and I have a son. I surprise myself when I suggest that he be named Joseph, but even more surprised when John agrees. "We should name him after his father," and then he tells me it was his father's name as well. We will call him Joe, a nickname I like, not wanting him to believe he has to walk in Joseph's footsteps.

Delivering a healthy son and enjoying the love and caring of a kind man, I find myself at times looking back at the sad times of my life, the tragedies I've endured. If I had been superstitious, I might have thought I was born under an ill-fated star, but there's nothing superstitious about me.

January 1906

"Pregnant again." I know I'm grumbling to the ladies in the sewing circle. I had tried to be careful, doing what I learned to do… pleading with John to stay away at certain times. I thought of standing on my head if that could make a difference. "How could this happen?"

Annie chuckles, "You mean you still don't know?"

Emma looks over at me with sad eyes. "Don't you want another girl?"

I often wonder why Clara is not the daughter I had imagined when I first heard the words, "It's a girl."

I rub my belly, "I would like another girl, but there's no way of knowing...."

There is sorrow on Emma's face as she gazes in the distance. She has had no children for years, and it doesn't seem likely that will change.

"I liked having my boys, such little men they were." She looks at Lucas. "He's gonna break a lot of hearts."

"So will Nicky," Ruth says. "Those dimples are so cute."

All the ladies know that Annie would have liked to raise another Sophia. Still, we all believe her raising a boy was best for everyone, even Annie. I remind her that a girl doesn't give you any guarantee. Look at Clara, and now Nick has the son he wished for. And her little boy adores her. His eyes follow her every move.

"He's like a puppy dog. In time he'll be at your heels, trying to please you," I say to Annie. That was something Sophia never did. She was always flitting about and doing what she wanted.

Gusts of wind blow in through the open window in the kitchen, throwing leaves all around. Then, hearing the rain, I rush to close the window as the rain begins to pound against the glass. Hail, the size of peas, bounces off the porch.

Annie sits back in her chair, face somber. “I guess hail is better than snow. I’ve got some news about Maria. One of our neighbor boys asked her to marry him.”

Ruth tries to chuckle. “So, if they marry, you’ll be feeding and cleaning up after him, and he won’t be paying room and board.”

Emma pipes up. “So, what did Maria say?”

“She said no, and I’m pleased she’s not gonna marry the first man who asks her. She likes workin’ and livin’ at home for now.”

Emma sticks her chin out with pride, “My Rosalie likes workin’ in the store. Doesn't want to marry. I know people are sayin’ she's gonna be an old maid. She sees how Violet is strugglin’. One child already. Another on the way. Not enough money to feed them. She's livin’ my life,” her voice dropping to a whisper, sadness around her eyes, her mouth in a pout.

Two years ago, Violet had married a young boy from the patch. Like Emma, she wants to have lots of children, at least until she sees the hunger on their faces.

I sigh. “Rosalie may still marry. Hopefully, when she wants. Not because she feels it's time. Look at men. They can wait until they're thirty or forty or even older.”

“This is your doin’ Josephine. Teachin’ the girls to write and do sums and talkin’ about a better life,” Ruth scolds with a smile on her face.

“I didn't say it would be better, just different. I'm delighted you're blaming it on me. I wouldn't have it any other way, but I don’t think it’s all my doing. I believe there is something that pulls women this way or that. Then if the path is clear…. strong enough to push ahead, they can travel it.”

Emma nods. “And they see our struggles. Some young girls want somethin’ else. I just wish there were more chances for them to get good work.”

I heave a sigh of happiness. Hurrah for Emma. “I’m just glad I’m here to see some changes for women. I just don't believe there will ever be a time when women won't have to plead and beg for a chance. They will always be prisoners of being women. The time in which they've been born will not change their choices that much.”

“But there aren’t many jobs I’d wanna do,” Ruth moans.

“It’s a beginning. I hope that one day women will be able to live the lives they want.”

Women live in a world that does not honor them. If a woman steps out of the kitchen and into the world, she is punished, mocked, often shunned. Women who don't marry are called old maids or spinsters. Men are called bachelors, and that's said with a wink. Many wives are treated as servants. Every way a woman turns, she’s trapped because she’s a woman. These thoughts make me feel so helpless.

August 1906

I gave birth to another son. We named him Michael. I'm thirty-eight, John is thirty-three, William is twenty, Clara nine, Lucas three, Joe just eighteen months, and Michael two months. Oh my!

I'm out in the garden with Emma and Annie, enjoying the sun and the breeze. The snorting of the pigs is the only sound in the distance. Joe and Michael and Annie's boy Nicky are asleep on a blanket.

"Lucas looks so much like Joseph," Emma says, smacking her lips on some cinnamon bread.

"Clara and three young boys at this time of life are going to put me in my grave early."

John doesn't have to be second-sighted to understand how worrying it is having three boys—one after another—in four years. Eleven years between William and Clara. One little girl died, and three I miscarried in between those years. Then another six years between Clara and Lucas. I could question why now and not earlier, but I don't. I could regret their births, but I don't.

Instead, I spend my day with my children, making sure they have food to eat and feel safe and cared for. Doing otherwise, whining and wishing for another life, will be using strength I cannot waste. But then, I remember I have John by my side—a kind and good husband and a father who plays with the children and helps me in any way he can.

Annie nudges my arm, looking at the boys outside in the garden. "I just can't resist Joe's break-your-heart smile. He definitely casts a spell over me. I often wonder how you can say NO to him. Then there's Michael's cherub face."

Unlike William, Lucas roams the fields, and Joe, missing his brother, tags behind, his little legs moving so fast, trying to keep up, stumbling and falling, yet still determined. Lucas can't wait to grow up to have a gun and hunt. But like William, Lucas helps me in any way he can, although at three there's little he can do.

"Your boys are devoted to you," Annie often remarks.

"What about Nicky? He's special, Annie! He's going to be handsome," Emma says with feeling. "So, have you ever thanked Josephine for bringing him into your life? He's surely your boy."

Annie lowers her head, taking in the breadth of those words. I know she loves Nicky. Maybe not as much as Sophia and now maybe Maria, at least not yet.

December 1, 1907. Thirty-two miners killed in an explosion at the Naomi Mine, Belle Vernon, Pennsylvania, owned by the Mellons of Pittsburg.

Friday, December 6, 1907 An explosion occurred in Fairmont Coal Company's #6 and #8 mines in Monongah, West Virginia, killing 361 miners. The deaths of children are unknown.

December 19, 1907 An explosion in the Darr Mine near Smithton, Pennsylvania, managed by the Pittsburg Coal Company and owned by the Mellons, killed 239 coal miners. Only one worker at the entry of the mine survived the tragedy. Miners were crushed to death, others suffocated, and the rest killed in the blast. Seventy-one of the dead men and boys share a common grave.

These mining disasters had several things in common: The miners had used black powder for blasting. Coal dust was permitted to accumulate despite warnings from England that it was highly explosive, and all of the mines were gassy and poorly ventilated. The miners claimed the explosions were due to management's disregard for safety and callous, wanton neglect. Management disagreed.

United Press Dispatch. Belle Vernon, Dec. 13, 1907 The coroner's jury investigating the cause of the death of 32 miners in the Naomi mine of the United Coal company this morning rendered the following verdict:

"We find the miners came to their death as a result of an explosion of gas and dust. The gas seems to have accumulated from insufficient ventilation and was, we believe, ignited from arcing electric wires or an open light at some point not definitely known. We condemn the use of electric use on return air currents, also the use of even lights in all gaseous mines. We recommend an air shaft be opened up where workings reach a point 4,000 feet from the main opening."

December 1907

Emma is sitting in the kitchen with the newspaper in her hand. Over the years, she has mentioned how grateful she is that I taught her and her children to read and write and do sums.

"Death is all around us, Josephine." She pauses and blesses herself. "My Violet's baby has died. Now this mining explosion yesterday in Darr. That's near here, right? The paper says over two hundred miners killed. Imagine those families.... It's so sad."

"And many of those miners don't have family in this country. Their mothers and fathers will never know what happened to their sons. Not knowing will haunt their mothers and fathers until they close their eyes for the last time."

"The foreman's wife said he had hounded the company about the gassy smell and poor ven—ti—lation. He wanted a new shaft sunk. The COMPANY had finally agreed. Twenty-four hours too late. They needed just one more day."

"Maybe all those lives could have been saved if the company had done it sooner."

"They're abandoning the use of open-flame lamps."

"They need to abandon them here too," I say just above a murmur.

Ω

After Joe and Michael were born, I wished my childbearing years were over, but once again, I'm pregnant. All those years without, and now one after another.

After breakfast, I ask Clara to wash the dishes. I'm on the back porch and hear the front door slam. When I peer in the kitchen window, she's missing, and the plates and pans are still on the sink.

With Clara, nothing changes. I breathe a sigh and think of William. He and I have the bond I wished for Clara and me, but then I have my three little boys who bring smiles to my face every day.

I'm lucky that the boys are more like William than Clara. Even at such a young age, Lucas does his best to take care of himself and his brothers so I can do my chores and teach and sew. Such a grown boy at only four. Joe is quiet and easy. Michael is tiny, with an impish grin, just like his father. I think there are horns under that mass of black hair, but he doesn't have a mean bone.

The snow has melted, so I sent Lucas to the slate dump to pick through the pile for pieces of coal with Joe tagging along. Just as I finish peeling and slicing the vegetables for a pot of soup, I see my two boys coming around the corner of the house. Joe is trying to help Lucas drag the wagon up the hill, and Lucas is pushing his little brother aside.

If I were going to raise so many boys in my late thirties, I couldn't have asked for more helpful ones. I pour out a glass of milk and cut a piece of berry pie for each boy just as William comes into the kitchen. I pour him a cup of coffee and hand him a bun.

"Ma, now that you have John, I'd like to marry Meg."

William is just twenty-one, and he gives me some money every week. Although, like me, he's been saving as much as he can.

"She can't be more than twelve years old." I stop. It isn't that I don't like her, but I believe they should wait a few more years. Waiting for what, I'm not sure.

"She's 17, and her family has said yes."

"Why not? It's one less mouth to feed," I say, regretting the words as I speak them. I guess I'm not ready to lose my son to another.

"We're going to move to Harrison City. I've taken a job in a store there, and we're renting two rooms in a house. Maggie will clean for the landlady to help with the rent."

I look into my son's pleading eyes and lower my gaze. "It's a good thing you won't be going back in the mine."

I could offer them Clara's little room on the first floor and put her in with the boys, but he hasn't asked. Besides, I wouldn't want Meg to feel that she must help me with all my chores, cook and eat what I think we should eat, or take care of my young children before she has her own. Doing chores in her mother's house, maybe, but in her mother-in-law's house. No, not a good idea.

"What can I do to make it a nice wedding?" Before I finish the word "wedding," Emma appears in my kitchen, tears in her eyes. I put my hands over my ears.

"Oh, Josephine," she cries. "Paul Evanich, only twenty years old, electrocuted. He was found by some men who were taking down some electric wires. He was friends with my boys."

Another young man with no family here in this country, no one to bury or mourn him.

January 1908

Twenty minutes after the whistle of doom rang out, Annie bursts through the kitchen door, with Nicky's spindly legs racing behind. "There was an explosion! The roof caved in, and two miners had their faces and hands burned."

I hand Nicky a piece of jelly bread. "You'd think they'd stop using open-flame lamps after the Darr explosion."

Annie flops on a chair, her face somber. "The mines will never be safe."

"Maybe yes. In today's newspaper, there's a story about a mining town called Marianna. They opened it last year. The mine is said to be the best in the world—the newest and best of everything. The houses are made of brick. There are indoor baths and fenced yards."

"Sounds like heaven. Are you sure you're not reading a fairy tale?" Annie looks like she wants to laugh, but no sound comes.

"The paper says everything's been done to make the mine safe. Men from around the world have visited and said it's safe and there will be no more accidents."

Annie shakes her head as she wipes Nicky's face. "I don't believe it. There'll always be explosions and roofs fallin' in. Silly to think there won't be an accident in that mine too."

Something about her words rings true.

March 1908

This morning I'm happy talking. Two days ago, I went into labor. Emma and Annie had stopped by to put together several baby quilts. They found me on my knees, unable to move. Bella said she could hear me screaming as she walked up the road.

I do remember John coming into our bedroom and kissing my brow. Emma was wiping the sweat from my face. Maria, my sweet girl, brought a cool cloth for my head, and Annie was telling me to push.

It took only about ten minutes before I gave birth to a baby girl. Maria brought in a small basin with lukewarm water and some towels. Annie sponge-bathed her, splashing water on her face, arms, and legs.

"She's perfect, Josephine. Ten fingers and ten toes. Everything in the right place. So, what are you calling her?"

"Margaret, after John's mother."

Maria brought me some broth to sip with a large slice of buttered bread. Annie toweled off Margaret and wrapped her in a blanket, warmed on the handle of the stove, and placed her in my arms. At forty years old, I have another baby—maybe my last.

John came in and cuddled beside me all night. I knew he loved me when he asked me to marry him, but now we are melded into each other with deep devotion.

From the moment we married, he knew I still had Joseph in my heart. My wanting to name our first son Joseph proved that. He had to win me over a little each day, and he has. He loves me, and he loves all our children.

June 1908

Margaret, who is almost three months old, was asleep in her bassinet. Nicky, Lucas, and Joe were playing with pieces of wood while Emma bounced Michael on her lap. I was hanging clothes on the line when the whistle of doom rang out. Even after Joseph's death, I still didn't run to the mine every time I heard that piercing sound. News would come soon enough.

About ten minutes later, I saw a figure out the corner of my eye. John's brother, his miner's hat in his hand, came towards me. I had seen that look too many times.

"Josephine, he didn't suffer."

I wanted to laugh at his words, how ridiculous that sounded. John suffered every minute of every day. You can't work in a mine without suffering.

"He died instantly. Nothin' anyone could do."

Frozen in place, my legs heavy, I couldn't' scream or cry.

His brother continued as I stood silent. "There was a fall of slate at the face of a rib. I wanted 'im to set a post, but he didn't."

This couldn't be happening again. Maybe this poor soul is the wrong John. I collapsed on my knees, my head in my hands. John was gone from our children and me, and just like Joseph, how he died could not ease my anger, my torment. I wanted to cry out, but crying would only scare the children.

The wagon with John's body arrived a few hours later. He was the right miner, the right John. My husband. His face and hands were blackened, and the blood had hardened. His body was not yet stiff, and his head and chest crushed. While waiting for John's body, I had sent word to the local undertaker to come for him. Preparing one husband for burial was enough for this lifetime.

Ω

I crept into my bedroom, where my four young children would spend the evening while friends and neighbors offered their condolences. The boys' hushed voices and Lucas's sobbing took my breath. Sadness swept over me as I looked at Margaret curled in a ball, her thumb in her mouth. She would never get to know her father, and in time his boys will not remember him.

Joe was sitting on the bench, his arms hugging his body. Michael was rolling a truck on the bed, that Joseph had carved for William. Lucas was sitting on the bed. His eyes filled with tears.

"Pa's not coming back, is he, Ma?" he said, rubbing his eyes with the back of his hand. As I sat down beside him, he buried his face into my body.

I felt nauseous and took a deep breath. I had no words. My three boys gathered around me as tears puddled in my eyes.

John had been a good husband and father. In all ways, loving and gentle to the children and me. He always thought of Lucas and Joe as his own, never favoring Michael. He fished with Lucas and told the boys stories about his time growing up in a foreign land.

"Why did Pa die?" Lucas asked, but I had no answer. I had believed that John and I would see our children grow up and marry, and we would play with our grandchildren. Then I had thought that about Joseph and me too.

I can still hear John's voice, deep and throaty, with the strong accent he never lost during his ten years in the states. I can feel his rough hands, though gentle, on my face. Although I had never wanted him around me minute after minute, hour after hour, I now miss those little touches.

July 1908

It has taken me several weeks to write about John's funeral. Maybe writing will help ease my sorrow, although writing about his death had not. I still cannot stop the tears from running down my cheeks, staining the page as I write.

During the service at the cemetery, Lucas's sadness shredded me into pieces. The only father he ever knew received the dirt that buried him. His lips quivered, and he held my hand tight. My three youngest were at home with a neighbor. Clara, now eleven, was under a tree talking to several young girls from the patch. I saw Bella drag her to the gravesite.

William was to my right, clutching my arm—his wife, Meg, next to him. William calls me brave since his father's passing. He told me in one of our mother-and-son moments, "You and the other mothers will do anything to keep your children from starving or shivering in the cold. You all deserve a place in heaven." Those years of making him read had given him those words.

As we arrived home, I sent the boys outside. Michael was clinging to my dress, and tears were streaming from Joe's face. Lucas cried out to me, "We don't want to go, Ma."

I sat them down in the kitchen with some sandwiches. The neighbors and relatives, including John's brother and my brothers, Frank and Fred, were sent into the garden by Annie.

In the past, I had thought I could do without the custom of welcoming family and friends back to the home. Seeing all the deaths over the years, I've come to realize that such gatherings are a way of letting others feel they are helping and doing what they can to comfort the family, and in some way, it does.

Ω

Most days now, I wonder how many losses can I bear until my spirit breaks. My parents, Gramps and then Gran, my baby girl, the children almost born, Sophia, Joseph, and now John. I know I'm luckier than most with a home and Emma and Annie and my children, so I get angry with myself when I want to cry out, "Why me?"

"Surely, I won't lose two husbands in the mine," I had once said to Annie after I had decided to marry John. Deep within, I wanted John to be my last husband, but now I have five children to raise. Will I do what other women do, what I've done before—marry? But then who would want to marry me with five young children? I don't think there is another John out there.

For several weeks after John's death, I've been trying to push my heartache out the door. I prowl my house, crocheting, baking, and scrubbing the woodwork, anything to keep moving. Several times each night, I awake and check on the boys. I want to make sure they are tucked in safe and not stirring. At least that's what I tell myself.

We are all sleeping in my room now. Michael, all arms and legs, is sprawled out in the crib on his stomach. I pull his thumb out of his mouth, pushing back the curls from his forehead. Margaret is sleeping at his feet, curled in a ball. Lucas and Joe, wrapped around each other, are topsy-turvy in the single bed they share. Clara is sleeping in my bed. I decided I needed her room to take in another boarder.

My sadness tugs at my heart as I watch the moonlight flickering through the window. Tonight, my mind is once again filled with memories of John. I was smitten… well, as much as a married woman can be, from the first time he walked into my kitchen, his hat in his hand.

He would talk to my belly and tease me and laugh and had cried when his children were born. He wanted his boys to learn and not have to work in the mine. He was patient with the children, even Clara. It was an easy marriage, if any marriage can be easy.

William had found comfort with John in the house to help raise Clara and Lucas. He also enjoyed having the three young boys and then Margaret around to bring smiles to our faces and laughter to our ears.

Oh my! Feelings and memories running through my head are landing on my heart. Maybe it's my way of remembering how important John was to my life, as though I need that reminder. I do know it's my way of keeping him alive.

After my parents had passed away, I tried day after day to see their faces and hear their voices. I didn't want to forget them or my few memories. I remember crying to Gramps, "I'm forgetting them."

He told me that I wasn't forgetting them. I was putting them into my memory. It would protect my heart so it wouldn't break day after day, year after year. At five years old, they were just words. Over the years, they have taken on meaning.

After Joseph's death, I tried to keep him alive by remembering our time together. Just as with my parents and grandparents, living my life had plunged those memories deeper and deeper. The same will happen with my memories of John, which causes me great sadness, but I know I can't live on memories.

I must think about the changes I will have to make in my life—a life without John. This time I have five children to feed and clothe, so I can't waste a moment feeling sorry for myself.

August 1908

Just as the sun is coming up, Maria comes to tell me that Annie woke up shivering with a high fever, gasping for breath.

When I enter the house, I hear deep coughing and turn to see Annie on a chair, her hair uncombed, dark circles under her eyes. The window in the parlor is open only a few inches, and a cool breeze is blowing through the room. Over the last few days, Annie said she was tired and had not visited as often. The front rooms are dusty and cluttered.

"Annie, I've brought some soup and warm bread. You need to eat something."

The gloominess bouncing off the walls makes me long to be in my kitchen with Annie, laughing and cooking. "All I want to do is sleep," she groans.

Ω

This illness kept Annie in bed for over a week, and it took another two weeks for her vim and vigor to return. That was a scare. I can't lose Annie.

November 1908

Just seven in the morning, and I've made breakfast for the boarders and six loaves of bread are rising. Green beans that I snapped and put in quart jars are boiling on the stove, along with a pot of vegetable soup. All the while, I'm humming one of Billy's tunes, and at times singing the words in my off-key voice. I want to bring joy back into our home.

I then gasp for air. I can feel John's lips on my neck, sending me into a trance. I have no idea how long I stood there, but when I awake, the bacon I'm cooking is burnt black.

Lucas is sliding down the banister as I walk into the hallway. "Didn't I ask you to take the sheets off the beds and bring them down for me to wash?"

He looks at me, his horns peeking through his hair. "Thought I'd shine the banister for ya' first, Ma." Oh, how he can make me smile.

Over the years, I've kept the same schedule—wash clothes, scrub porches, and bake on Monday, iron on Tuesday, sew and bake on Wednesday, clean the upstairs on Thursday, clean the downstairs and bake on Friday, wash windows, dust and clean floors downstairs on Saturday.

I used to spend all day Sunday making dinner, either plucking, gutting, and cooking a chicken—an all-morning job—or roasting a piece of meat. Now that John is gone and money is scarce, I make a casserole of little meat with vegetables and lots of bread.

I'm about to check on the boys when Annie walks in. "Guess what? I baked a cake." Still asking and answering her own questions. "And there's more bad news. Two hundred dead."

"Yes, I heard about the Marianna Mine. You were right. No mine is safe."

When I heard the news, it reminded me of how often I asked Joseph, "Can they make any mine safe?"

I open the front door and see Clara and two of her friends sitting on the front porch. "Clara, I asked you to do the dishes."

She pretends she has not heard me, so I march out and grab her by the hand.

"I wanna' play. Let the boys do the chores. I'm a girl."

"So am I. I do chores. So will you." I pull her into the house while she screams and tugs.

Only yesterday, I had said to Annie, "I've got to do something about Clara. I let her bully Joseph and me, and then John, heaven rest his sweet soul. He was just putty in her hands. She's driven me crazy long enough. She's going to do what I ask."

Annie just nodded, and I knew she doubted whether I could carry out that promise to myself.

I drag Clara to the kitchen sink. "Now wash those dishes!"

"Let Helen do it. That's why she's here."

"She's washing the sheets. If you want nice dresses, you can work for them."

"Hey, Ma," Lucas yells out, "Can I get the eggs?"

"Yes, but be careful. Several of the hens are brooders, and they will not give up their eggs without a fight."

"I'll feed them too, Ma."

When I look around, Clara is walking out the front door.

March 1909

Tonight is the first time since John's passing that I will be going out for fun. One of the young girls in the patch has just celebrated her fourteenth birthday and is rushing to the altar.

For the reception, I selected a blue dress that was John's favorite. I hold it in front of me and look in the mirror. At forty-one, I look too young to wither away. While I still have desires and dreams, I have no desire to marry for the third time. Rarely have my desires and the needs of my life matched.

I pin up my hair in a chignon with a pearl comb. Before starting to dress the boys, I change Margaret's diaper. What am I thinking, taking all these children to this wedding? Then what other choice do I have? I cannot leave them with Clara, and all the young girls want to go and have fun. Four little ones tagging along with a twelve-year-old, oh my!

I place Margaret in Lucas's arms and Michael and Joe together in the wagon, Clara walking ahead. As we walk into the patch, neighbors come out of houses dressed in their best Sunday clothes. Children race to greet each other, and men and women separate into two groups.

I'm soon swept up in the festivities inside the social hall, tapping my foot to a polka. Out of the corner of my eye, I see Bella walking towards me with an older man with thinning hair and beady eyes. "I have someone who would like to meet you. This is Carl."

The man holds out his hand. "Would you like to dance?" he says, with a heavy accent.

I turn to Clara and shout above the music, "Watch your brothers and sister," as I step onto the dance floor.

"So how many children you 'ave?"

"Six but five are at home," I say as I glance at my children. "My son William is married, and they're soon going to have a baby."

Carl shoots me a puzzled glance.

"So, tell me, Carl, where do you work?"

"Denmark Mine. Live at boardin' house down the road. Bella told me you 'ave boarders."

"I have six."

"That's a lot. 'eard your 'usband killed in mine."

"You know a lot about me. You must have been asking questions, or someone has been doing a lot of talking."

Carl smiles. "Little of both."

The polka ends, and I hurry back to my children. Carl goes for a beer. Within seconds Lenis, one of my boarders, asks me to dance. It's a slow dance, and he holds me tight as he whirls me around the dance floor. We dance, but we do not speak.

I look over at Emma, Annie, and Ruth. As I approach their table, dragging my little ones, I hear Annie say, "She's gonna marry him."

I walk up to them. "So, what are you talking about?"

Ruth laughs, "We're talkin' about that young buck you were dancin' with. There's somethin' about him."

Yes, there's something about him.

Annie shouts, "He's young enough to be your son. He's the same age as William."

"No way," Emma squeals. "He looks much older."

Ruth sighs. "That's what workin' in the mine can do. Josephine is one of the lucky ones. She always looks young."

Emma pinches my cheek. "That's because she's so little. I don't want to hurt you, Josephine, but why isn't he chasing after the young girls? Why not marry someone sixteen, seventeen years old, someone who can give him children?"

"Who says he wants to marry me or wants children? He just boards with me. He's just being nice. Wants something extra in his pail."

Emma shrugs her shoulders. "There are men who like older women, even their wives when they get old. They don't see age."

"That's plain crazy! It's men who are always older, not women," Ruth crows.

Emma says in a calm voice, "So, whatever you decide to do, Josephine, we'll go along with it."

"Decide to do about what?" I shout over the music.

April 1909

The night of Lenis' proposal, I paced in my bedroom. I think of Joseph and then John, but mostly William. I'm sure William would wonder why a man near his age would want to marry a woman my age and be with me in that way.

When I tell William about the proposal, he says, "Look, I know he's always laughing, nice to you, but Ma, he's got a temper. His fists fly without much goading. John and Pa didn't beat you, but I think Lenis will. He says things about women—things I can't repeat. They're dirty, and they shame women."

I'm stunned by William's words, surprised by these tales.

"Ma, he'll spend all the money you worked so hard to save. You don't need him! I can try to help out when you need something done."

"How can you help out? Your baby will arrive soon, and that may be the first of many." There's a tremor in my voice.

"Marrying Lenis is not what you want to do, is it Ma?"

But when have I been able to do what I want? Instead, I've always done what I needed to do. When I don't say anything, William bows his head. It's not for him to decide.

Ω

With five children to raise, marrying should be a decision of the head and not the heart. Yet, I can't leave my heart out of it, but my head must decide. I must ask what troubles would emerge for my family if we married? He wouldn't be a father to the boys, although he does seem to like Margaret. He wouldn't be a husband in all ways, could he?

Some would say he's a pretty boy with fire in his belly and a bad temper. Others would say it's a marriage for a paycheck, and so it would be… might be if he's willing to share. The young girls may think why me and not them.

Some would probably wonder how long it would take him to stray and have an affair with a younger woman. Others would ask how long would it take him to spend all my money.

Well, all that blather makes me realize I've made the right decision. This Sunday, Lenis will be moving out.

Ω

The following week William's wife gives birth to a daughter, Carrie. William is a father. I'm a grandmother. Oh my! A little girl to fuss over and make sweaters and booties. Someone to be a friend to Margaret.

Since 1883 trade unions had tried to organize the miners in the coalfields of Westmoreland County. Not enough miners were willing to join the union because the coal operators threatened eviction, but in February of 1910, miners in Westmoreland County met with the United Mine Workers of America (UMWA). The miners were angry about the decrease in wages and a new deduction from their pay on immigrant workers.

On March 7, 1910 UMWA vice president came to Westmoreland County to finalize negotiations and form a local union. Four hundred miners signed up and paid their dues.

The company fired one hundred miners for going to union meetings. They had ten days to move out of their homes. The other miners walked off the job, and the strike swiftly spread throughout the Irwin Basin near Claridge.

Twenty-five tent communities were set up by striking miners and their families. More than one-hundred temporary huts and tents were built overlooking the a dam in Export, the largest tent community. Other camps were located at Irwin, Westmoreland City, Blackburn, Herminie, Adamsburg, Penn Station, Wendel, Rillton, and Yukon.

The coal companies used the Coal and Iron Police, commissioned by the state and paid for by the coal operators, to protect their property and the strikebreaker, known as "scabs." This police force was commissioned by the state and paid for by the coal operators. Striking miners called this police force, "yellow dogs" and the Slovak miners called them "Cossacks."

April 1910

Coal mining patches throughout Westmoreland County are being awakened like Rip Van Winkle from their usual routine of work, sleep, work, sleep. The invisible fortress around the coal patches is starting to crumble, invaded by the outside world.

A strike was announced on March 9. Over fifteen thousand miners in over sixty mines went on strike, toppling their lives and that of their families. About two thousand strikers marched through the streets of Greensburg. Brass bands played. Young boys and girls led the parade. Boys carried dinner pails and wore caps with lights. Girls carried banners with "Give us our daily bread" or "All we ask is justice" or "Equal rights for all men." It wasn't only the miners on strike. Every family was.

Annie collapses into a chair, concern on her face. "The union says we need to march. It's the only way to keep the strike going. The companies say the marchers are threatenin' the miners crossin' the picket line."

"The marchers are not causin' problems. They haven't hurt anyone," Emma snorts, her voice louder than usual. For the last few weeks, the strike has put her on edge.

Annie loosens the knot on top of her head and lets her hair cascade around her face. "Yeah, but the strikebreakers walk by the miners and their starvin' children. They're callin' it in-tim-i-dation. The mine owners are trying to get an injunc—tion. It's to stop the marchin' and the picketing."

The miners are asking for an eight-hour day and wages equal to those paid in the nearby Pittsburgh coal basin. Since miners are paid by the ton and the wagons are not weighed, they want all coal wagons to be the same size to make sure they get paid fairly.

The strikers also want to be paid to mine fine coal, called slack, lay track, shore up tunnels, pump out water, and remove slate and clay. Often the miners spend several hours or even a day doing that work for no money.

Annie's face is a twist of distress. "Companies keep screamin' that the marches and the picket lines are illegal. But how else can the miners get them to listen?"

Emma clears her throat and sighs. "They're brave, and they've suffered so much. They're choosin' to suffer more. It's not right!"

Annie snipes, "But when do the coal barons do what's right? Families have been thrown out on the streets with all their belongings and no place to live. It doesn't have to be this way if only the mine owners had some heart."

I move towards the stove, my feet dragging. "The miners' demands are just. The big wigs just want to squeeze every drop of blood out of them."

Emma opens her mouth and looks like she wants to speak. Then she stutters. "So… you… agree with the strike?"

My thoughts about the unions and strikes have taken many twists and turns in my mind over the last twenty-five years.

"The miners are in the right. I always believed that, and I have always known it's the only thing they can do. Yet, I know the coal barons will never agree to any demands. In the end, the miners will lose. Nothing will change! Those in charge want to keep the miners down. They have the money and power to do that. They believe once they give in to any demand, miners will make more demands."

Emma looks at me and then Annie. "You're sayin' we are all suffering for nothin'…."

"No, maybe not for nothing. Some miners are going to lose their lives, maybe women and children. If men want to be miners, then until things change, their families will suffer and they will suffer. I guess the drums have to be heard again and again before something is done."

May 1910

The miners have been on strike for almost two months. Two months too long, but then one day is too long.

"May I have milk, Ma?" Margaret is holding up her cup. Her twinkling eyes and puckered lips make me want to hug her.

"Yes, you may."

Annie sits at the kitchen table with her feet propped up in the air while flipping through a tattered newspaper. "The UMWA is spendin' lots of money on tents and shanties for the miners and their families."

I can't help but sigh. "If they're doing' that, then they believe the strikes going to last a long time. The union's got to do more. If it lasts through the winter, the families will not only starve, they will freeze. A tent is hardly a home."

Emma picks up Margaret and bounces her on her lap. "We're lucky you took us in. In Export, a hundred tents are up. It's the most tents put up, and right in our backyard! Imagine livin' in a tent, cookin' over a fire every night. Maybe through the winter."

Annie chuckles. "I think the boys would like that. That's if there is somethin' to cook."

"So, how are you doin' with all of us in the house?" Emma says. "I just thought the strike shows no signs of endin' soon. You'll have us for a long time."

I mop the sweat from my brow. "Well, I guess it's been good having two more women in my kitchen. I do miss the boarders and their money, but I'm happy to have your husbands' doing repairs and feeding the animals." I regret my words as soon as I hear them.

"I'm sorry we can't pay you," Emma speaks above a whisper.

"I didn't mean it that way. I'm happy to have all of you here."

Emma, Annie, Margaret, and Clara are sleeping with me in my room. My boarder Mike, who I could not turn out, the two husbands, and Emma's two boys, now young men, are in the boarders' room. Nicky is in the bedroom on the first floor with my three boys. Maria is boarding with three other girls nearby and shares any pennies she can spare.

"We'll be fine." I try to assure them with my voice. "We can kill a chicken now and then, and we have plenty of eggs. Nicky and Lucas have set traps to catch rabbits. We won't have a lot to eat, but no one will go hungry. I'm more concerned about getting coal and wood for the stove."

Emma feigns a shiver as she starts peeling a few carrots. "It's going to be a cold winter."

Annie looks out the kitchen window. "Let's send the men and boys out into the woods for any branches that have come down. The men can cut down some trees."

I shake my head. "The wood will be too green. It will just smoke. Although if this strike lasts, it may be dry enough to burn." I try to smile, but the thought of being on strike for more than a few months….

Annie claps her hands. "We can pick a lot of berries and make a lot of jam this summer to put on the bread," her voice trailing off and then adds, "It will be bitter, and without sugar, it won't thicken, will it?"

I jingle some coins in my pocket. "Let's can them, and they can eat them as a snack. Maybe we can find a few pennies for sugar, but I'm sure the children won't care. We can have a bigger garden. Put in root crops that we can store in the cellar and don't have to can. Put in lots of cabbage. Cabbage and noodles will keep their bellies full."

Annie stands up and smiles at me. "Emma and I have saved money from our sewing."

I put the dress I've ironed on a hanger and sit down with a cup of coffee. "You know Bella is now living in Yukon. She's frightened for her son and husband. Thirty people were injured, and one man was killed on the picket line there."

"Nick told me that in Irwin, they're bringing in workers from Slav countries to do the mining. Paying their way here and building houses for them. They're calling it Scab Hill."

Emma yells, "They're taking food out of our mouths."

I don't want to talk about the strike, but I must. "The sad thing is the immigrants need work, like our men. No one told them that they would be taking jobs from others. They came here to live the American dream, not to hurt the miners. The company wants to break the strike. They'll do it any way they can. Bringing in other men to mine the coal is one way."

"I'm afraid for our men. All the beatings and gunfire," Emma cries.

"I am too. Mike told me that in Export a small group of miners was walking home from a meeting. Twenty deputies and State Police troopers attacked them. All those men with guns attacking a few miners. Some beaten almost to death, and one killed."

Annie frowns and yells out. "That's only a few miles away. Why are they afraid of the miners? There's no need to beat and kill poor people! And what could a miner be doing to be killed?"

I take several deep breaths. "They do it because they can. Who's going to stop them? And you're right, Annie, they are afraid of the miners. They want to keep the poor down. If there weren't poor and uneducated, they couldn't use them. They're beating and killing so the miners will call off the strike. That's the intimidation you mentioned earlier, Annie."

Emma pulls at her cross—something I see her do several times a day when we talk about the strike. "I heard that a miner was trying to protect the child he had in his arms."

I nod. "Put a gun in a man's hand, and it's anyone's guess what he'll do with it. I told you long ago that the government has given the companies a license to kill."

Our silence seems to be saying more than our words.

I collapse in a chair and press my lips together. "There's no way the mining companies are going to give in. They have so much money that their families won't suffer or starve. The miners and their families will!"

Nobody wants to talk about the fact that the strike won't change a thing. None of us want to share our doubts with Emma and Annie's husbands. They are sure the miners will win.

Emma sighs. "Over and over, we hear that America is a melting pot. They make it sound like a good thing. Yes, they let people like us come here and slave away. We're only allowed in so we can be used."

I would smile at Emma for her knowing if it weren't so true and so sad. The country needs people who will work for little pay so that the rich can prosper from their labor. At the same time, many people and the industrialists in this country don't think much of the immigrants.

"We're a melting pot under protest," I groan. "Those running things don't believe that immigrants add anything to the country but blood and sweat, and they don't care about the tears."

To end the Westmoreland Coal Strike and break the union, the coal companies began importing thousands of immigrants from Eastern Europe.

The Penn Gas Coal Company built about 30 two-story, wood-frame houses on Adams Hill at Hahntown, in time named Scab Hill, to house immigrant workers. The company recruited them with the promise of a job and housing for their families and paid for their passage to America. They never told the immigrants they would be strikebreakers. They came to this country to work and provide for their families.

In Export, Westmoreland Coal Co. built barracks behind St. Mary's Church to protect the strikebreakers. The building next to the church served as temporary police headquarters and as a store since it was too dangerous for the strikebreakers to purchase items from other Export stores.

When many of the immigrants discovered what was happening, they wanted to quit the mine. The Coal and Iron Police stopped them by telling them they would have to pay back their passage to the United States. Some were beaten and forced to work, and the companies had fences built to keep them from escaping.

The abuse got so much attention that the U.S. federal government held hearings on whether the coal companies had used illegal force.

July 1910

Miners are tired of the strike, women are tired of the strike, of living without. It's only July.

"Well, it's happened," Annie shouts. "The people with guns are killing the miners!"

Emma looks up, confusion on her face. "Are you hurt? What happened?"

"The miners had a permit to march in Greensburg. Deputy sheriffs and the Coal and Iron Police came at them, swingin' clubs. The marchers tried to walk away. A deputy fired into the crowd—killin' a miner. The Chief of Police tried to arrest the deputy who shot the miner. Then other deputies arrested the Chief. The citizens of the town were so angry they mobbed the sheriff's office and demanded his release."

I scowl at her. "At least one policeman tried to do the right thing! But, Annie, there's going to be more deaths and people hurt. You have to be careful on the picket line."

Annie looks grateful for my concern. "All we have are our voices."

Emma lowers her gaze, her face filled with gloom. "In the end, that's not going to be enough."

DEPUTY SHOOTS STRIKER—Altoona Tribune

July 13, 1910

Jacob Patla, a carpenter, and another man were stopped by John Snelling, a Coal & Iron Police deputy employed by the Penn Gas Coal Company. Snelling shot Patla and ran away.

The shooting took place at the junction of the Claridge-Jeannette and Bushy Run Roads. He is survived by four children and his wife, expecting a fifth child.

July 14, 1910

Snelling, a deputy sheriff, 30 years old, was found hiding in the woods near the Claridge mines, near where he shot and killed Jacob Patla, a striking miner, late last night.

Patla's body was found by the side of the road with four bullet wounds. The miners said that Patla was shot from ambush. According to the police, Snelling confessed to killing the miner and claimed self-defense.

August 1910

Annie walks into the kitchen, her hair hanging loose and clothes soiled with dirt from the garden. I start to chuckle, although I want to yell "outside." But instead, I say, "Is there any dirt left in the garden?"

"I've some good news. I've decided I want to be a mother!" Laughter echoes in her voice.

Emma's eyes fill with surprise. "No, not you."

"Yeah, me! Pray for the dead. Fight like hell for the living."

"What?" Emma says, a smile breaking on her troubled face.

Annie is scrubbing her arms in the sink. "That's what Mother Jones says."

I put a bowl of potatoes in front of Emma to peel. "Yes, I've heard about her. She's been fighting for the rights of workers for years. They say she's barely five feet tall with sparkling blues eyes and a crinkly face. There was a story about her with a picture in the newspaper."

Annie nods, "She looks like someone's grandmother, snow-white hair twisted in a knot here." She points to the base of her neck. "She came from Ireland. Her husband and her children all died in a yellow fever epidemic over forty years. He was a union activist. Before she married, she was a teacher and then a dressmaker. I guess she joined the labor movement at some point."

"But has it made any difference?" Emma sighs.

Annie splashes water into Emma's face. "So, Emma, you're saying we shouldn't try?"

"I'm saying the miners and their families are suffering! We can make all the noise we want, march, scream, yell. No one will listen. No one will care."

"Oh, Emma!" Annie cries. "But I must try to do something. Isn't it wonderful? A woman who's fighting for the miners."

I nod in agreement. "It's a miracle Mother Jones has a voice in a country ruled by men. She is considered the most dangerous woman in America. Hurrah for her."

Annie's eyes flash a glint of imp.

Emma whispers with a soft smile. "So, does that mean we won't have you in the kitchen?"

I throw my head back and chuckle. "We can only hope."

Annie throws a towel at me. "I'll be out with other women, but not all the time."

"Being a nuisance, and you think that'll help?" sighs Emma.

Annie puts a pot on the table for the potatoes. "Well, every coal patch has at least one mother. Mother Jones is seventy-three, and yet, she has come to our back yard, to rally the women."

"I heard that miners' wives got arrested for harassing scabs and the police," Emma moans. "So, you want to be one of them? I think it's dangerous. You could land in jail."

"I've got you two to take care of Nicky if that happens."

I glare at her. "Do you think that'll happen?"

"It has. In Greensburg, women got arrested. Mother Jones told the women to bring their babes and small children. The judge sentenced them to pay a $30 fine or serve thirty days in jail. They couldn't pay, so the women were jailed."

I shout, "That was silly of the judge. Doesn't he know the strike is because their families have no money and are starving?"

Annie laughs. "Mother Jones told them to tell the judge they had to bring their children along with them to jail because there was no one to take care of them."

I race to the stove and lift the lid from the pot of soup I'm making. "So, the government had to feed the children as well, and they had a roof over their heads. How clever."

Annie shakes her head. "Probably didn't feed much to the women. But Mother Jones told them, 'You sing the whole night long. You can take turns singing if you get tired and hoarse. Sleep all day and sing all night. Say you're singing to the babies.' She brought the babes milk and fruit. 'Just sing and sing," she said. 'Don't stop for anyone.'"

"What a clever woman."

Annie giggles. "It gets better. The sheriff's home, the hotel, lodging houses were next to the jail. The singing kept most of the local people awake. So, after about five days of going without sleep, the locals insisted that the judge release the women."

"So, he did?" I shout.

Annie looked over at me with a big grin. "What choice did he have? It's been our only victory. Isn't it great? Women who sang their way out of jail!"

A wince came across Emma's face. "Women can march, sing, picket, go to jail, die.... No one asked them if they wanted to strike!"

Annie, noticing the tears in Emma's voice, touches her hand. "But many did want to strike—tired of seein' their children hungry, their husbands hurt and crippled."

I gaze into her eyes and see resolve. "So, what's your job?"

Annie bounces onto her feet. "I'm to gather the women together. We're to stop the scabs from crossing the picket line, make a lot of noise, banging pots and pans to frighten the mules, do anything to disrupt the work."

"And get arrested?" Emma snaps.

Annie's face brightens. "Wouldn't that be fun?"

September 1910

We are six months into the strike. Emma is in the barn helping the boys feed and water the pig, chickens, and cow. Annie and Nick are still on the picket lines with Emma's husband.

Earlier that morning, Annie reported that seven shots were fired into company house #14, just down the street, near the Claridge mine. Twenty-seven miners were in the house at the time. Four of the bullets passed entirely through the building. Two hit the beds where the boarders were sleeping. It was a miracle no one was hurt or killed.

I guess the police have more than a license to kill. It's more like an invitation. This strike is going to last a long time with more bloodshed. I'm happy William's not in the mine.

November 1910

Gusts of wind are swirling the snow in all directions. Outside the back door, I'm sweeping the white powder that has blown on the porch, soon realizing my time is wasted. It's time to start making the soup anyway.

Now that the days are colder, I invited Ruth and her son to join our merry family in the house. They are sleeping on the floor in the sitting room. Her husband passed away earlier this year.

I also invited Gerhard and Billy to stay in the barn with their wives and young children. I can give them a few eggs and milk, but the warmth of the cow and the pig will be better than sleeping in a tent. Billy shot a deer that we are all sharing. On freezing nights, I will invite them to sleep on the kitchen floor.

Today all the children are outside playing in the snow. The house is quiet. Annie, Ruth, and her son are on the picket line. Emma has another cold, so I told her to rest. I look out the window and see Joe and Lucas rolling balls of snow for a tiny snowman. A warmth comes over me as I look out at the children. Such few joys in our lives, so we must make the most of the little things.

Ω

Two days later, the temperature is in the 50s. Joe and Nicky ran outside to play. In a few seconds, they rush into the kitchen. Joe is in tears, "Ma, the snowman ran away. He's gone. Why did he do that?" Such sweet boys.

Greensburg Journalist wrote: I have just received a letter from Mother Jones, "the angel of the miners," who has gone into Westmoreland County, Pa., to lead in the unequal fight of the impoverished men, women and children against the gigantic corporations.

Thursday June 29, 1911
Mother Jones Tells of Women and Children in Rat-Infested Jail
"There were three generations in jail because they could not pay $10 apiece in fines to a corporation squire, who might as well have demanded $10,000 as $10. There was a mother, her three months' old baby and a grandmother besides two little children who could not walk, huddled together in a foul prison fighting off rats.... The men of this nation who permit such outrages are cowards."

Sadie Baker, aged 14, was sentenced to 20 days for laughing at a scab and singing, "Will there be any stars in my crown."

Mrs. Dot Smith, aged 19, and Her Three-Months-Old Baby, Sentenced to 20 Days in County Jail For Beating a Tomato Can and Making Sarcastic Remarks While a Scab Was Passing Her House.

From the Evansville Press of June 29, 1911
PETER POWERS TALK--WOMEN AND CHILDREN FIGHT JAIL RATS.
Gilson Gardner's stories of women and girls thrown into a vermin-infested rat-hole called a jail because they "disturbed the peace" by beating a tin can and singing at a strikebreaker in Westmoreland-co, Pa., is not overdrawn.

July 1911

The strike ended on the first of this month—more than sixteen months after it began. The miners got nothing. No shorter hours, no increase in pay. NOTHING!

I see black clouds hanging over the sixty-five coal patches and the fifteen thousand miners and their families. They have endured those months with no work and no pay, hungry bellies, freezing in the cold. It has been reported that sixteen miners and their family members were killed. I heard they were mostly women, but no one wants to dwell on that.

Our not-so-merry band is sitting on the back porch and enjoying the quiet of the day.

Annie stands up and throws her darning on the chair. "I guess it's gonna be good havin' your house to yourself again."

I haven't confessed to them that I have found comfort and a family I had never known with them in the house. I get up to fold the rugs hanging over the porch railing.

"What a tragedy this strike has been. All these months of not working. No money. They got none of their demands," I sigh.

Emma puts down her head, sorrow written on her face. "It's been nice being together."

I can hear the sincerity in her voice. We are sisters like sisters should be. Always there for each other, accepting each other for what we are and what we are not.

"That it has. The husbands caused the problems." I chuckle, knowing that isn't true. They have been kind and helpful, grateful they didn't have to pitch a tent and thankful for the meals we put together with very little.

Annie begins to fold the clothes and put them in the basket. "The strike endin' like it did… the men are angry. Still a nine-hour day and low wages. Nick hasn't said more than a few words to Nicky or me for days."

"I'm glad Joseph wasn't here. He would have hated that I'd been right all these years."

During the strike, I often wondered what Joseph would have said. Even during my marriage to John, Joseph was in my head. Sometimes he was like a ghost, trying to lend a helping hand.

I often wonder why Joseph came to guide me after his death when I seldom agreed with him when he was alive. Then one day, I realized that other than Aunt Rosie, Joseph had known me most of my life. Now, it's Emma and Annie.

"I heard the big wigs spent $500,000 on security," Annie says, drawing out the dollar amount. "Why couldn't they give that money to the miners?"

Emma snarls. "Because it means they would lose. They didn't want to lose!"

I nod an approval. "Coal production decreased by almost fifty percent no matter how many men they brought in. They still wouldn't budge even after spending a half-million dollars on security. Plus losing all that money on the coal not mined."

Emma starts pacing back and forth across the garden. I know she's worried about the next few months. "It's not a lot of money to them, but it's a lot of money to all of us."

Annie sits down and rubs her knees with her hands. "All those miners going out on strike couldn't make one of those thirty companies agree to one demand. They stuck together. Not one person had a heart. Not one person cared about the suffering of the miners and their families."

Emma lets out a sigh, "I'm just happy our husbands got their jobs back."

"The union leaders got theirs," Annie shrieks. "Over three hundred were denied work in the mines. Many of the immigrants blame the failure on the union leaders."

Emma studies my face for a moment and then clears her throat. "They didn't trust them. The union people couldn't speak their language."

We walk back into the house, Annie with clothes in tow. I look around the kitchen as though in a daze. "The union has worse problems. It'll be a long time before miners are willing to strike again around here. That's why the companies didn't give in to any demand! They wanted to break the union and shut them down. They had the money and the law on their side to do it."

Emma looks over at me, tears starting to form in the corners of her eyes. "I just don't understand the meanness in people."

Something I've been saying and thinking for years. I walk towards Emma and touch her hand. "Their money has blood on it. Will their children and grandchildren be proud of them? How will they feel about inheriting blood money?"

"But if they're like their fathers and grandfathers and great-grandfathers, they won't care," Emma says, choking on her words.

Holding Emma's hand, I look over at Annie. She walks over and grabs my other hand saying, "So, will you miss us?"

"It's like having the sisters I never had. It was nice sharing my days with people I love."

Annie squeals. "You love us."

Embarrassed, Emma sighs.

August 1911

Footsteps coming down the hallway surprise me right before supper time. I look down the hallway and Clara, now fourteen, puffing on a cigarette and her latest boyfriend, Frank. She is pressing her body against him. A few days ago, she told me they were getting married, and I haven't been able to change her mind. They walk into the kitchen, grab a donut off the table, and run out the back door.

Emma arrives a few minutes later. "Isn't it good Clara is getting married?"

"I'm not like you, thinking that my daughter should be married," and then regret my cheek. "I'm sorry, Emma."

Emma recovers from the shock of my words and, after a few seconds, she murmurs. "I don't think every woman should be married. Look at my Rosalie. She's still single, living with girls just like her who don't want to marry."

"There are worse things." I pause. "I just don't like Frank. He carouses and drinks too much. That saying about you're not losing a daughter but gaining a son is just plain crazy. I've got four sons and don't need another! Besides, she's only fourteen."

"Lots of girls get married at her age."

I pull out a tray of cookies. "Clara doesn't have to be one of them."

Many mothers worry their daughters will lay down with the first man who comes along. Many girls believe that life would be better out of their home, not having to live on top of each other and taking care of their parents' younger children. Too often, they are just replacing one bad situation with a worse one.

"She's hell-bent on settling for a man—any man. Why not look for a man with some promise?"

Joseph or John or any of my friends' husbands didn't have much promise either, though they worked hard. With both husbands, I had been the one taking care of the days and months and years ahead and any happiness we could have. Then I was able to do that. I know Clara cannot, but I wanted her to live a better life than me.

"So, are Clara and Frank going to move in with you?" Emma chuckles.

That's something Emma would want. I bang the cookie tray into the sink. "Not while I've got breath in my body. Oh, please tell me something funny."

Emma chuckles. "I read in the paper yesterday that fifteen women working for a publishing company in New York City got fired for dancing the Turkey Trot during their lunch break."

"What did they do—strut around like a turkey?" I say, bursting into laughter. "But why would they be fired?"

"It's a silly time."

"No, it's because they're women working in an office. Men will grab at any reason to get rid of them. Women frighten men, although they would never say so. I bet they were making the men look bad or they fear women will take their place."

I glare at Frank as he walks into the kitchen with Clara. I shout out, "No hat in my house."

He hesitates, then swipes his hat from his head and passes it in front of his body. I want to smack him. He then sits down at the table, takes out his tobacco, and rolls a cigarette with his calloused fingers.

"Take that smoke outside. No smoking in my house!"

He stands up, bows from the waist, and walks out the kitchen door. What a cheek!

"Clara, I don't know what you see in him. He's never going to amount to anything."

"You keep saying that. Did Da when you married him? Did John?"

"No, but your father and John worked hard every day. Not like Frank. He's just plain lazy. You're only fourteen, and you have nothing but what I choose to give you."

I hesitate. I'm trying to save Clara from marrying a man who will give her a life of suffering.

"You were sixteen when you married. Many girls in the patch marry as young as thirteen."

"They don't think they have a choice. I didn't have a choice. I had no mother, no father, no Gramps, and there was my Gran. There were few opportunities for women then. It's different now. You could get a job in one of the nearby towns and live with other young girls. You could do what Maria and Rosalie are doing. You could wait for a better husband."

"I don't want their life. I don't want the life you didn't have!"

"It's your life I'm talking about. Why would you want to live in a company house and have baby after baby?" I pause, biting my lower lip.

Clara walks out of the kitchen and slams the door. There's no point running after her. There's nothing I can say or do to change her mind.

"I could hear you fighting with Clara way down the street," Annie yells out, making me jump. "You don't want her to marry Frank?"

I slam a frying pan on the hot stove, wishing it were Clara or Frank's head. "If she were more like me, I wouldn't want her to marry at all."

"But she's not like you. You can't force her to live the life you didn't get to live." Annie's face wilts. "Oh Josephine, I'm so sorry. I shouldn't have said that."

That's the second time I've been accused of forcing on my daughter the life I wanted.

"Mothers talk to their daughters about marriage and children, often when they're only thirteen. So, why can't I caution her not to marry?"

With my apron, I wipe the tears that begin to stream down my cheeks. I turn and look away from Annie and Emma. My tears are for myself—mourning the life I didn't have a chance to live.

Emma flashes me a blank expression. "What's wrong, Josephine?"

I inhale and force myself to speak. "What Annie said is true. But, it's also true that if Clara marries, she'll have a horrible life."

"But if she doesn't marry, she still could have a baby. You can't lock her up."

"She could have had other choices if she'd only wanted to learn."

"And if she wanted to do more than sit on her backside or run around," Annie yelps.

"Marry Frank, and she'll only live a life of wanting more."

Annie pauses and breathes, looking flushed. "We've all lived a life of wanting more, even you.... Well, maybe for you, it wasn't about more."

Yes, she's right. It was about something different.

I shake my head. "Clara's one of those damsels you read about in fairytales—the girl that needs to be rescued by a man, the girl that needs a man by her side to live happily ever after."

Emma and Annie exchange puzzled looks. Oh my, they probably think they are those women.

"I know you'll give her a beautiful wedding!" Annie sighs with excitement, happy to plan a wedding—a wedding she had been denied by Sophia's death and Maria's choice not to marry.

"And Clara did ask if they could move in here with me. It was the first time I wanted to...." my words trail off to almost a whisper.

"So, what are you going to do?"

"All these years I've put up with her... but asking to live here. How could she ask that? If I say no, it'll be another reason for her to hate me? If I say yes, I'll be a slave to her, Frank, and any children that come along."

I hear my words bouncing off the wall. At that moment, I decide I have to save myself.

Clara walks in and shouts, "So, will you let us live here?"

I turn towards her, trying to keep my anger hidden. "You've made your bed, so sleep in it. I don't want Frank under my roof." The knife I have been using to cut bread is still in my hand. "You've never done any work in this house. You want me to take care of you and him and any children. Never!"

I cringe at hearing myself say those words. But Gran had a saying, "You give someone one finger, and they take a hand."

There are givers, and there are takers. With takers, there is never an end to what they will take. I now believe that mothers aren't supposed to turn themselves inside out to be liked by their children. They are to love their children without conditions, keep them safe and fed, and teach them how to live a good life. Doing and giving beyond what is needed gets mothers a life sentence of doing and giving.

Your children don't necessarily think better of you for the doing. That will not always make you closer to them. They won't love you or love you more. Clara gives me proof of that every day. I've had enough.

The Pennsylvania State Police, although not paid by the companies, took the side of the coal companies. There were claims made by the miners and bystanders that they used the same brutality as the deputies and Coal and Iron Police. This was the same throughout the nation.

Those who investigated the 1910-11 Coal Strike reported that violence increased considerably after the State Police arrived. Citizens testified that troopers charged on horseback onto town sidewalks or into crowds. They trampled and severely injured men, women, and children whether they were strikers or not. They did so without cause.

The State Police broke into homes without cause, beating citizens and miners. They fired into crowds or tents, killing and wounding sleeping women and children. Sexual assault, including rape, was typical. Six striking miners, nine wives of striking miners, and one bystander were killed, and thousands of strikers and members of their families were severely beaten or wounded. The local police could do nothing to stop them.

The coal operators sanctioned both the shootings and abuse.

September 1911

Emma walks onto the porch, her eyes beaming. "So, you're finally doing it. You've talked about this for years."

"I thought I would build in the porch and put a doorway into Clara's bedroom since she's leaving. We don't use the front porch now that I've added the back porch."

Annie lets out a whoop. "You can sell the eggs, milk, and cheese you've been peddling for years."

"I've bought two more pigs, so I'll have meat to sell next fall once they are fat enough. I'm not going to sell the peeps. I'll raise them and sell the male chickens live, so I don't have to clean them. The females will give me more eggs to sell." Whew! I finally stopped. I've been bursting with ideas these last few days.

Emma heaves a sigh. "Smart lady, but then I knew that the first time I dropped by to buy the peeps."

"I thought I'd put up signs on the road to get people here from town. Many might want fresh eggs, milk, cheeses, and meat. The prices will be lower than in the store."

"Who's going to run the store? You've got enough taking care of the boys and the boarders," Annie bellows and then chuckles. "I know. You're gonna hire some girls to run it."

"For once, your answer is partly wrong. I'm going to hire boys if I can. Maybe I can keep them out of the mine, at least for a while. Then, once Lucas and Joe are old enough to help, they can run the store."

Emma claps her hands. "You're going to kick Clara out of her bedroom before the wedding?"

"I have her sleeping in with me. It's an omen for her of things to come. Let's go in."

The banging of the kitchen door makes us jump.

"Lucas!" I stop, looking at the coal dust covering his clothes and his face.

"There's some hot water on the stove. Take it outside and wash your face and hands. Then come in and get yourself some milk and a sandwich."

"How's he doing?" mutters Emma.

I lean back on the chair, my expression somber. "Lucas is…."

"Good looking," Annie shouts. "His looks are…." she shakes her head, her eyes going in many directions. "He's the apple of your eye."

"He helps me all ways he can. He's most like Joseph in looks and bad temper. One day he's going to come to blows with someone. I'm just not sure he'll win."

Ω

I am a grandmother again. William and Meg have a second daughter, Frances, nicknamed Fern. She is so tiny, and her sister Carrie is enjoying playing Mommy. My heart is so happy for William. He deserves all the good things that come to him.

Seven coal companies in Westmoreland and Allegheny Counties sued the leaders of the 1910-11 strike. The coal companies claimed they had suffered economic losses as high as $500,000 due to the strike and strike-related property damage.

Twenty-eight officers arrested strike leaders in Westmoreland County on conspiracy, intimidation, violence, and general lawlessness. Local labor unions helped the forty-five men post a bond of $300 each and instituted a special per capita assessment to form a legal defense fund. The public outcry was so loud that the coal companies dropped the suits.

October 1911

I wake early to the promise of bright sunshine on the day of Clara's wedding. After making breakfast, the ladies who had helped me prepare the food for three days swarmed the house to take everything to the social hall.

After carrying casseroles and roasters, putting tables and chairs in place, and decorating, I hurry home to get Clara and me dressed.

We are in the bedroom, and there's a knock on the door. "Come on in." William pokes his head inside the room. He will be walking his sister down the aisle.

"Clara, you look nice," he says.

How handsome he is in his dark suit and tie and haircut. He steps nearer, and I can smell his bay rum aftershave, a reminder of his father. He kisses me on the cheek. "So sad Pa is not here."

He hasn't mentioned his father in many years.

"You could be mistaken for the bride, Ma."

Clara frowns. "Maybe a bride the third time round."

William ignores his sister and walks toward the door of the bedroom. "Ma, I'll see you in the parlor."

I put on my shoes and look at myself in the mirror.

"Are you coming?" Clara asks, awakening me from my troublesome thoughts.

"I'll be down shortly." My voice sounds far away—something I wish for on this day.

A few minutes later, I walk out of my bedroom. My thoughts are about Clara. Although I disapprove of Frank, getting her out of the house will be good. I hate having that thought, but there it is.

Making my way down the stairs, I wonder if this marriage will make a difference in Clara—make her caring, not so mean.... My body goes limp at the thought, knowing she will never change.

Ω

I put on a smile and walk into the church on Lucas' arm, casting my eyes over the flower arrangements. William is shaking hands, welcoming the men, and kissing the cheeks of the sewing circle ladies, making them feel important, which they are.

Clara walks down the aisle on William's arm, dressed in an ivory satin and lace bridal gown with a high-necked bodice. The veil cascades over her shoulders and almost touches the ground. It's not worth the money it cost me, but she looks lovely.

I hear a neighbor say, "Josephine could have made her dress."

Not true, but nice to hear, but then she didn't have to insist on the most expensive one in the store.

Another neighbor replies, "Why did she have to buy it in a fancy store?" Yes, why?

"Yeah, but you know Clara," came the reply.

A twinge of sadness sweeps over me as I watch my daughter take her vows, imagining her hardships and heartache.

Ω

After the reception, I walk home alone and flop down in a chair in the parlor, slip off my shoes, and collapse like a wet noodle. I don't even have the energy to scream or cry. But I do feel a sense of pride in bringing some joy into the lives of my neighbors and friends. It was a great party, if not a great wedding.

March 1912

My sweet Margaret is ill once again. Since her birth, she has always been so thin, so frail. She catches anything that comes around. Leaving the kitchen in disarray, I race up the stairs to check on her. Lucas is reading her a story as I walk into my bedroom.

"Does she still have a fever?" He touches her forehead and nods.

Getting closer, I see a rash on her face. As I pull a long flannel nightgown, warmed on the handle of the oven, over Margaret's head, I see a rash on her throat and over her chest and arms.

"Now, go to sleep."

"But Ma, I didn't say my prayers."

"You can say them in bed instead of kneeling tonight. The room is too cold."

Margaret recites just above a whisper, "Now I lay me down to sleep," stopping every few seconds to catch her breath. I touch her face and her hands. Her entire body feels too warm but not hot.

"Now, you go to sleep, and don't let the bed bugs bite," I say, pulling the curtains closed.

"What are bed bugs?"

"I'll draw a picture for you tomorrow. Now go to sleep."

That night, sleeping beside my daughter, I kept repeating, "Please make her well," not sure who I am speaking to or who will hear.

Ω

The following morning, I awake and pull back the curtains, filling the room with the morning sunlight coming over the hill. I sit down on the side of the bed and touch Margaret's forehead.

"Get up, sleepyhead." She opens her deep black eyes and then squints to block out the sun. Her lips are dry and cracked. Her cheeks are hot when I touch them. I call out to Lucas.

"You need to get the doctor. Margaret is burning up with fever. Hurry, please hurry."

In coal patches, the company doctor's care is seldom available for the miners' families, and I'm not a miner's wife anymore. But I have no other choice. He knows I'll pay him, so he will come. I follow Lucas down the stairs and head for the back porch. I chip off a block of ice, wrap it in a towel, and race back upstairs.

"Oh, Mama, that's coooold."

"I know, but you need to keep it on to cool you. Now, stay in bed while I go down and make breakfast. I won't be gone long."

I tell Mike to cut some bread and make the coffee. "I don't have time to get you more. I've got to get back to Margaret."

Mike, who always brings Margaret some candy when he gets paid, nods. His expression is one of worry. He knows that if I'm concerned, he should be too.

By the time Lucas has returned with the doctor, I've got her to drink some hot milk with sugar. The doctor hobbles into the bedroom with Lucas at his side. Margaret is cuddled against me, listening to a story that I'm telling her.

"Thank you for coming, Dr. White. She's burning up, and she's got a rash all over."

He sets his worn leather bag down and looks into Margaret's eyes. He then places his fingertips on the side of her neck. "Ouch, that hurts," she cries out.

The doctor shakes his head. "Open your mouth."

Her tongue is white with tiny red pimples. "It's scarlet fever," the doctor whispers.

I don't want to believe the doctor, but denying his words won't change his words. A shiver goes down my spine.

"What can be done? How can her tiny body fight this?" As I say those words, not one for hoping, I hope there is an answer to give Margaret a chance.

Dr. White casts his eyes downward. "Make sure she stays in bed. You can give her a salt bath. If you have honey, lace it with whiskey. That might ease her throat."

I can't move or think. It takes several seconds to realize what the doctor is telling me.

"Will she get well, Doctor?" I have to ask, but my body quivers as I remember stories of other children. There's a blank stare on his face. He shakes his head, telling me without words that he cannot give me any comfort. He doesn't seem to understand that he has to give me something to do. He cannot just leave me feeling helpless. I need to do everything possible to save my sweet girl.

He speaks just above a whisper. "I can't lie to you. There have been many deaths from this horrible fever. You must keep your daughter in bed and make sure she gets lots of rest. Keep everyone out of her room, especially your other young children."

The doctor leaves me sitting on the bed watching Margaret. My eyes fixed on her baby face and pink lips. Her breathing is short and labored. Lucas comes into the bedroom. Throughout his life, Lucas has seen the suffering of others and the death of two fathers. I caution him to keep his distance, but he brings her such comfort.

Ω

It is almost nine at night—a time when the shadows of my life press down on me. I keep a vigil by Margaret's bedside while Lucas, Emma, and Annie stay nearby.

Ω

The doctor comes by to see Margaret the following evening, but he has no words to ease my fears. I walk into the bedroom with a cold cloth when her little body starts to convulse. I pull her to me and try to calm her. Her entire body is burning up as though it will turn into ashes. I curl in beside her, trying to take away the fire in her.

I coo into her ear, "Ma is here. Stay with me." I keep repeating the Lord is my shepherd and pray for mercy as she cries and gasps for breath.

June 1912

It has taken me several months to sit down and write about Margaret's passing, but I must. Maybe….

Three days after the doctor's visit, she slipped into a coma. That morning of her final day was sunny. Still, within five minutes after she took her last breath, the cloud cover hung low on the horizon. Rain started slashing against the window.

I wanted to scream, but there was no sound. My body buckled from the sorrow. I collapsed on her body and sobbed, "Ma loves you."

The whistle of doom rang out within seconds. Oh no, more sadness, but then there are times when we live in endless sorrow.

Lucas walked in and found me wrapped around Margaret's lifeless body, my lips pressed against her cheek. He touched my hand, and I looked into his tear-filled eyes. Grief, mixed with love, flowed over me. Such a young boy who had endured such losses and a little girl who had brought me such joy lost to me. I thought of Annie's words to Emma, "Why would God want my little girl?"

On the day of the burial, Annie and Emma clung to my feeble body, keeping me from crumbling to the ground as we walked into the cemetery. I stopped to place a rose on John's grave. She will now be with her father.

My footsteps quickened as I walked to the gravesite. My friends and Maria stood around in a circle, creating a safe haven for my sorrow. I stared into the hole in the cold ground that would now be her home. William stood across from me, holding his baby girl Fern in his arms.

His wife, Meg, would care for the boys and their daughter Carrie at home. I didn't want my boys to see their sister buried in the ground. Clara and Frank were absent, but then that was expected.

An altar boy held an umbrella over the peppered-gray hair of the priest. With his surplice flapping around his legs, he raised his prayer book in one hand and a cross in the other.

I watched the raindrops bouncing off the wooden box. Those gathered recited, "The Lord is my shepherd." The words evoked pain in my heart, hearing my little girl's voice. A bitter taste rose in my throat. Annie braced my arms as I stepped forward, tears stinging my cheeks, and placed a bouquet of baby's breath with tiny pink rosebuds on top of the casket.

I walked away as they began to lower it into the ground. I could hear the dirt hitting the pine box. I walked, not caring where I was going, losing myself in the space around me. I did not want to return to the quiet and gloom of my home.

Many close to me knew that Margaret's birth was one of the happiest times in my life. My little girl's passing was one of the most tragic. Although funerals are a chance for neighbors to gather and reminisce and comfort the living, only my close friends and family returned to the house to mourn with me.

I clutched my hands to my chest as I collapsed in a chair in the sitting room. Echoes of Margaret's sweet voice rang in my ears and pierced my heart. The only time I reacted was when someone told a story of Margaret, especially with Daisy, who she taught to roll over and give her paw.

Known to everybody for being a good cook and welcoming, I never moved. Instead, I sat there while memories of Margaret swirled in my mind, providing me some solace and, at times, bringing a smile.

I walked out onto the porch and sat down on the swing that Margaret had enjoyed. I unlaced my shoes and stretched my legs before me. I was staring into space when awakened by the sound of the siren filling the air with doom. Bad news travels fast, and I could not face any more bad news. I've had enough for several lifetimes.

I caught a glimpse of William. As he opened the door, tears formed in my eyes. I gulped, trying to swallow the lump in my throat. "She gave me so much happiness," I stuttered, hoping to feel something other than the ache in my heart. The flood of tears stung my cheeks and blurred my vision. William wrapped his arms around me. No words passed between us.

I sit here now and close my eyes to hear her laughter, listening for the sound of her footsteps. I picture her tiny hands kneading dough, her giggling at the snorting of the pigs, and her grasping a needle in her little fingers as she embroidered. I remember how she played teacher banging a spoon to get her brother's attention as she held up words for them to recite.

Gone are the days of spending time with Margaret, embroidering, making cookies, cuddling her in bed, and reading a story. She was the daughter I had wished for, but she was more than that. For one so young, she was kind and caring, curious, and fun. She talked to the chickens, greeting them every morning. And patted Daisy ever so gently and chatted with her as I had done with Pallie.

My grief is made more painful, not only because of the special bond between us but because Margaret was and would be my last baby. I would not marry again, and even if I did, my monthlies had stopped after her birth—a time I had celebrated—ever-lasting birth control. Then, I had my little girl to cuddle and love.

At times I'm stuck in place—waking up and finding myself sitting in a chair, flour and eggs waiting for me to make into bread.

The store is doing well, and the two boys I've hired have taken it out of my hands, which is a good thing. It holds no interest for me.

Buried with Margaret is part of my heart, and for now, I'm spending every day remembering. My memories are all I have left, and I want to keep them as vivid for as long as possible.

On February 13, 1912, during a strike in West Virginia, Mother Jones was placed under house arrest for inciting a riot. She was suffering from pneumonia at the time.

On March 4, Governor Henry D. Hatfield, also a physician., personally examined her and decided to keep her under house arrest for two months or longer.

April 16, 1912. After spending two months in prison for inciting a riot, the authorities released Mother Jones due to public outcry. Nothing dissuaded her, and she was once again traveling the country, going wherever she was needed.

For all of her social reform and labor activities, she was considered by the authorities to be one of the most dangerous women in America.

She said, "My address is like my shoes. It travels with me. I abide where there is a fight against wrong."

November 1913

At 2 a.m., I awake, Lucas by my bedside. "What is it? What's happened?"

"Someone's at the door."

I jump out of bed and pull a dress over my head. I know the Smolic's baby is coming soon. Although I've been a midwife for years and birthed dozens of babes, my heart still pounds.

Three of the Smolic's four children greet me when I arrive. I see the look of relief on Paul's face.

"Go get me a clean towel or sheet and a lot of hot water."

Paul starts to walk to the kitchen, shouting, "I already have the water on. It's gonna take a while. The fire was out."

I race up the stairs to the bedroom, where I hear the cries. "How far apart are the pains?"

"Every few minutes."

"Then it won't be too long."

"I hear that every time. Every time it takes too long."

"I know. Oh, how I know. Maybe we can make it a little easier for you. I'm going to put this pillow under your back. I want you to start taking some deep breaths."

In less than an hour, Anna's baby girl arrives. I'm grateful it was an easy birth, but I feel a sadness holding a babe in my arms. And then I think about Clara's first babe, a boy named Frank after his father and called Frankie. He is now two months old. Clara was not speaking with me at the time of his birth and still isn't. Angry with something I did or didn't do. I bide my time. That will change when she needs the store bill paid.

April 1914

Lucas runs in yelling that the Pittsburgh Pirates had a 5-3-7 double play.

Not knowing what he's talking about, I say, "That's nice."

All I know about baseball is that Pittsburgh has a team. Men hit a ball, run around a field, and try to score runs.

Out the corner of my eye, I see Andy, a boarder who is not as good-looking as he thinks he is. He winks at Jelena, my latest girl for the day. Then opens his mouth to speak, but I talk first.

"Ready for dinner, Andy?"

Andy cannot miss the scowl on my face and sits down at the table with the other boarders and my three boys.

Lucas reaches to take a piece of chicken from the platter. Andy lunges toward him and stabs his hand with a fork. "The meat is for the men!" he snaps.

"There's no need to do that, Andy. I've made a piece of chicken for the boys." I want to add, "I raise the chickens, and I can decide who eats them," but decide to lower the heat in the kitchen.

Andy stands up, his fist clenched, but he sits back down when I rush towards him. His eyes tell me this isn't over. He glares at Lucas. "In my father's house, the men got the meat."

Lucas sneers, anger in his eyes. "This is my mother's table, her house, not yours," he shouts. For a young boy almost eleven, his words surprise me.

Mike yells out, "Did you hear that Henry Whiteman is dead?"

"I thought he was in the hospital," I say, still upset by Andy, but grateful for Mike's friendship for almost thirty years.

"Yeah, he was. That fall of slate mangled his leg, and he refused amputation. Gangrene set in, and they couldn't save him."

There is silence, and after a quiet meal, the boarders leave for the social hall. I cut each of my boys a piece of cake I hid in the cupboard. As they chomp away, smacking their lips and licking their fingers, I explain that, in some homes, the men eat the meat, and the children eat what is left. "They work hard all day, so they believe they should have the meat. But, just know that you'll not go hungry."

Ω

That night I keep thinking of Andy's attack on Lucas, and I find myself comparing him to my other boarders. They were always grateful for a clean bed and good food, but then I had Joseph and John and then William for a short time. So tomorrow, I will ask Andy to leave after work on Saturday.

December 1914

Not much happening to ponder these days, so I seldom sit down to write. I don't want to bore those who might read this once I'm gone. Yet sometimes I have to share my thoughts, if it's only on this page.

Most days, the boys are easy to raise, especially Joe, who is gentle in his ways and soft-spoken. Michael is a bit of a scamp with a devilish grin. It's hard not to hug him. Lucas, my helper, is feisty and full of life. I more than miss Margaret, but she is still by my side as I do my chores. She tugs at my heart remembering the moments we shared day after day.

Time passes like a dripping spigot, and there are still accidents and deaths in the mines and sadness. I live most of my days not thinking about what I'm doing from one minute to the next.

I wake at the same hour, prepare meals for the same hour, and cook the same things. I even take my walk into the patch at the same time. I do all this without pondering whether I should or not. I'm not complaining. The sameness of my day keeps me from thinking or deciding about much of anything.

I have always liked change. In the past, change was a gift I gave myself. Since Margaret's death, I'm finding wisdom in keeping things the same. Nothing is nudging at me. Now, jumping off that roof doesn't seem like a gift, so I will stand still until the pain is too great. Then, I will have to jump.

March 1915

Clara gave birth to her second child, a girl, a week ago. Two children in less than three years with a miscarriage in between, and she's only eighteen. Oh my! If she keeps going like this, she could have twenty children.

She has named the babe after me and is calling her Josie. I guess she's trying to flatter me somehow. But because of my life's struggles, I now look at little girls and imagine what they will have to suffer because they were born female.

August 1915

In the distance, I hear footsteps and look up to see Maria running down the street. "Josephine, it's Ma! She's so sick. Ruth is with her, but she's asking for you. Hurry!"

Racing down the road to Annie's home, memories of Betty dying before I got to say goodbye flash before my eyes. I slap my face with the palm of my hand, trying to remove that image. Annie is stretched out on the divan, face flushed, and perspiration on her forehead and cheeks. Ruth is coaxing her to drink some warm broth.

"I think she's got pneumonia, Josephine. When she puts her head down, she can't stop coughing."

Maria takes her mother's hand. "She's having trouble breathing, and her hands are hot and clammy."

Annie starts to shiver. I put my head against Annie's back and listen while she struggles to breathe. "There's crackling and rattling. We need to call a doctor, and we need to do it now."

"The doctor can't come now. Men got injured, and he's patching them up," says Ruth, pacing back and forth.

"Let's make a tent over her. Maria, get a sheet and start boiling water. Ruth, send Nicky to the train station and ask someone to call a doctor in Harrison City. Here's the money." I take some money from my handkerchief and stuff it in her hand.

Annie looks up at me, tears in her eyes. "Now Emma will have you all to herself."

My heartache is mixed with sadness. I never knew my friendship with Emma hurt Annie.

"Emma is a good friend, but you have a piece of my heart. You are my very best friend."

Annie weeps, tears running down her cheeks. "I wish I believed in Emma's heaven. If I did, I would see my Sophia there."

I want to hold back the tears now streaming down my cheeks. I don't want Annie to believe she will be leaving this earth, but I can't always keep my feelings buried. I finally eke out the words, "I'm sure if she's up there, you'll find her, but you're going to be fine."

November 1915

My heart is broken into a thousand pieces, and I'm not sure when and if it will ever be put back together.

Memories of the first time Annie and I met come flooding over me. Maria and Sophia were holding on to her dress, and her body was shaking with laughter when she spoke. Now, there is stillness all around me most days, and in those moments, I look around expecting to see Annie standing in my kitchen with bits of news to share.

I surprised myself on the day of Annie's funeral. I had admitted to Emma that Annie's passing was more crushing to me than the death of my two husbands. And in some ways, as much as the death of Margaret, although Margaret had so much life yet to live.

Maria and I sat together through the three days of mourning. We seldom spoke to each other or to the friends who came to say goodbye to our dear Annie.

Over the last weeks, Emma's mission has been to console Annie's family and me. She takes care of Nicky, who misses tagging after his mother and helping her with chores. She brings Nicky to play with my boys while we cook and bake and sew together.

Maria cannot be consoled, and both Emma and I think it's a blessing that she has started a new job. Nick tried to coax Maria to come back home and take care of him and Nicky, but Maria kept silent. She has gotten out, and she is staying out. Her mother is in heaven applauding her.

Sometimes Maria comes for Sunday dinner. After Annie's passing, I invited Nick and Nicky to live with me. No sense renting a home. It may make people wonder and cause some gossip, but so what. He helps with chores around the house, and Nicky has my boys to play with. I cannot replace Annie, but maybe I can ease their sorrow.

Annie had been a gift I had given myself the second she arrived at my front door with her twins in tow. She had been sent to me by someone who loved me and knew I needed a friend who would make my days happier and light. The passing of Margaret and my two husbands have made me numb, and at times angry. Annie's death has left me broken.

July 1916

Nick and Nicky lived with me until a month ago. It helped to be together, to remember Annie together, for Nicky to be with my boys. Then Nick met Ruth's sister, who had been widowed for two years.

I thought it would sadden me to see him with another, but I knew Annie would want her son to have a mother and Nick to have someone by his side to live out the rest of his days.

My only concern is that Nicky will never love his new mother. Annie will always be his Ma, and he will always have me telling him stories about my best friend.

October 1918

Without as many tedious chores to keep me busy, my mind wanders to places of sadness, losses, and to a life unlived. I have picked up my diary again, and I cannot stop my pencil from flying across the page.

Since Margaret's passing and then Annie's, my life has been quiet, and I've spent my days just putting one foot in front of the other. Gran's advice. After all these years, I still heed it.

Last year in April, Clara gave birth to another daughter, Caroline.

The last six years have gone by at a snail's pace. Lucas is fifteen years old. My little boy is almost a man. Joe will soon be fourteen, and Michael is twelve. Three boys, almost ready to step into the world.

Now with my granddaughter, Caroline, in my life, I feel like my clock is no longer stuck and is ticking once again. Thanks to Clara. I never thought I would say those words.

A few days ago, William, who had bought a car a few years ago, took me to visit Clara and see the new baby. I wanted to deliver some food, diapers, flannel pajamas, dresses for Josie and Caroline, and one-piece pants for Frankie, the little boy. I had also crocheted a blanket for baby Violet, Clara's most recent. I continue to help the family, no matter how often I tell myself I'm done. It's not for her that I do it. It's for her children.

Watching Josie and Caroline play with the newborn in the cradle brought tears to my eyes and memories of Margaret.

While sitting at the table, I noticed Clara's bulging stomach.

"Clara, you've got to stop having all these children. Four in seven years and three miscarriages. You can't afford to feed yourself and those you have, let alone more."

Josie glared at me with her piercing dark eyes as I spoke, making me regret my words.

Clara scowled. "Well, you can help me out. You have money."

"I've given you money, but it's never enough. You and Frank drink it up. You don't spend it on food for the children or pay the store bill. Feeding your children has to come first. You're a mother. When are you going to act like one? I'll bring you food but no money."

Clara stared into my face. My years of hard work have started to show—gray in my hair, plumpness of my body, drooping of my breasts.

"How about taking Caroline off my hands?"

"You want to give me one of your children?" Yet, as I said those words, I realized that the idea might be a blessing for both of us. I looked at the babe and then at Caroline with her fair skin and big gray eyes as she watched over her baby sister. Their faces were dirty. The baby was wearing only a diaper that needed changing. Caroline had on a tattered, dirty dress and no shoes.

"You keep on about me havin' too many babies. Takin' her would be one less."

I smiled at Caroline, who is eighteen months old and walking. A toddler, she wouldn't miss her parents and siblings, and soon, like my brothers and me, she would not remember them. She laughs easily, just like Margaret, and having a little girl sharing my days could give me a reason to get up in the morning. I know Annie would be happy for me, so I will raise Caroline for both of us.

"Come here, Caroline," I said in a whisper, placing the toddler on my lap and twirling her straight hair around my fingers.

"Caroline, would you like to come and live with me?"

She smiled, and her eyes twinkled. "Kin I eat buns every day?"

"Yes, you can."

I wondered what the boys would say when they learned they had a sister. I wondered if they would remember their time with Margaret.

William and I drove home in silence, although he smiled when he saw me put her in the car. Less than thirty minutes later, we arrived home with Caroline. I could hear in my head distant voices, "Your sons are almost raised. Why do you want to do it again? She will never be yours! Why do you want to raise someone else's child?"

My answer to anyone who will ask and my answer to myself, "She's not someone else's child. She's my granddaughter, and I'm going to raise her as mine. Clara gave her away, and my sons are almost grown, so why not? I just want to take care of her, give her a better life."

Ω

Emma arrives just a little past nine in the morning to meet Caroline. "I heard you had your granddaughter here."

"Yes, Clara asked me to take her. I think she wants me to raise her."

"Raise her? Oh my! Why did she give you this one?"

"Josie and Frank don't need much care. At least, I'm sure that's what Clara thinks. They can help out with the chores and dress and feed themselves. The baby still needs to nurse, and there's another one on the way. Caroline is the lucky one. She got out of that house!"

"She'll be more work! You're not getting younger."

I lower my head so Emma does not see my anger. Why isn't she happy for me? Glad I have a little girl to care for. Finally, I say, "Work I'll enjoy. Besides, Caroline is not like Clara!"

Emma touches Caroline's head and smiles. "She's got lovely skin. Well, I'm off. Violet is coming by with her girls for dinner."

I take Caroline by the hand and walk her upstairs to my bedroom. Having Caroline in the house will give me what I was secretly longing for—another little girl.

Ω

"This is a promising beginning," I say to Lucas after tucking Caroline into bed. "I thought she might sulk or ask about her parents. But, it's almost like she already knows she's in a better place."

Lucas grins and lowers his head, "Well, it's quieter and cleaner, and she won't go hungry."

Ω

Over the next few days, Caroline delights me as she chatters about the chickens and the cow. She asks questions about the names of the vegetables I have in jars and what I'm cooking. She often wanders around in a daze, looking at the quilts and crocheted and embroidered scarves.

November 1919

Caroline doesn't ask about Frank or Clara, nor does she cry or say she wants to go home. It's like she knows this is where she should be. I have said that to Lucas and Emma again and again, hoping they will show some sign of agreement. I know they're happy that I'm happy, but some words are unspoken, "When will Clara take her back?"

That thought is in the back of my mind too, but with a fifth child on the way, it's only a matter of time before Clara asks me to take another one. She has forgotten there is a Caroline. As for Caroline, memories of life with her parents are being washed away by being well-fed, clean clothes, brothers who play with her, and the hugs I give her daily. She is a joyful little girl.

The sewing circle ladies arrive early. Ruth has brought her grandson, thinking he could play with Caroline. "She doesn't get in the way, and she's always happy. Where is she?"

"Michael took her to the store with him. I think he likes having her around." I didn't say what we were probably thinking that it's like having Margaret again.

Emma says with some approval, "She is so sweet."

Although she had never said anything nasty about her, she hasn't said much good about her either. Emma has no grandchildren to smother. Her boys are still single, Violet and her children are not close by, and Rosalie, according to Emma's words, is going to be an old maid. Hurrah for her!

"All my boys like having a little sister about."

Emma nods. "They probably still miss Margaret."

At the beginning of the 1920s, post-war demand for coal continues to decrease. As a result, the coal supply was more than the demand, so coal operators lowered the miners' wages and reduced their working hours.

The strikes that had erupted throughout the country in 1919 continued but with no effect. With a coal surplus and no reason for the mining companies to meet any of the union's demands, many coal patches were steadily declining. So, the United Mine Workers of America was rendered powerless in area after area.

March 1920

When I hear that Congress has ratified the Nineteenth Amendment, granting women the right to vote, I think of Annie. I close my eyes, and memories of her sweep over me.

The sewing circle ladies still meet, but we don't get many requests for handmade quilts and scarves. We still make baby sweaters, booties, and baby quilts, which we all enjoy doing. We meet most weeks just to sew clothes for grandchildren and quilts for our own beds.

The sound of voices awakens me, and I look around to see Emma and Ruth and someone I don't know.

"Josephine, I invited Jenny to join us. She likes to sew," Emma says. Before me stands a woman with hair the color of russet fall leaves. "She and her husband moved in a few doors from me last week."

"Good to meet you, Josephine. I heard a lot about you."

Tears well up in my eyes, remembering Annie's greeting the first time we had met.

These last few days, I asked myself where had all the years gone. Some were throw-away years. Years filled with chores, with nothing good or nothing tragic happening.

Some were filled with contentment, even joy, others with heartache. Today I've been trying to block out the heartache of the loss of Annie. Yet, everywhere I turn, there she is.

"You have a big kitchen. Do you like to cook? Sure, you do." Jenny giggles and I have to smile as Annie's face appears before me, remembering her answering her own questions.

"Josephine, are you going to vote in the upcoming election?" says Jenny, as she twirls her hair in a knot.

Ruth chuckles, "I know Annie would be first in line." Her face becomes frozen. Everyone is careful not to bring up Annie in front of me, but it is difficult. For over thirty years, she had been in our lives.

I smile and hug Ruth. "Yes, she would, and I'd be standing right behind her."

"My husband is against it," Ruth shouts. "He said I should stay where I belong, in the kitchen."

I throw my arms in the air. "Are you going to OBEY him?"

"Hell NO! Why start now? We've been married for over forty years. In all that time, he just huffs and puffs, and then I do what I want," Ruth giggles.

"We've got to vote!" Emma bellows. "Women have worked hard to get us that right. Jailed, beaten. If we don't vote, they will have suffered for nothing."

I nod. "I'm also tired of men running things. They rarely get things right."

"So, women should be in office, too!" Jenny cries.

"Don't you? I think they should have the right to do what they want."

Jenny grabs my hand. "I never thought about it, but yes, why not?"

Ruth collapses onto a chair, stretching out her legs. "We run the house, take care of the money, and some days we do ten different things. Who can stretch a dollar better than a woman? Most of us make sure everything gets done."

I nod. "And we don't have to tell everyone about it or expect a thank you and praise."

I'm proud of the new woman in America fighting for women's right to vote. They fight against child labor laws and young children working in factories and mills for twelve hours a day, six days a week....

"So, let's all go to vote together and get as many women as we can," Jenny declares.

Joy flows over me. "I think Annie would approve."

1920 Census: Josephine Potocar, 52; sons, Lucas Sauntner, 17; Joseph Potocar, 16; Michael Potocar, 13.

1920 Census: Frank Weicker, 35, head of household; Clara, 23; Frank, 7; Josie, 5; Violet 2.

It is significant that Caroline's name, born in 1917, does not appear in either report of the 1920 census. She was three years old.

August 1922

The loud voices of the boarders in the hallway racing to the outhouse awaken Caroline. The bird in the tree outside our bedroom window is singing to us. Caroline rubs the sleep from her eyes that seem too big for her face. She stretches her body as she looks around the room, her eyes gazing at the pink-flowered wallpaper. I have made pink and white gingham curtains and a patchwork quilt with a cutout design of a doll in shades of pink, blue, white, and yellow for our bed.

"Good morning, sleepyhead. Did you sleep well? Did you have a pleasant dream?"

This is my usual morning greeting to Caroline. She probably never wonders whether she slept well or had pleasant dreams. All she knows is that I care about her sleep and her dreams, and that is enough to send a warm glow through my body.

At this age of fifty-something, I am still five feet in all. Now a little rounder than I was at forty. I pull on a light cotton dress, the same color as the cucumbers that I will put in canning jars later.

Caroline runs to the chest at the foot of our bed to find the blue dress I made for her. The smell of mothballs seeps into my nostrils and jolts me wide awake. She jumps into her dress, forgetting to pull it over her head.

Before I can say, "Brush your hair," she grabs an old hairbrush and brushes her straight brown hair away from her pink cheeks. She tries to look at her image in a streaked, speckled mirror hanging on the wall, jumping up and down until she sees that she has no hair sticking out, and then looks back at me for approval. Her once-sad eyes are now bright.

We race along the hallway to find Bert and Henry coming up the stairs. We have secretly named them Twiddle-dee and Twiddle-dum. I had nicknamed the previous two boarders High and Low. One was over six feet, and the other about a foot shorter.

We enter the kitchen just as Michael runs out the door to clean the kitchen coop—his morning chore before leaving for school. Caroline yells to him, "Don't get the eggs. I want to do it!" She wants to run after him but also wants to help me.

I nod at her. "Go get two plates."

She brings the plates and holds them high above her head as I pile the eggs and fried bread on them. The boarders' eyes get larger as they watch the little girl walk towards them, balancing the plates, hoping not to drop a morsel on the floor.

"You can go collect the eggs now, Caroline. I can do the rest. Make sure Michael gives the chickens water."

She bolts out the door, always excited to see how many eggs the chickens have laid since yesterday.

A few minutes later, she walks into the house with her basket.

"Look at those huge eggs. The chickens only lay big eggs if they're happy and like you," I say, smiling at her.

"What are we doin' today, Ma? Is it gonna be fun?"

"We'll make some loaves of bread, and we'll save some dough to make some fried donuts."

Just as my boys had done when they were young, Caroline follows me around the house like I'm a pied-piper. While I prepare the yeast mixture, she measures the flour, trying not to get it on her pretty dress and face. "Four," she almost whispers.

"Now count three more. Four and three make seven."

Caroline smiles. "One… two… three cups."

I throw in some salt. "Now, push the flour to the side like this." I show Caroline how to move the dry ingredients to the side of the bowl.

"Good. Now break the eggs into a bowl and beat them with a fork." Caroline bites her lower lip as she tries to twirl around the eggs in the bowl like she has seen me do.

"Good. Now, we'll add the eggs and water into the hole we just made."

I add the yeast mixture and a scoop of lard, and a pinch of sugar. Then I gradually pull the flour into the wet ingredients and knead the dough.

"Now, we don't want to play with the dough too much. It'll only make it tough. You know how you like soft bread."

When it has been kneaded, I cover it with a gingham cloth. I put some hot water on the stove to blanch the tomatoes. As we work together on our morning chores, Caroline cannot resist peeking at the dough every few minutes, willing it to rise.

Our time passes quickly as I wash and she dries the dishes. It is finally time to loaf the bread and make the donuts. There is a simple grace to the motion of donut-making.

"Pull a little ball of dough about the size of your fist." Caroline plunges her tiny hand into the bowl and pulls out a piece.

"That's good. Now pull it apart into any shape. Think of clouds in the sky. That's what we're going to make."

Caroline attempts to mimic me. "That's right. Now we're going to put them in the pan and fry them."

Her eyes grow large as she watches the dough puff up and turn golden brown. As I take them out of the pan, I caution, "Don't touch. They're still hot." I wait a few seconds and say, "Now!"

Caroline starts dipping them in the sugar and then begins feasting. "Oh, mmmm! How many kin I have, Ma?"

"Just two. We need to save some for your brothers and the boarders." I look at Caroline, who has sugar all over her face.

"Why don't you finish that donut and clean your face."

"I will, Ma," she mumbles, her mouth full.

October 1922

Two months ago, Clara gave birth to another son, George. Such a beautiful baby boy. Almost three years and no miscarriages in between the births of her last two children, so she says.

I had Lucas take her some food and clothing for the children. I only visit her once or twice a year. It's easier that way. She can't ask for anything if I'm not there, we can't have words, and Caroline doesn't have to see the poor children's faces.

April 1923

Caroline's first recollection of her young life seems to be of me holding her and reading her to sleep. She mentions it almost every night when I pick up a book. I do not believe she has any memory of life before she came to live with me, which makes me happy.

"Caroline's lucky livin' with you," Emma sighs as she beats the icing for Caroline's birthday cake. "She's never had a single day she's been sad or hurt or hungry. You two are joined at the hip, never apart."

We both know it is much more than that, but Emma still has difficulty being happy for Caroline and me.

"She's happy. That's all I care about."

"Are you ever going to tell her that Clara is her mother?"

My body stiffens, surprised by this question from Emma. I have wondered the same thing over the years but put it aside. After George was born, Clara suggested that I take Violet into my home. Giving birth to her babes is where the mothering ends.

"She calls me Ma like my boys. I'm the only mother she's known. She's happy here, and telling her the truth will only…."

The devil in me is delighted that Clara and Frank's visits are rare. If they do stop by, it's for a good meal. They never talk to her or show any concern for her.

No matter how upset I was with Clara, I always gave her attention and care. Neither Clara nor Frank asks about Caroline, which gives me hope that they will never want her back. I cannot imagine my days without her.

I will tell her the truth in time, but not until she is much older. Her mother has abandoned her, and abandonment is ever-lasting, difficult for a child to forget. That scar I do not want Caroline to carry with her at such a young age, although in time she will. For now, or as long as forever is, I want her to feel wanted and loved. I say this, again and again, to convince myself that I have made the right choice. More than anything, I know Caroline is happier living with me. If anyone asked what made my days joyful, I would say, "Spending them with Caroline."

During the night, I watch her sleep. She is the daughter Clara had never been, and, like Margaret, she is the daughter I have always wanted. Yet, it tortures me that I do not have the same feelings for Clara as I had for Margaret and now Caroline.

I want to shake Clara every time she yells at her babes with meanness, the frequent smacks she plants on their faces and bottoms. "She can't be the daughter I raised," I say to myself and sigh, knowing that indeed I had.

"Clara only shows up with her brood when she needs money or my canned goods or something from the garden," I grumble to my boys and friends. I am happy to give her anything, but it would be nice to be appreciated and thanked.

Caroline walks into the kitchen after feeding the chickens.

"So, would you like chocolate or white icing on your birthday cake, Caroline?"

"I get a whole cake. Just for me!"

"Well, I hope you'll give me a piece."

"I will, Ma."

The miners continued the strike until August 1923, their families starving and many homeless. The union finally accepted a settlement that did not get them their demands. The seventy-five thousand non-union miners who joined the strike felt the union had not fulfilled their promise.

The mayor of New York City appointed a committee to investigate the situation in the coal mines. The report stated that the conditions in the coal patches were "worse than the serfs of Russia or the slaves before the Civil War."

July 1923

The fragrance of cloves and pickling spices fill the air, wafting out onto the street as we sit on the front porch mending some socks.

"Luke, Luke," Caroline cries out as she sees Lucas, now twenty, approaching with a wrapped parcel under his arm. She runs to meet him, eager for the pretty doll she hopes he has brought.

"How do you keep winning these dolls?" I yell out as Caroline traces the eyes and mouth painted on the doll's face.

Lucas grins. "I seem to be quite lucky at it."

Every two or three weeks, Lucas comes home with a toy or a doll in his arms for Caroline, who screams with delight. The punch-boards had become a craze in the early 1900s. It's a game of chance, and Lucas likes taking chances.

I tie the dolls to the backs of the chairs around the kitchen table or place them on the bed in the room we share. They are never a nuisance or too many—and there is always room for one more.

"Lucas, would you like a piece of bread? It's still warm."

The three of us walk into the kitchen, the fragrance of cinnamon and baked bread filling our nostrils. As I cut a piece of the nut bread, Lucas's favorite, he snatches a bun from the counter.

"So, what are the men saying about the strike at the mine?"

Lucas starts to answer with his mouth full. Then stops and swallows hard. "The older men are saying it's another failure, just like 1910. President Harding has wired the governors of over twenty states to give the coal operators protection. We never get any backing from the government."

"I heard the governor of Pennsylvania ordered state troopers to the mines, but the miners wouldn't give in."

"It's hopeless."

"I started telling that to your father in 1885. He talked and talked about needing a union and then about striking. I told him then it would never work."

"I know, Mom. William told me you wanted him to learn so he wouldn't have to go into the mine."

"I wanted him to have a choice," I sigh, bowing my head. "To me, it would have been wonderful to have been able to choose." Again, I heave a sigh. "Well, never mind. You're like your father. You'll do what you want. I just want to live long enough to see the day you walk out of the mine and never return."

September 1923

During this century and the last one, there are three constants in the lives of the coal miners and their families—births, deaths, and hardships. Yes, in between, there is hard work and some good times—the hard work is always there, while the good times are now and then.

Now, I have two sons out of the mine. Joe has gotten a job at a glass factory in Jeannette. Although he has not always heeded my warning about the mine, I am grateful that the coal surplus has forced him to look elsewhere for work.

August 1924

Life is good. I have Caroline, and Lucas and Michael are still home with me. They pay me something from their pay each week. I'm happy I have only two boarders.

Emma's husband passed away earlier this year. Her two boys have not married, and she still enjoys being their mom.

September 1924

Caroline walks into the kitchen. Her eyes spy the loaves of bread on the counter. Every bit of her thirty inches comes alive, her eyes darting to each corner of the room. She looks spellbound within a world that for her is always full of wonder, with something new to learn, something yummy to eat, something nice and warm to wear. This is her world now. She is not just visiting. At least that's what I keep telling myself.

I bring from the oven a roasted chicken with onions, potatoes, and carrots and place it on the table. "Caroline, go get six forks and six knives and six spoons." Then I open the kitchen door and yell out, "Supper's on the table."

As the boarders and my boys take their seats, I look over at Caroline's big eyes, her face with an easy smile. "What part of the chicken do you want, Caroline?"

"I want the wings."

"Why the wings?"

"They're little and soooo good."

"Just like you."

Caroline giggles, a light shining around her. She is always happy and talkative and makes me smile. I hope to teach her how to stand on her own two feet. She is already caring and kind. I write about our time together, so I can relive our moments together as the years go by.

October 1924

Rust, red, and yellow leaves swirl in the wind. Autumn has come early, and it's time to make sauerkraut in the crocks. Michael and I are in the garden cutting the cabbages off their stems. Caroline is picking them up and putting them in a wooden cart.

As I stand up to straighten my back, I feel older than my fifty-four years. It seems I have aged more in the last few years than in the previous fifteen. My hair is now more salt than pepper, and the bounce in my step is gone.

"Michael, go into the shed and get the barrels so we can wash them out."

With the last head of cabbage tossed into the cart, we wash them at the well. Once they are patted dry, I put them through the shredder I have fixed on a makeshift table. Michael stands by my side, dropping the shredded cabbage into the barrels that had been half-filled with water. He then tamps the cabbage down with a wooden mallet while Caroline sprinkles salt and pepper. I smile as I watch Caroline working alongside Michael, her face scrunched up.

"When can I do that, Ma," Caroline cries out to me.

"When you are eight."

She counts on her fingers. "Ma, that's another year!"

It takes less than two hours to fill all four of the four-gallon barrels. "Michael, let's put them in the shed," I say as I put the lid on the first barrel. The sauerkraut will stew for weeks. After it has fermented, I will remove the brine.

Three of the barrels I will sell by quarts in my store. The other one I will put on the back porch outside the kitchen door. It will be there for me whenever I want it for a pot of navy bean soup or around a piece of roast pork or share with the sewing circle.

"Well, we're done. Michael, go on and meet your friends." He smiles and runs down the street.

Emma comes around the corner of the house as the whistle blows. "I just heard that Joe got married. Of all your boys, I hadn't expected him to be seeing someone."

"I didn't expect that either, but they say, 'It's the quiet ones to watch out for.' I did think they'd wait a few more years, but she's going to have a baby. So last weekend, they said I do in front of a Justice of the Peace."

Caroline cups her hands over her ears. "Ma, why does that whistle blow so long? It's scary."

"Caroline, let's sit on the front porch with Emma and do some embroidering. I have a couple of doilies with a pattern of pretty flowers."

I drop the needle as Nicky's voice breaks the silence. "Josephine! It's Pa, Josephine! He keeled over and was rushed to the hospital. I just got back. He's gone! Just like Ma!"

November 1924

About four months ago, Clara gave birth to another boy named Joseph. I'm surprised she's honoring her father. So sad that he is so frail and tiny. I hope he can live out his life, and if he does, without pain and heartache.

This same year Joe's wife, Celia, died in childbirth, and the baby passed away a few days later. Joe returned to live with me, taking a job in the McCullough mine alongside Lucas, Michael, and Clara's husband, Frank. Sadness all around for my children.

December 1924

Christmas has always been a holiday our family celebrated with little fanfare. Every year we put up a small tree on a table, hung stockings, and made a good meal. Sometimes a much-wanted toy was given to William and Clara and then the four little ones that came one after another. This year we are going all out.

I have asked Lucas to cut down a tree for the family to decorate. "I want that tree at least seven feet," I shout as he goes out the door that morning, delighted that all my sons will be spending the day with me.

Michael went with Nicky to pick up Maria, who lives nearby with two other women and works in a clothing store. Nicky has been one of my boarders since Nick's passing. He is working in the mine, but I'm doing my best to change that. I'm not his mother, I'm not his stepmother, but we are bonded by our love of Annie.

Clara will not be with us. Once again, she's not speaking to me. Why I'm not sure. I became aware of this last tiff at a wedding we had both attended. Every time she saw me, she turned and walked the other way. I would have laughed if it weren't so silly. It's her way of getting me to do what she wants, giving her what she wants, or punishing me for something she has decided I should have done.

I have said to William, who knows her as well as I do and for years has ignored her, "Does she think she's so perfect? Does she think she's never harmed or hurt anyone? Why am I always the bad one?" But then that is Clara.

Caroline walks in, wearing only a slip, her hair in rag curlers and her mouth bent in an impish grin. I lift the dress I have just ironed, wave it in the air to cool, and then slip it over her head.

"Now, take those rags out of your hair, and I'll comb it. Then let's make the nut bread and peel the potatoes and carrots."

I pull out the old meat grinder that my Gran had used and screw it to the side of the wooden kitchen table. Then I pop one walnut in my mouth as a taster and pour a handful of nuts into the grinder.

"Ma, why do I have to sleep in those rags? They hurt my head."

"With your eyes so big, you look pretty with curls around your little face."

"I look pretty? Really, Ma?"

I smile and nod. "Now, while I'm getting the nut mixture ready for the bread, why don't you read to me."

Caroline bites her lower lip as she starts to read.

The clock on the wall tells me it's time to pull out from the oven a tray of buns and two loaves of poppy seed bread. After making the nut mixture with hot milk, sugar, and vanilla, I spread it on the flattened-out dough. I then roll it up like a jelly roll and place it in a pan to rise. I score the skin on top of the ham in a diagonal window-pane design and push cloves into the skin. Then I coat it with brown sugar and put it in the oven.

Ω

Right before noon William and Lucas arrive with a tree. I had invited William and Meg and their three little girls to decorate the Christmas tree and have dinner.

Meg touches Caroline's face. "She's growing up fast. Such a sweet face."

"So are your girls. They're so good together. Can you and William help me decorate the front door? The girls are playing with their dolls. They'll be quiet for a while."

Using the branches Lucas has trimmed off the tree, William frames the outside of the front door while Meg and I make bows from leftover cloth. Pleased with the festive results, we take our shivering bodies back into the house.

"Let's start putting ornaments on the tree."

Caroline gets on her tiptoes to peek into the large box I put on the table. Her face lights up.

"Lucas, William, you picked out a beautiful tree."

The children clap their hands. "I'll put the hooks on the bulbs, and you three," I say, looking at the girls, "can hang them anywhere you wish, only where you can reach."

William takes the baby from Meg. "After a day of baking and cooking, Ma, and you still want all of us around?"

I hear the front door open and hear Joe and Nicky's voices. Maria rushes over and hugs me. Tears come to our eyes.

January 1925

Emma has stopped by with news that her youngest son is getting married. I can still see him hiding behind his mother, those twinkling eyes bursting with wonder. Her other son has taken a job in the Yukon mine, boarding with a family.

"Well, are you happy for your boys? I know how much you love them."

Emma lowers her eyes. "Violet's husband is working at the McCullough Mine. She asked me to move in with them. That way I can help her out. She's not well at times."

"So, finally, some grandchildren for you to dote on."

"How's Lucas doing in the McCullough Mine?"

I chuckle, imagining Lucas trying to pull his mule along in the dark, cold mine. "He complains about Barney like he's a person instead of a mule. I'm hoping he'll get a job in a factory and get out of that darn mine. But, Michael... he will never get out of the mine."

My eyes glaze over—the image of Joe beneath rubble appears before me, and tears form in my eyes. I wish something else for him too. He has a tender heart and is not meant to be in the mine. I shudder. At this time in my life, I wonder why I have a tendency to imagine only sorrow.

"The pig's here!" Michael shouts, running into the kitchen.

Caroline's eyes twinkle. "You mean Oinkey's back."

I glare at Michael. "No, it's just pork, Caroline. Not a real pig. I told you that Oinkey had to go away. He was needed by another little boy and girl."

The Keystone Coal & Coke Company closed several of its mines and reduced operations at several others. The Claridge Mine is one of the properties the company decided to abandon and ceased operations in 1923, forcing the miners to look elsewhere for employment.

The nearby Kew mine continued to be in operation, and in 1924 over 68,000 tons were extracted. In 1925, its last year of operation, the Kew Mine produced about 13,000 tons of coal, employing just twenty men. The Denmark mine was still operating.

June 1925

While I'm sitting on the porch shelling peas, Lucas brings Clara and Frank with their five children for a visit. I'm being kind. It's probably for a good supper. Caroline is with the chickens, and the children run to join her.

While Clara sits at the kitchen table, Caroline walks into the house.

Caroline tries to smile, "Ma, look at these big eggs. Three double yolks."

I look into the basket, beaming at her. "Why don't you put them in the pantry."

As she walks away, Clara blurts out, "Why are you allowing her to call you Ma? You're her grandmother."

This was the day I had dreaded. I try not to shout but say with anger in my voice, "Then, who's her mother? Certainly not you. You left her with me some six years ago. Not as much as a word. You rarely see her. When you do, you don't even talk to her."

Since Clara married and had her own children, I've tried to put aside the anger and regret I felt all those years. She has never forgiven me—but for what I still don't know. Our chats usually end in a fight—nasty remarks from her about what I did and didn't do. I wonder what her children will say about her when they get older.

"You're jealous of her and me. Just like you were jealous of Margaret!" I cry out.

"Well, I know you'd never cry for me if I died like you did for Margaret."

I clench my fists. “My heart ached when Margaret died. It might have ached less if you'd been a loving daughter like she was. You've never shown me any kindness.”

“I knew I wasn’t your favorite. You never cared for me the way you did her and William.”

“And you think that's my fault? You believe I hurt you in some way. For that, you've never forgiven me. You never once thought that you caused some of the problems between us, that you hurt me. You've always been mean, and you always will be.”

I stop, shocked by my words. I’ve kept them inside all these years.

Clara stands up, towering over me. Her face is red, and she comes towards me. “She's still my child. I gave birth to her.”

Over the years, I had allowed her to beat on me. Maybe I should have taken her on a long time ago, but this time….

“Lying down with a man doesn’t make you a mother. You never cared about her and never will. You don't care about your children. You just give birth to them. Besides, I'm more of a mother to her than you've ever been to any of your children. So, what, if she calls me Ma? You don't want her. You never did.”

As Caroline puts away the eggs, she hears me yelling. This is one of the few times she had heard me raise my voice, other than shouting to the pigs, broom in hand, when they won't go into their pen or at the neighbor boys who chase the chickens.

When Caroline walks back into the kitchen, Clara glares at her and yells, “Caroline, why are you calling my mother, Ma?”

Caroline shrugs her shoulders and looks at me. I remain silent. Caroline's eyes get big as the moon. She probably thinks she is doing something wrong, but she just doesn't know what.

August 1925

It is a rainy, stormy day, two months after Frank and Clara's last visit. Caroline and I sit at the kitchen table. A voice awakens the sleeping dog that I had recently gotten from the farmer nearby. I named her Bonnie.

Clara and Frank are coming up the path just as thunder rumbles the sky. I'm amazed at how much Caroline's face resembles her mother's, but that's where the resemblance ends.

Hoping to keep the visit pleasant, I say to Clara. "So, you came just in time for supper?"

She walks into the kitchen without saying a word. It is quiet except for the bubbling of soup on the stove.

She barks at me, "I want you to pack Caroline's clothes. We're takin' her with us."

I brush back the hair from my face. "No, you're not. You can't feed the children you have. So, why do you want another one?"

Frank's dark brown eyes glare at me. "You're getting too old. If you die, who'll raise her?"

I had thought about that too, although I had never been ill a day in my life.

"I've talked to William and Meg. If anything happens to me, they're willing to take her. Caroline would have two sisters and a good life. You can't do that for her."

"The truant officer is after us, askin' why she isn't in school. They've threatened to jail Frank. Then he won't be able to work."

I know Clara is lying—one of her better traits. Caroline looks at me, waiting for me to say something. "You're doing this because you're jealous of her. You're jealous she calls me Ma. You want to hurt her, hurt me."

Clara glares at Caroline and screams. "Caroline, go get your clothes. Put them in this bag. You're leavin' here."

I want to tell Caroline to run, but where could she run, where could she hide? A feeling of helplessness comes over me. I watch Caroline out of the corner of my eye as Clara continues to rant about her rights to take Caroline.

"Why do I have to come with you?" Caroline whimpers.

"Because I'm your mother!" She points at me. "She's not. She's your grandmother."

I sink into a chair and motion for Caroline to come to me. "Caroline, all these years, we've been playing a game. I've been playing at being your mother because your real mother, Clara, couldn't take care of you. Now, she wants you to go home with her. Frank is your father." I pause, tears forming in my eyes.

"Why can't I stay here?" she cries out to Clara. "You got other babes, and Ma only has me."

I smile at Caroline, trying not to show the pain deep within my heart. Caroline speaks the truth. Clara doesn't need another child. But she wants someone to do the chores, take care of the younger children and the ones still to come, and she wants to hurt me once again.

Caroline's pleading eyes tear my heart apart as I beg Clara to leave Caroline with me. Caroline nudges into my body, her hand pulling on my dress. Caroline does not know I have no right to keep her. In a few years, she will be asking, if only to herself, why was she the one sent away. That will be a stain that will hurt her all her days.

As Frank drags Caroline to the car, she keeps looking back at me, the only mother she would ever have who would treat her with kindness and love. On that day, I cannot know how long it will take her to wonder if she will ever be happy or loved again.

Ω

Over the next few days, in the deep sorrow I know all too well, I try to make sense out of what happened. Maybe I should have told Caroline the truth—that I wasn't her mother, but I wanted to be. Yet, I never lied to her. I had just not told her the whole story. That is what I keep telling myself, so it might release my guilt. Yet, there is no way to take away the overwhelming loss I am feeling deep inside.

But more than my sorrow, I wish I could take away the pain in Caroline's eyes as she was dragged away. Living with Frank and Clara, Caroline must think she stepped into hell.

When I'm not in tears, I'm angry with myself. I should have adopted Caroline legally, but that was not done among families. It was common for children to be swapped back and forth without any papers. I should have fought Clara for Caroline, but I had no claim. Or maybe I did, but not knowing how, or maybe it was fear of what Clara would do.

I was also afraid of Frank—afraid he might strike me or harm Caroline. I've seen bruises on Clara's face and arms. Begging Clara would only make her more determined, and my relationship with her already has so much bitterness. In the end, I would still lose and maybe I would never be able to see Caroline again. I should have.... I should have.... but I cannot live with "should haves."

Clara once again is harming the one person who always wanted the best for her. But there's one thing she cannot do. She cannot take away my heavenly days with Caroline. They will be with me until I close my eyes and hopefully into eternity.

January 1926

Michael is now working in a mine in Green County. Not sure why he chose to go that far away, but he is determined to make his way on his own. Joe, who needs to be married, has married again. He lives in Yukon with his second wife, another Celia, and works in the mine there.

William and Lucas inherited their yellow hair and blue eyes from their father, but that is where the similarities end.

William is thoughtful and quiet. He works in an office, busy taking care of his wife and two girls. His second daughter, Florence, passed away. Lucas is the only son still living with me and working at the McCullough mine. He is dating a young woman named Isabel—Bella—who is going to the University of Pittsburgh.

All different—all make me proud.

My days now are humdrum. Caroline had given me a reason to get up in the morning. The last flame of inner fire that had kept me going was put out the day she was taken away.

My two husbands are gone. Margaret is gone. Annie is gone. Mike is gone. Caroline is gone. I am looking all of my fifty-eight years. I am now a very private person and stay to myself most days—living with those memories that had lifted my spirits.

Never one to live in the past, I find all I have is the past, and I'm locked in my memories.

Time is said to be a healer. A hopeful sentiment. But what is hope when your life is filled with so many losses, and losses are never forgotten?

If Caroline could have imagined her pain and suffering living with Frank and Clara, she would have frozen herself in time with me. If Caroline could make a wish, she must wish that Clara would give her back to me.

For Caroline's sake, I still wish that Clara would be a kinder daughter. That wish gives me hope of Caroline's return, although I never believed in hope, but what else do I have.

Sitting on the front porch, I'm gazing into the distance, but I'm not seeing what's right in front of me. I want to talk to Annie, but there is no Annie—only the Annie who still lives in my heart.

Overwhelmed by losing Caroline, I am reminded once again that my fate had been cast the day I was born. All I could do these many years was the choosing. My regrets are few, and those I have never served me well. The choices I can make now, what happens next, hold little meaning.

For now, I keep putting one foot in front of the other, helping my children and Annie's children when I can. I will walk every day until my death uttering the words, "too many losses." In my quiet moments, I sit and wait to be reunited with those I have loved and lost.

Acknowledgments

I am indebted to David, my husband, who encouraged me to keep writing and fell in love with Josephine's story. He read the novel, again and again, commenting where necessary, listened to my ideas, provided insight, and worked on the nitty-gritty. I was sustained every day by David's love and support throughout my journey and wish to express my gratitude to him.

I wish to express my thanks to friends, John and Linda Mracko, who opened their home to me when I returned to the Pittsburgh area to do some research. I also want to thank a distant cousin, James Santner, another great-grandchild of the original Josephine. He shared with me a collection of some family history.

A special thank you to Raymond A. Washlaski, Editor, of a website, *patheoldminer.com*. From his site, I gathered historical information and became aware of the miners in the area who lost their lives or had accidents. Where I could, I used their names and the particulars throughout the novel. I wanted to honor them and their struggles and sacrifices. Mr. Washlaski passed away in 2021, but I did have a chance to thank him for all the information he had gathered that was so helpful.

I also want to offer my appreciation to those in the writing group I facilitate, Sarah Holler, Sarah Moreno, Carole Shimko, Anne Louise Feeney, and Joanne Wright, who listened to several chapters of this story and inspired me to keep writing. Last, but no less important, I wish to thank Nancy Robinson, one of my readers who gave me valuable insight into the heart of my characters, and countless others who encouraged me to "get it written!"

Writing is thought to be a solitary act, but it isn't.

Author's Notes

My parents were the driving forces behind the writing of this novel. Growing up, they regaled me with stories of the coal mines and coal patches scattered throughout Westmoreland County in western Pennsylvania. The family Sunday outing was a drive to one of the many coal patches in the area. They pointed out the houses they lived in and told stories.

As a child, I never questioned why they would want to relive that time. At times there was bitterness in their voices, and some of the tales ripped at my heart. Other stories made me celebrate their strength and courage. I came to believe they shared their stories not to reminisce but to say they lived through it and survived, and I applaud their indomitable spirit and bravery. Although my parents are no longer on this earth, they walk by my side daily, inspiring me to fight for injustices and speak up.

My mother also told stories about her grandmother, Josephine, the woman who inspired this novel. She said two things about her grandmother. "She was my real mother," and "There wasn't anything she couldn't do." I used those two statements to channel Josephine's indomitable spirit, as well as a few stories of family life and her relationship with my mother, as I cobbled together this novel.

The story and traits and incidents of her friends and family members are products of my imagination and experiences with the human condition. As far as is what is accurate about the characters, Josephine was my great-grandmother. Her first husband's name was Joseph, and her second husband's name was John, and they were both immigrant miners and passed away in the years recorded in the novel. How many miscarriages she had and babies she lost I have no way of knowing, but she did give birth to six children and Margaret did pass away as recorded. The year of Josephine's marriages are accurate as my resources.

There were many primary sources, reports, newspaper and magazine articles, and websites that were invaluable, as I wanted to include historical events, especially those that impacted the lives of the coal miners and their families. Those historical events scattered throughout are only as accurate as the sources, only the timelines may vary.

I could have continued to write this novel ad infinitum. I was captured by researching the historical events of the time period in which the novel is set and creating the characters that burst forth on the page. I hope you enjoyed reading it. Please contact me, if you wish, at www.thedancingbridge.com.

It was a pleasure sitting with Josephine throughout the writing of this novel. She was someone my mother loved deeply, and she and my mother inspired me throughout.

About Elizabeth Rodenz

Elizabeth Rodenz was born in a coal patch near Irwin, Westmoreland County, Pennsylvania. She grew up listening to her parents tell stories about the life of coal miners and their families. Since she left that coal patch, she has traveled many roads—that of an educator, editor, executive coach, workshop facilitator, management consultant, entrepreneur, and author.

Living and traveling throughout the United States and many parts of the world, she has never forgotten those stories. That time in her life helped shape her thinking and ease and prepare her for her many journeys. She did not live a fairy tale life, but it was the life she believed she was supposed to live. *Josephine* is the story she was destined to write.

In 2005, Elizabeth authored a fictional tale, *Odd Ducks and Birds of a Feather,* to introduce readers to personality types, based on the work of Swiss psychologist Carl Jung. Her forthcoming book, *Samson and Delilah: My Two Loves,* is the heart-warming memoir of two beagles Elizabeth and her husband rescued hours before being euthanized.

She now lives with her husband, David, and their precious dogs in the Pittsburgh area. She spends her time helping people build bridges in their lives through their writing and the study of Swiss psychologist Carl Jung's body of work, as well as writing her own memoirs, poetry, and fiction.

One of the miners

Immigrant miners

Coal Miners and family, coal patch, 1910

Mother Mary Harris Jones, Strike of 1910-11, Westmoreland County, Pennsylvania, Women Who Sang Their Way Out of Jail

Coal patch children, 1910-11 Strike

Miner and his son—the family legacy

Miners' wives doing the laundry

Young boys working in the mine

Young breaker boys

Miners' families living in a tent—Strike of 1910-11

Made in United States
North Haven, CT
10 October 2022

25251506R00193